The Forces' Sweethearts

Also by Rosie Archer

The Girls from the Local
The Ferry Girls
The Narrowboat Girls

THE MUNITIONS GIRLS SERIES

The Munitions Girls
The Canary Girls
The Factory Girls
The Gunpowder and Glory Girls

THE BLUEBIRD GIRLS SERIES

The Bluebird Girls
We'll Meet Again
The Forces' Sweethearts

ROSIE ARCHER

The Forces'
Sweethearts

First published in Great Britain in 2020 by

Quercus Editions Ltd
Carmelite House
50 Victoria Embankment
London EC4Y 0DZ

An Hachette UK company

A CIP catalogue record for this book
is available from the British Library

HB ISBN 978 1 78747 407 9

10 9 8 7 6 5 4 3 2 1

Typeset by CC Book Production
Printed and bound in Great Britain by Clays Ltd, Elcograf S.p.A.

Papers used by Quercus are from well-managed forests and other responsible sources.

For Mollie, Betty, Joan, Maureen,
Veronica, Ronnie and Rosa.
Friendship is precious.

Prologue

April 1942

Bea, on stage, looked proud, beautiful and unafraid. Her glittering black evening dress with the tight bodice emphasized her full breasts and her blonde hair cascaded in tousled curls over her creamy shoulders. She appeared untouchable.

He'd change that, thought Melvin. He watched from the shadows; saw how her smile at the audience eclipsed those from the girls either side of her.

The Bluebirds, three English vocalists, practically at the height of their singing careers who had volunteered to cheer and entertain troops in the Libyan Desert, North Africa.

He imagined his hands roving over that exquisite body. Already he could feel his arousal growing . . .

Chapter One

May 1942

Three dusty, battered three-ton army trucks, accompanied by a jeep, pulled into a scrubby palm clearing where several tents were already erected only miles from the Libyan front. As the vehicles stopped, out spilled a motley crew of entertainers, including three weary girls.

Some of the occupants of the vehicles were wearing ENSA uniforms, the garb of the Entertainments National Service Association and not, as some wags said, 'Every Night Something Awful'. Some of the men set to building a makeshift stage, using ammunition boxes, petrol cans, planks of wood and oil drums.

'Not much like the Palladium, is it?' the blonde girl said, laughing. Her khaki uniform, 'drab' they all called the colour, of shirt and trousers was crumpled; her silk tie which had to be worn at all times when not on stage was knotted defiantly in a bow around her neck. Much as the performers loathed the ENSA uniforms, they were all well aware that if enemy action occurred they could get left behind by the armed forces if they were in civilian attire. Possibly they would be shot as spies.

'No, Bea, but I'll bet the audience will cheer just as loud, maybe even louder.' The voice belonged to Rainey, who had jammed her long auburn hair beneath a headscarf in an effort to keep it dust-free and out of her eyes; she hauled a bag containing stage costumes as she clambered down from the lorry.

Bea could see the sadness etched on Rainey's face. Charlie Smith, the photographer Rainey loved, had had to return to England after news that his shop in Gosport had yet again suffered bomb damage; this time staff and customers were inside.

'Cheer up, Rainey, you can't go on stage looking like a wet weekend! Keep yourself busy until you hear from Charlie again. It could be worse – he could have been inside the shop when the bomb fell. Why don't you check our frocks are still intact and sand-free?' There was so little room in the trucks for costumes, props and actors. Bea was relieved to see Rainey duck beneath a canvas awning that had suddenly been strung up, hang the ancient and damaged clothes bag on a wooden strut, unzip it and begin her examination of the black glittery dresses. They were designed slightly differently for each of the Bluebirds. A black high-heeled shoe slipped from the bag onto the sand. 'I bet that's one of mine!' shouted Bea. 'Make sure you shake it, the sand's a bloody nuisance.'

'Stop telling me what to do,' Rainey yelled back, 'or I'll put sand in your knickers!'

Bea smiled at her. Rainey's cheeky reply showed she hadn't quite lost all of her sense of humour. Bea didn't like to see Rainey listless. The travelling and the performances over the past months had been relentless; they were all tired.

Charlie Smith had toured with them when they'd been sent to Burma. It had taken four weeks on a troop ship to get there; longer to accept the great heat, the jungle wildlife and the country's water-logged ground. Its contrast to India's brightly clothed inhabitants and dusty streets with wandering cows had amazed Bea. Scotland, by comparison, had been wet too, but cold, and the troupe had shivered in Aberdeen, despite piling on extra jumpers. Charlie had become part of the company, sending photographs of the show back home to the English newspapers and doing all he could to promote Blackie Wilson's Bluebirds and Bombshells Show. Rainey was crazy about Charlie. Not that he was anything to look at, thought Bea. Five foot and a fag paper tall, hair that was pepper-and-salt and thinning. He could also be quite abrasive when speaking with anyone except Rainey, who treated him as though he was Clark Gable's double. And Charlie? He was besotted by the auburn-haired beauty, lovelight practically beaming from his eyes.

'Where can we change?'

Bea watched Ivy jump lightly to the sand. Beads of sweat clung across Ivy's forehead making her fringe damp. The heat didn't agree with Ivy. Small and dark, with her blunt black bob she reminded Bea of a modern-day Cleopatra. There the resemblance ended, though, for Bea knew Ivy missed the cold crisp days of Gosport on the south coast of England. But, like the other artists in Blackie's show, plus his assistant, Jo, who was Rainey's mother, wardrobe assistant and the girls' chaperone all rolled into one, they were there to entertain the brave boys who were fighting the war against Hitler. For this, the Bluebirds and other cast members were each paid the princely sum of ten pounds a week.

'Not sure yet,' Bea answered, then opened the battered leather music case that was her job to take care of.

'Side of the truck, Ivy,' called Blackie who must have

heard her shout to Bea. 'Follow Rainey, a tarpaulin's being set up.'

Blackie Wilson was helping steer the scratched upright piano on its way down from a lorry before it careered off the two wooden planks and swerved to its final demise in the sand. Bea saw the canvas shelter that had now been erected to give the players privacy and relief from the gritty sand that swirled in the light wind and ferocious heat.

Now Bea continued checking the music sheets were in the order Blackie would play them throughout the show. The piano was his prop and when the performance was ready to start he would remove his uniform of khaki shorts and matching shirt and slip into his black dinner suit.

'All right?' Blackie enquired. He looked tanned and fit, and his dark curls were tinted almost to gold at the front where the fierce sun had caught him. Bea was struck anew by how his odd-coloured eyes, one blue, one brown, only enhanced his good looks. Ghost eyes some people called them – lucky, others said.

Bea said, 'I could kill for a cuppa.' She was hungry and tired as well.

The word 'kill' made her suddenly remember the makeshift graves they'd driven past in the dunes. Sticks with helmets on top, stuck above the mounds to mark where fighting men had died, and been buried.

'Tea'll be ready in a minute,' Blackie said. 'We'll eat properly after the show. The army has prepared food and a tent for us to sleep in and rigged up private showers . . .'

'The lack of water is something I never thought about before coming out here,' Bea said to him. She knew now it was rationed for everyone. 'I'll get ready.' She turned to walk away.

'Bea!' Blackie called and she turned. 'I've already been asked by one of the Forces' spokesmen here if you'll sing "Always In My Heart"?'

'I will if it's all right with Rainey and Ivy.'

"Course it is,' he said. She worried, she had more and more requests to sing that brand new song. Of course, she was flattered to be asked to sing solo but she didn't want her friends to get upset about it.

It had all started when the Bluebirds had had to improvise and pad out the show because half the concert party had gone down with a stomach upset. Surprisingly, Ivy told a few jokes! Rainey and Bea had heard them before. They were old chestnuts they'd heard Bert come out with in the café. The men had loved her! But Ivy said she was relieved when the outbreak of sickness had passed and the cast was on its feet again and she could get back to singing.

'You're here to make the men happy,' Blackie stressed. 'No one's ever thought it strange that Ivy with her sultry Billie Holiday voice sings alone.'

Bea smiled. 'You're right. You play and I'll follow,' she said as she went in the direction of the makeshift tent where the actors were changing. The smell of sweat, fresh and stale, greeted her as she pulled back a corner flap.

Selma the snake woman had propped up a small mirror and was trying to glue her fake eyelashes in place. She looked over to Bea, shrugged and said, 'I think these look more like dead spiders every day. What d'you think, love?'

'You can work wonders with them, Sel, you always do.'

Make-up was almost non-existent now. War shortages had taken care of that. Already Selma was zipped into her shiny green outfit that Bea decided made her look more snake-like than the real thing. Soon the contortionist would keep the audience's eyes glued on her as she curled herself fluidly into shapes that Bea thought impossible for any human body to attempt.

A sharp exchange of voices took her attention away from Selma.

'I saw you!'

'Have it your own way, then, I did stare at her!'

Bea's heart dropped like a stone. The Dancing Duo were at it again! She couldn't see Leonora or Len. They were behind the rails of costumes brought down from the trucks. The couple's bickering was gaining momentum as if their lives depended on it. They probably did, Bea thought. Leonora's jealousy was legendary. Len only had to glance at a woman and his middle-aged wife insisted he wanted her as a fancy piece. A few days ago Leonora had apparently caught him chatting to Old Olive, who was really a gorgeous-looking brunette aged twenty-five, and she obviously wasn't letting that matter rest. Blackie had long since given up warning the Dancing Duo if they didn't desist in upsetting the rest of the crew, they'd be sent home in disgrace. Alas, their rows often fluctuated into full-blown throwing sessions but always ended in weepy recriminations and apologies. Golly, could they dance though, thought Bea, and the audiences loved the glamour of their act.

Leonora's frocks were dreams of tulle, lace and sequins that she guarded with her life. She insisted on changing halfway through their act, coming back on stage in another cloud of a dress while Len finished a solo tap dance. The frocks she wore were now impossible to buy. Even if she had coupons, the materials just weren't available. The audience was transfixed by the dancing couple's film-star qualities. Perhaps they conjured the glamour and memories of times past.

Leonora was now tying Len's black bow tie, the argument seemingly forgotten or, more likely, put on hold. Bea smiled. Len might once have been a Lothario but it was rumoured he now preferred the bottle to blondes. Still, jealous Leonora couldn't help the way she felt about her man, could she?

'Can you zip me up?' Rainey moved in front of Bea, who sealed her friend's slim body into the stage dress. Earlier in their careers the girls had started their act wearing Air Force uniforms, then left the stage to change into the glamorous creations provided by Madame Nellie Walker, Blackie's mentor. When they were in India, Bea had suggested their audiences had had enough of drab uniforms and deserved as much glamour as the girls could provide. Rainey turned and smiled at her.

'Thanks,' she said. Bea noticed her pallor. 'You all right?'

'Of course!' Rainey's voice was sharp.

Bea put Rainey's tetchiness down to her missing Charlie.

Her thoughts were disturbed by Jo, who thrust a make-up bag and hand-mirror in front of her. 'Come on, get ready.'

A tiny gold camel glinted from the collection of charms hanging from the chain on Jo's slender wrist.

'Is that new?'

Jo blushed and then smiled. Blackie had declared his love for Jo before they'd left England. After presenting her with the bracelet, he'd promised to buy her a charm for every country they visited. So far, he'd managed to do just that, even though Bea knew he'd had to pay extortionate prices for some of them. Jo held out her hand to display a miniature temple from Burma, a heart from England, a pyramid from Egypt and a tiny gold thistle from Scotland next to India's tiger. She shook the bracelet and the gold jangled. Bea put her arms around Jo. 'I'm glad you and Blackie have an understanding,' she said. 'He's lucky to have you.'

Jo pulled away from Bea, 'I'm the lucky one,' she said. 'Because of Blackie, I've travelled to places I never thought possible and I so love being with you all.' She paused and smoothed her fair hair back behind her ears. 'But to tell the truth, I can't wait to get back to England, to Gosport. I bet you miss your brother and little Gracie.'

Eddie, Bea's brother, had recently become a father to Gracie, the result of a one night-stand. Sunshine, Gracie's mother, had died giving birth.

'Gracie's rolling over now and sitting up,' Bea smiled.

'I know, your mum is daft about that baby. Maud tells me all about her in her letters. I miss my best friend.'

'Yes, I miss Mum. In the last letter I had from Eddie he was telling me that Grandad Solomon was again taken to a séance given by that Helen Duncan, the spiritualist. Gertie took him to Portsmouth . . .'

'That Gertie's always carting him off to places like that,' Jo said.

Bea's grandad Solomon, who lodged in Lavinia House where Gertie also lived, was captivated by the spritely elderly woman whose company seemed to have given the old man a new lease of life.

'Didn't that Helen Duncan tell everyone about HMS *Barham* long before it became common knowledge?'

'That's the woman, Jo. Gertie says she's ever so good. She informed people that the ship was sunk ages before it was announced to the public last January.'

'I don't really know much about it,' Jo said.

'Well, we're on tour and we don't get to hear much about what's going on back home. I wish I could go to Helen Duncan and ask her what's in store for me,' said Bea.

'Maybe you wouldn't like it if you did,' said Jo, stepping aside as a large man tried to push his way into the tent.

'I can't find my bleedin' shoes!' The top-hatted, bulbous-nosed comic's voice was loud. He had pulled back the sheeting and was staring glassy-eyed inside the tented area. A waft of spirits came from him and mingled with the stale sweat from his very grubby checked suit.

'Probably still in the back of the lorry,' Jo said. 'No rude jokes tonight, Titch, you know the rules.'

There was a long list of forbidden material the players were advised not to use, and Blackie could be called upon to produce this rule book at any time. Lewd jokes and offensive acts were frowned upon by Basil Dean, the man responsible for ENSA. The comic swore and withdrew.

Jo shook her head. Bea wrinkled her nose; she disliked Tiny Titch, the comic, as well. He danced wearing enormous long shoes and his act could be very funny. The audience loved him but like most comics he was a solitary and morose man when off the stage.

'A lorry-load of the British Eighth army has just arrived,' Ivy shouted from where she'd been watching the proceedings from behind a tear in the canvas sheeting. She let the tarpaulin fall again. Bea could hear raised male voices.

'I wonder how many . . .' Jo began.

'Doesn't matter,' said Bea, 'the more the merrier. They

all deserve a bit of cheering up for all they're doing for England, don't they?'

'I forgot to ask, Ivy, did you get a letter from Eddie?' shouted Jo. 'I must write back to Syd Kennedy as well.' Syd was a friend of Jo's who owned a garage in Alverstoke.

Ivy reappeared. 'I did. And I've got a letter to go back to him this time.' Then she was gone again.

Bea shrugged. It was good that letters from home were forwarded on to the various tour stops. Not that she received many. Her mum occasionally wrote, and sometimes she received a few words from her brother, Eddie. Bea was happy that Eddie and Ivy were on an even keel again after the shock of the unexpected baby. Ivy had had feelings for Eddie since her schooldays. Bea was sure Eddie reciprocated but had kept his feelings hidden from Ivy until recently; mainly because she was around seven years younger than him. Now they were both older, though, the age difference didn't seem to matter.

Gracie's birth had opened a chasm between them but slowly it was narrowing. How could it not when Gracie had melted Ivy's heart? Bea remembered how Gracie charmed everyone.

Eddie had been heartbroken when he'd been turned down for active service on medical grounds. However, because of the war his building firm was thriving; repairing and renovating bomb-damaged houses and premises was big business.

'Fifteen minutes,' announced Blackie, pulling back the tarpaulin and stepping inside with a tin tray filled with steaming enamelled mugs.

'You're a life-saver,' said Bea, helping herself, her smile a mile wide. 'Come and get it,' she called, so he could dole out the tea to the rest of the thirsty actors who were in various stages of undress.

'There's about five hundred men out there now,' said Blackie, 'and they're still turning up, ferried in on all modes of transport.' Bea saw the wink he gave Jo. He'd changed now into his suit, his dark curls just touching his collar. Maybe she'd tell him later she thought he needed a haircut!

There was a sudden burst of far-off gunfire. The occupants of the tent became hushed, the atmosphere tense.

'Don't worry about that,' Blackie shouted. 'Those machine guns are in the distance and most of the lads here are carrying rifles.'

'Is that little speech supposed to make everyone feel better?' Bea asked.

Blackie glared at her but didn't reply.

Olive was now at Blackie's side. She was swamped by a ragged dress and wore scuffed, high-buttoned boots. Her ill-fitting apron was deliberately grubby. The black straw hat with a rose that threatened to fall from its brim was pushed forward over one eye. She'd used dark make-up to give the appearance of eye bags and wrinkles. Looking like an old crone, she carried a paint-speckled birdcage with a large stuffed bird hanging upside down from its perch. Bea gave her a big smile. 'Want a cuppa?'

Olive nodded. 'I'm fair parched,' she said, setting down the birdcage and taking a mug from the tray.

Olive opened the show. Her repertoire of comic songs soon had the men laughing. She began with 'The Biggest Aspidistra in The World'. Then with knowing winks and suggestive body movements she told the story of 'My Old Man'. After that came 'Everything Stops for Tea'. Bea was always surprised that the men showed how much they appreciated that song. She supposed it was because there was something very English about cups of tea. 'It's a Bit of a Ruin That Cromwell Knocked About A Bit' came next. Olive kept the best until last when she had the audience wiping tears of laughter from their eyes with the Marie Lloyd song, 'I Sits Amongst The Cabbages and Peas'. Olive always received thunderous applause and she deserved every handclap, thought Bea, for the way she handled the suggestive but innocent song.

'I'll get by the side of the stage behind the curtain,' Olive said to Blackie, replacing the tin mug on the tray. Blackie handed the tray of remaining teas and empty mugs to Jo with a grin and followed Olive, saying, 'You can't start without me.' He then called louder, 'Fifteen minutes, everyone.'

Bea loved watching Olive who had a naturally suggestive way of signalling words so that every man in the audience felt she was singing just for him. Bea worked hard at her own act, memorizing Olive's effortless communication with the audiences.

Sometimes Olive would descend from the stage, select a likely candidate and sit on his knee, perhaps slide her fingers through his hair. This interaction with the men made the audience laugh, sometimes quite shyly, then they would call out to each other good-naturedly. The troops liked Olive. Bea, however, didn't want the audience to like her, she wanted them to love her.

'I'd better get ready,' Bea said.

'I'll collect the rest of the mugs,' said Jo.

Bea went to join Ivy and Rainey who were putting the finishing touches to their make-up and hair. The fifteen minutes before show-time that Blackie had mentioned didn't actually apply to the Bluebirds. As the last act on the bill, Bea appreciated dressing without the rest of the cast milling about in the confined space.

The sand grazed against the tarpaulin as the wind tossed the grains about.

Rainey, busy applying mascara, said, 'There's a small bowl of clean water there I've hoarded for you.' She pointed to an enamelled bowl covered with a towel, then went back to coating her lashes and staring at herself in a foxed mirror hanging from piano wire tied to a wooden strut.

Bea smiled at her. 'What would I do without you?' She was pleased to see Rainey had a bit more colour in her cheeks now. Bea proceeded to wash as much of herself as she could with a wet flannel and a sliver of soap. The meagre supplies of washing materials they'd managed to bring with them had pitifully dwindled. It suddenly occurred to her to wonder whether Basil Dean, the creator of ENSA, had ever imagined how his entertainers would cope with the privations they suffered as they were driven through sun-bleached deserts and wet tropical jungles.

Dean, as well as Leslie Henson, the actor, producer and film director, both great friends of Madame Nellie Walker, could never have foreseen the difficulties from the elements associated with their scheme to bring entertainment to the brave men fighting for their country.

Dean and Henson were pioneers, especially in film. Henson's company, Associated Talking Pictures was a huge success and both men had launched the film careers of celebrated stars like George Formby and Gracie Fields. Would the Bluebirds ever feature in a film? Bea hoped so. Above all she wanted fame and fortune, wanted to prove to everyone that a Gosport girl could shine among the stars like any other actress or singer. She stared at herself in the hanging mirror. She would do it! She would become a star!

But now she was more concerned with giving her heart and soul to making a difference in raising the morale of the troops during wartime. She picked up her toothbrush.

'There are hundreds and hundreds of men out there, now,' Rainey said stepping back from peeping out from behind the tarpaulin and helping to fasten Bea into her dress. Bea shook off grains of sand from her skirt. Suddenly, she froze.

'Can you hear that?'

'I'd be deaf if I couldn't,' said Ivy. Bea knew she was trying to make light of the fresh gunfire.

'Ignore it,' said Rainey. Then she said brightly, 'That piano wants tuning again.'

Bea knew Blackie would be cursing the erratic notes issuing from the upright.

He was well aware that a finely tuned instrument couldn't be shoved in the back of a lorry and trundled in and out of it daily without some kind of mishap. Sometimes he got lucky after asking, as he often did, 'Is there a piano tuner in the house?' Then the instrument would sound wonderful for a while after the talented ministrations from some soldier who'd had another life before fighting the enemy.

Bea applied lipstick, using her fingernail to gather as much as she could from the diminishing colour in the tube. She dashed a brush through her blonde hair, frowning as it encountered tangles.

There was a hush, then a sudden huge, united gasp from the men outside watching the show.

'Melvin,' said Bea. She felt shivering fingers creep up her spine. 'The men are wondering how he does it.' Stop it, she told herself, it's all in your imagination. But sometimes, just sometimes, she wondered if the man really did give out the actual evil vibrations that she felt whenever he was near her.

'Marvo the Magician and the Amazing Margo,' said Ivy. 'Up to his tricks again, conning the audience into thinking he really can play mind games.'

'Should be named Slippery Sam and Sleazy Suze,' sniffed Rainey. 'I can see it now: Suze in her sparkly leotard is holding up some poor bloke's last letter from his sweetheart, and blindfolded Melvin, with his back to the audience, is telling everyone what it is. They're marvelling at his clever ability to read her mind, not realizing Sue's careful choice of words as she asks the magician what's in her hands is revealing to Melvin that it's a letter.'

'They never seem to realize it's a con trick,' said Ivy. 'But he is good-looking. He's dead clever with card tricks . . .'

'Yuk!' said Bea. 'I hate his pencil moustache and Brylcreemed hair and the way he looks at me . . .'

'You sure that's not in your imagination, Bea?' asked peace-loving Ivy.

'I hate it when it's dark and he does that creepy bit in the act when he pretends to change from Doctor Jekyll to Mr Hyde using that torch beneath his chin.' Rainey shivered.

'Bea, you hate him because back in England there's a wife and three kiddies waiting for him and over here he acts like he's Douglas Fairbanks Junior . . .'

'No, Ivy, it's not that!' said, Bea. 'But I do think he entertains out here because it's a way for him to get out of serving for his country in the forces.'

'Children, children,' intoned Rainey. 'Play nicely, now. Calm down, we're on in a couple of minutes.' She suddenly swallowed and put her hand to her mouth.

'You all right, Rainey?' Bea was worried.

Rainey removed her hand. 'Drinking that cup of tea on an empty stomach wasn't a good idea, I just feel a bit queasy. I'll be all right in a minute.'

Bea nodded at her then took a deep breath. She knew she shouldn't let Melvin get to her but the man made her cringe. Bea heard the cheering die down.

Blackie was now introducing them. He would then sit down again at the piano and begin to play a popular song, one that they had recorded on the Parlophone label. They would walk out onto the stage . . .

'Bluebirds, Bluebirds, Bluebirds,' chanted the men. However many times this happened, Bea was always genuinely surprised, humbled and excited. As usual, Rainey led them onto the stage.

Out now in the open air, Bea saw the best of the day had gone and dusk was fast approaching. She could smell cordite in the air. The audience's eager faces were turned towards them. The stamping, yelling and whistling was so loud and frantic that for a single moment she worried the makeshift stage would topple because of the noise. Below was the piano and standing next to seated Blackie, Jo beamed up at them – she believed in them implicitly.

When all three girls were on stage, Bea put up a hand to quell the noise and amazingly a hush fell over the sea of expectant men.

Bea wriggled her way in front of the centre microphone

and said, 'Thank you all for being here and for what you're doing for us all.' The crowd again went wild.

Blackie began playing 'All The Things You Are' and immediately the crowd was silent as the girls began to sing. As the last notes were played, hats and caps were being tossed in the air amidst the sound of stamping feet and cheers. But again the audience immediately calmed as Ivy stood in front of the microphone and began singing 'God Bless The Child'. Bea knew Ivy's smoky voice wasn't simply singing the words: Ivy was being the character, pouring her heart into the words of the song. Next came 'I Don't Want To Set The World On Fire' and then they sang 'You Made Me Love You'. 'I'll Be With You In Apple Blossom Time' was a tremendous hit, sung with audience participation. Bea loved the way the men let themselves go, chanting at the tops of their voices. She could see from the expressions on some of their faces that the words meant hope for them all.

At the end of that song both Rainey and Ivy stepped back so Bea had the microphone to herself. She smiled at them then looked down at Blackie as he began playing the introduction to 'Always In My Heart'. The men were very quiet as Bea began to sing. There was no doubt in anyone's mind that every word, every note, came straight from her heart and was directed to the brave troops in front of her.

As her final notes died away the chant of 'More, more' began, then grew louder.

She spoke directly into the microphone, laughter in her voice.

'Thank you for your great kindness. We hope you liked our little show. We love being with you.' The clapping started up again but Bea held up her hands and quelled it. 'Now, you sing along with us to our final song!' She gave a broad, exaggerated wink, put her hands on her hips and added, 'This really must be our last song because the whole gang here, the Bombshells as well as us, are spitting feathers for another cuppa and then we all want to come amongst you, the audience, to chat for a little while.' Bea nodded to Blackie, then waved Ivy and Rainey forward into their places either side of her. Bea glanced down below the stage where Blackie's Bombshells, the rest of the actors, were waiting for them to finish, ready to drift amongst the audience to have the usual conversations with the troops that the men were so grateful for.

Blackie struck up with 'You Are My Sunshine' and everyone's voices rang out happily, loudly and clearly.

Bea glanced down again and caught Melvin's steely gaze upon her, and she shivered.

Chapter Two

Eddie saw the crocuses had withered to brown husks. A smile still lingered on his face as he waved at another friendly guard while his papers were checked at the main gate of Gosport's St Vincent Barracks. He was well known, being an employer of prisoners of war, but protocol had to be observed. He was there to sign up more men to work on repairing bomb damage caused by their German countrymen.

A young man staggered into step beside him. The large white letter P for prisoner decorating his trouser leg denoted his position at the holding unit.

'You want more workers?' The young man's voice was reedy and Eddie could hear the difficulty he had in breathing.

'Yes, Hans, you buggers don't let up on trying to blow us off the face of the earth, so I have to keep on repairing damaged homes.'

Hans tried to laugh but the effort was too much for him and the result was a wracking coughing fit that had the young German bent double. Eddie stopped walking and waited until Hans recovered.

'That don't sound good, mate,' Eddie said. He wanted to commiserate but knew that would do more harm than good. 'I see the crocuses have told Max's story?' He looked back at the dying remains in the overturned earth facing the entrance to the barracks. Hans' breath rasped as he said.

'None of our men would dig that garden over after Max had planted all the bulbs to resemble the swastika when they flowered . . .'

Eddie laughed, remembering the tall blond flyer who had escaped from the holding camp the previous year but was caught in a café in town.

'One of the guards forked it over in the end . . .' continued Hans.

'Yes, but not before the people of Gosport saw the distinctive enemy symbol in full flower,' Eddie laughed. 'The *Evening News* came and took a photo and published it on their front page! Gave us something to talk about.'

'That Max, he was a cheeky man,' said Hans thoughtfully.

'Yes, but a bloody good worker. Any news on where Max was taken after he got caught?'

Hans shook his head. 'Some say Winchester prison, but who knows? I believe Max intended to escape the moment he was incarcerated here.' Hans gave another phlegmy cough. When he'd calmed he said, 'They do believe he had an accomplice but so far that person hasn't been found. And no one wants to voluntarily take over Max's gardening job. He's a hero.''

'He was a clever bugger,' admitted Eddie.

Han's face suddenly looked downcast. 'I wish I could offer my services to you, it would be nice to get out of this place . . .'

'Sorry, mate. I'm not in a position to take you on.' Eddie hated himself for admitting that Hans would be useless working for him. But he thought Hans realized Eddie couldn't afford to pay the young man simply because they had become friendly. It pained him to think it was doubtful the young man would see the year out. Eddie raised a hand in farewell and made his way to the office where he knocked on the door then took a letter from his inside pocket.

'Come!' a voice from inside called.

Once in the office that smelled of polish and cigarette smoke, with pleasantries out of the way, Eddie showed the officer the letter.

'As you can see, I've been granted salvage rights on the Ritz picture house in Stoke Road.' He sighed, remembering the death toll at the late afternoon showing of a Bing Crosby film. 'I need to start pretty soon before the looters take what they want. I'd like to employ two more of your prisoners, making six in total on my payroll now.'

There was no surprise on the officer's face. He merely reached for a wooden pen, dipped it in the open bottle of ink and began filling in a form that he pushed across the table for Eddie to peruse then sign.

'There will be another couple of men waiting when your transport turns up tomorrow,' Mr Pontin, the officer, said. Eddie nodded. Since most of the eligible men had been called up, Eddie had been using prisoners of war as employees. Pontin added, 'It'll suit us all when the war's over and shops and building supplies get back to how they were before. Maybe then the public will stop referring to buildings, new or otherwise, as "Jerry-built".'

'Until then,' smiled Eddie, 'families need their homes repairing and I'm sure they don't really mind who tackles the job.'

The officer nodded, shook Eddie's hand and he turned to go. Eddie knew Hans would be waiting for him outside. Sure enough, he was.

'I wish I could take you on but you know I can't,' Eddie repeated. He tried to ignore the huge dark eyes that looked

as though the young man never slept. Hans, his disappoint-
ment weighing him down, shuffled nearer.

'How's the baby?'

Eddie paused. Gossip was rife in Gosport, even in the
holding camp. He turned to face him and said, 'Of course,
you knew Sunshine, Gracie's mother. She worked part-time
here in the kitchens, didn't she?'

Hans nodded. 'Everyone liked her. She was a happy girl.
Max adored her . . .'

'Everyone adored her,' cut in Eddie. He'd so far ignored
rumours that she and Max had been more than good friends.
Besides, this place was a prison, wasn't it? Fraternization
between staff and prisoners was totally forbidden.

He thought back to that night when he and Sunshine had
hastily made love around the back of the Criterion picture
house. Sunshine had said it was her first time and he'd had
no reason to disbelieve her.

His Gracie was the result of that coupling; Gracie the
blue-eyed, blonde-haired child who was the light of his life.
The little girl whose face would light up with a gummy smile
when he got back to Alma Street. He remembered the night
his mother had arrived home with the tiny child wrapped up
against the elements. Sunshine had given birth at the guest
house where his grandfather lived, and where Sunshine also

lived and worked. Maud had been visiting Solomon at the time and had been called in to help. Sunshine herself, before she died, had begged his mother to take the baby to Eddie. She had grown up in a selection of undesirable foster homes and didn't want the same for her child.

'I'm not saying it's easy with a baby in the house and I couldn't manage without my mother.' Eddie thought of Maud, who lived for his daughter. 'You know what grand-mothers are like,' he smiled at Hans. 'Gracie's the spitting image of our Bea when she was little.' He pushed away the memory of Max's blond good looks and replaced it with his and Bea's white-gold hair colouring. 'I'd better be on my way.' He shook the young man's hand. 'Maybe I'll see you tomorrow when I pick up the men,' he said kindly.

Eddie was looking forward to salvaging whatever he could from the bombed picture house. There should be tiles, bricks, wood, sanitary ware, even electrical fittings. The war had put paid to buying new goods – the shops were empty. Food was a priority and rationing was rife. Salvageable materials, however, meant bombed homes could be repaired. It meant homeless families could be rehoused.

The duty guard unlocked the side gate, allowing Eddie to walk out onto Forton Road. He paused at the door of his van. The air smelled of cordite and burning after the hammering Hitler had doled out to Gosport the previous night.

The main road out of the town had been cleared; rubble lined the pavements. The spaces where houses and shops had stood reminded him of the toothless gaps in old men's mouths. Dust had settled anew on his van.

With tomorrow's work planned in his head, he drove into the centre of town. His next job was to make sure Bert and Della and the Central Café had escaped the Luftwaffe's rage. Of course, he could just have easily telephoned to make sure they were safe, but he enjoyed a chinwag with Bert.

A smile lifted his lips as he pushed open the door and he was greeted by the pungent smell of bacon frying. Ivy's mother, Della, looked up from her stance at the gas stove, turned, and waved a fork at him across the Formica counter.

'I'll do one for you an' all,' she grinned. 'Bert's upstairs polishing his walking sticks, go on up.'

Della was a pretty woman, he thought. It was easy to see who Ivy got her looks from. Eddie would go so far as to say Della was the spit of Hedy Lamarr, the film actress. Bert had given Della, an ex-prostitute, a home when Ivy was a mere child. Della had given up that life, content now to be cared for by Bert. Eddie gave a quick glance around the café. Della was coping easily with the few customers tucking into fried breakfasts and mugs of thick brown tea. He thought of Bert's arrangements with mates in the black market that meant the café was just about the only place in town where such plentiful breakfasts still existed, and the officers from the cop shop in South Street who benefited from those arrangements. Everyone, it seemed, held an interest in amiable Bert.

He took the uncarpeted wooden stairs two at a time. Here the smell of San Izal disinfectant was strong.

Through the open door of a first-floor room he could see Bert, his battered prize-fighter's face thoughtful as he examined a leather-strapped stick so slippery-looking Eddie thought at first it was wet. As he moved closer, he realized the stick was just very highly polished. At Bert's feet and at his side on the single bed were other sticks and canes waiting to be rubbed and cleaned. On a white sheet nearby was a collection of walking sticks shining and glittering with polish and his elbow grease. The Bakelite wireless on the bamboo bedside table was turned on and Frank Sinatra was singing.

'Della told me you were up here,' Eddie said.

'Well, she was right.' Bert smiled at him.

After Della, Ivy and the café, the next love of Bert's life was his sticks. He was a rabdophilist, a collector. The weapon he loved best was hanging behind the counter downstairs: a swordstick he had removed from a German officer during the Great War. It was a sharp-bladed, fearsome object that had ended many a drunken fight in the café below.

'Not often I get the time to look through this little lot,' Bert said. A striped apron covered flannel trousers and a collarless shirt. He passed the shiny stick to Eddie. 'This is an Irish shillelagh, a fighting stick and it's made of black-thorn,' he said proudly. 'That could tell a few stories.'

'I daresay,' said Eddie, running his finger along the stick's immaculate surface before passing it back to him.

'You heard from Ivy?' Bert asked.

Eddie could hear footsteps coming up the stairs. Della entered the bedroom with two plates, one on top of the other. Bacon and brown sauce poked out of doorsteps of bread. In her other hand, she carried two mugs of tea.

'Get your laughing gear round this little lot,' she said. The smell caused Eddie's mouth to water.

'Well, have you? Heard from Ivy?' With her hands now bereft of plates and mugs, Della stood with her hands on her hips. Without waiting for a reply she added, 'The cheeky mare only said she'd buy me a house when she comes home.' Della puffed out air from her cheeks. 'As if I'd ever move from here!'

Bert shrugged. He'd reverently laid the stick on the

white sheet and now he took a mouthful of tea. After he'd swallowed he said, 'She's got money going into Lloyd's bank regularly from them BBC shows and record deals. She only wants to share her good luck with us because she cares . . .'

Della sniffed and whirled her way back down the stairs.

The bacon sandwich melted in Eddie's mouth. He sat down beside Bert, licking his lips and picked up his mug of tea.

'I'm expecting a letter from Ivy any day,' he said. 'That sandwich hit the spot, Bert.'

Bert eyed him without speaking for a moment then he said, 'I know Ivy's doing what she's always wanted, singing and all that, but that don't beat settling down and being happy with a husband and family . . .'

Eddie knew what Bert was referring to. Ivy loved the bones of him and hoped Eddie and she would marry. Eddie aware of the age difference between himself and Ivy didn't want to tie her down. He wanted her to explore her dream. He knew what Bert was expecting him to say and instead, replied, 'I can't see her being content back in Gosport after leading a life of excitement . . .'

'We all ends up beneath the ground eventually, you got to grab what happiness you can, especially in this bloody war.'

Bert put his empty mug on the floor at his feet. 'Nobody knows what's around the corner, Eddie my boy. Anything can happen before this war ends.' Bert stared at Eddie. 'I'm telling you, Ivy is one young lady who definitely knows her own mind. Me and Della knows you thinks the world of Ivy. You want to tell her so, snap her up before someone else does . . .'

Eddie said a hasty goodbye to Bert and carried the empty plates and mugs down the stairs and left them on the café counter. Della was wiping tables.

'Did he tell you what we was talking about?' She emptied an overflowing ashtray into an old biscuit tin and faced Eddie expectantly. Customers' tobacco smoke swirled in the air. 'Not just us, your mother Maud was only saying the other day she wished you and our Ivy would stop messing about and settle down.'

'Oh, yes,' Eddie said, still smarting from Bert's advice. He turned towards the door. 'And I've probably got as much chance of Ivy saying yes as we all have of this war ending tomorrow!'

He left the café deep in thought. Much as he loved Ivy, would it be fair for him to expect her to become a mother to his and Sunshine's daughter? Could she love the little girl as much as he did? He wanted what was best for his daughter, Ivy and himself, though he had to admit Ivy seemed besotted with Gracie whenever they encountered one another. Would Ivy even consider marriage to him when she had a busy career that promised success and travel all over the world? Proud though Della and Bert were of Ivy and her talent, did they really believe marriage to him was what Ivy desired above all else? He thought of all the letters he and Ivy had exchanged while she'd been travelling and how he wished he'd been brave enough to tell her what was really in his heart. Instead he'd kept every letter brief and friendly. One thing Eddie knew for sure, there wasn't much he could do about anything while Ivy was in Libya! His next stop was Albert Street. While Jo and Rainey were overseas it had fallen to him to regularly check their terraced house was still standing. He let himself in with the key, picked up the letters that had accumulated behind the door and strode into the kitchen.

As usual the small house had a calming effect on him. Jo and Rainey had arrived here at the beginning of the war and had made the scruffy place into a home, a safe place to escape from Jo's quick-fisted husband. Then they'd both joined a school choir. That had been the stepping stone to today's success for the Bluebirds.

Eddie climbed the stairs and checked the bedrooms for

damage. The windows were criss-crossed with tape to minimize blast damage; everything was as Jo had left it before they started travelling with ENSA. He was on his way down the stairs when a knock on the front door disturbed his thoughts.

'Hello, Mrs Fellowes, fancy seeing you.' He didn't step aside in the passage so the neighbour could enter. She reminded him of a Gosport sparrow with her metal curlers tightly rolled like feathers above shiny, sharp, dark eyes.

'Fancy a cuppa before the buggers start dropping bombs on us again?'

'All right, love. I'll just lock up in here,' he answered. His eyes travelled down her wraparound pinny to her bobbled slippers with the holes cut in the sides to allow her bunions to breathe. She was a nosy, lonely old baggage who lived on her own. She smiled and shuffled back to her own home. After a look around the downstairs of number fourteen, Eddie locked up and followed her.

Jo mightn't approve of his familiarity with Mrs Fellowes, but Eddie was a labourer who worked outside for a living and depended on the kindness of elderly ladies with their cups of tea and slices of home-made cake. A bit of harmless gossip did a great deal to brighten their days, and sometimes his, he thought.

Number sixteen looked too small to accommodate all the furniture that was jammed inside. He sat down on a settee that protested at his weight, squashing in next to a large black and white cat that fixed him with a malevolent stare. He could hear the rattle of cups and saucers coming from the scullery. There was a strong smell of mothballs and honeysuckle polish.

Presently Mrs Fellowes stepped back inside the kitchen holding a large crockery-filled tray.

'Need some help?' Eddie bounced to his feet. He saw the cat's eyes narrow as he moved.

'Comes the day I'm too old to make a cup of tea, I'll be in my grave,' she said. Eddie decided he'd better not offer to help again. She began arranging cups and saucers then asked as he sat gingerly next to the cat again, 'How's that sister of yours?'

'They're in the Libyan desert,' he said. 'She's been hob-nobbing with George Formby.'

'Well I never,' came the reply. 'He's a big star. What's he really like?'

'She reckons no one can get near him. His wife's a Tartar; right jealous woman.'

'Fancy that,' Mrs Fellowes looked over at him. 'Still, I bet that funny bugger makes everyone laugh, wife or no wife.' Her face fell. 'I'm sorry, lad. I got no sugar. I hope you can take tea without.' She passed him the flowered cup and saucer, then said, 'I got Saccharin tablets for sweetening, if you want?'

'I like it fine without,' he replied. 'I think Saccharin makes the tea taste of iron filings!'

The woman laughed. The war was a bugger with its rationed ounces of sugar and tea that lasted no time at all. 'When they coming home?'

'No idea, Mrs Fellowes. Our Bea's seen a few different countries . . .'

'And do the authorities put them up in nice hotels?'

'No! Bea's told me about the creepy crawlies, the snakes, the dirty tents and huts they get to sleep in. Sometimes they're lucky and kip in an army camp. Sometimes a deserted house with no water or sanitation.'

'Oh, my,' The old woman frowned. 'But she's an entertainer . . .'

'Maybe so, but they're out there to entertain, not to be pampered.'

'Oh, my,' she said again.

Eddie drained his cup, set it back on the saucer and said, 'I really can't stop long. My mother's looking after Gracie and she wants to go to the jumble sale at the church hall and it starts at four,' he looked at the wooden clock on the mantelpiece and added, 'I'd better get back. Is there any little job you need a hand with?' He was well aware elderly ladies often couldn't open jars or tins or reach items from top shelves.

'Bless you, but I'm all right, lad.'

The cat pushed a paw forward onto his knee and Eddie expected it to claw him. Instead the feline stared at him, its eyes changing shape as only a cat's can.

'I won't be a moment, I've got something for you,' the old woman said, turning towards the door.

She twisted through the closely packed furniture and he heard the front-room door open then close again before she returned, a small tissue-wrapped parcel in her arthritic hand.

'This is for Gracie. It's old, it belonged to my Eric but of course he's long gone now. Your little one must be ready with some teeth . . .'

She pushed the small offering into Eddie's hand. He remembered that her husband had died in the Great War and her only son had copped a bullet in 1941.

'You're doing good looking after that baby,' she said.

'I can't take this,' Eddie said automatically.

'You'll upset me if you don't.'

He unrolled the tissue to reveal a hallmarked silver rattle complete with a bone teething ring.

'I know there's precious little in the shops for babies

nowadays and your tiny one'll be growing like a mushroom,' she said. 'Them teeth causes kiddies pain like nobody knows.'

'Thank you,' he muttered. He was touched by her thoughtfulness, her kindness. He stood up, the cat rolling into the sudden warmth he'd just left. For a single second Eddie expected it to jump from the sofa and haughtily walk away. Instead, it lay where it had rolled, glaring at him. Eddie leaned across and kissed the woman's papery cheek.

Before he reached the front door his eyes were misted with tears.

Chapter Three

Eddie poured the boiling water into the sterilized baby bottle, then added the required amount of National Dried milk powder. He shook it well before pulling the teat onto the bottle with his clean fingers. Then he dropped the bottle into a bowl of cold water to cool down. Another good shake and a drop of the milk on his wrist to test the temperature, then the meal would be ready for Gracie who was, no doubt, still screaming at the top of her lungs down in the Anderson shelter at the bottom of the garden.

Hitler's bombers had wasted no time in coming over tonight for another visit.

Maud had only just returned from the jumble sale and daylight was bleeding into night when the siren had gone. Then it was all haste, grabbing the carrycot containing Gracie, who wasn't due another feed for hours, the flask of tea, a few sandwiches and the book he was reading, while Maud sorted out terry nappies and her knitting.

The raids were upsetting Gracie's sleep and feeding patterns. Maud had been getting her to eat mashed potato with gravy and sieved vegetables. Sometimes she was quite successful.

'I'll make her another bottle,' Maud had said a few minutes ago.

'I'm perfectly capable,' returned Eddie. His mum and Gracie were safer in the shelter. 'You stay here.'

Now he stared through the scullery window. He'd already pocketed his fountain pen and the air mail letter he'd purchased today to write to Ivy. He wondered what she'd think of her mother's and Bert's matchmaking. Eddie knew you couldn't rush these things.

The rooftops of the houses at the bottom of the garden stood out against the orange glow in the sky. His nostrils were still stinging from the acrid soot and red brick dust billowing across the yard as he'd run back into the house to prepare a bottle for his daughter. The searchlights illuminated the huge plumes of smoke, drifting and spreading over Gosport.

We're certainly getting a real bashing tonight, he thought. The chilling scream of a bomb cried overhead followed by the loudest blast he had heard all evening.

'Shit!' he said to no one in particular, ducking his head automatically.

He grabbed the cooling bottle, wrapped it in a clean napkin, opened the scullery door and made a run for the shelter. Another ear-splitting crash showered him with dirt and fragments of debris. He shoved open the shelter's door and fell inside.

'Cor, that's beautiful!' Ivy fingered the pink-fringed silk shawl. Already particles of sand clung to its softness.

'A soldier gave it to me. He got it in the marketplace. It's for Maud.' Bea allowed the slippery material to trail across her fingers, and she smiled at Ivy. Then she looked out of the back of the lorry where she could see anchorless balls of brown vegetation bowling along in the wind. 'I thought she could make a dress for Gracie.' She shook the shawl then began folding it carefully. 'I'll stick it right down at the bottom of my kitbag,' she said. 'I want to keep it as nice as I can. The authorities at checkpoints don't always like digging their hands too far into our mucky belongings.'

'I never knew Maud was fond of sewing.'

'I'm not sure about that either, Ivy,' said Bea. 'But I know she has access to Sunshine's old Singer machine.'

Just then the lorry gave a lurch and the occupants sitting

on the hard wooden-slatted benches cried out and grabbed at each other for stability.

'Sorry about that,' called back the harassed and apologetic driver. The back of his neck was dripping with sweat. 'I just clipped something sharp in the sand.'

'Don't worry about it, Bill,' called Blackie. He was feeling around on the wooden floor for the pencil he'd dropped.

The driver shouted back, 'You sure you're all right?'

A chorus of voices yelled back something that sounded like 'Yers'.

Bea flapped a hand in front of her face, trying to create a cool breeze. She could feel the sweat running down her backbone.

'Sunshine used to make some lovely clothes,' said Ivy. 'Mostly out of jumble sale throw-outs,' she paused. 'But a sewing machine's a bit heavy for Maud to have taken home in her shopping bag.'

Bea laughed. 'The landlady at Lavinia House told her to collect it when she wants it.'

Ivy suddenly looked serious. 'Do you think that's why Eddie fancied Sunshine? Because she was . . .' She paused, 'Clever, talented?'

Bea stared at her. 'That was a fling he had with her, you know it was. He's only ever cared about you.' The torn canvas cover of the lorry flapped noisily. Bea looked over to where Jo slept. She'd been oblivious to the lorry's mishap with the stony object. Her mouth was slightly open, her head was resting against her kitbag. Next to her was Rainey, scribbling away furiously, a notebook on her knees.

'Not another letter to Lover-boy?'

Rainey stopped writing and looked at Bea through her curtain of silky auburn hair. Rainey looked tired and pale. She poked out her tongue then went back to her scribbling.

It must be wonderful to love somebody and have that person love you back, Bea thought. She doubted it would ever happen to her. That awful episode when that sailor had assaulted her in the back yard of the Fox public house in Gosport came back to her. She had been stupid that night to have allowed herself to become so drunk that all her inhibitions had flown out of the window. Even now, years later, just thinking about it made her feel sick.

Highly strung, her mother called her. Told her she was too choosy, a tease even. Why? Was it because she had no use for male relationships that weren't, long term, going to be useful to her? Was that what being highly strung was? Being determined never to let a man get close enough to dominate again, to hurt her? She sighed. Whatever vibrations she sent out they never stopped men trying one way or another to get close, to talk to her, to possess her. She knew she was called the Ice Queen by some of the members in the troupe. She didn't care. Rainey, Jo and Ivy were her special companions and they understood her. She knew it was because she never followed through on what her stage body language promised. In truth she was scared of men, scared of their physical strength.

She wanted to focus on her stage career. Not turn to props as she had in the past. Alcohol had been one such prop. She rarely touched it now. Food had been another; ballooning her body size so that she could hardly fit into her stage dresses. Bea seldom ate sweet things these days, even when she could get them. Her determination, and rationing, had seen to that.

Thank God for Jo and the girls. They'd pulled her through, made her see success could be the Bluebirds' prize if they gave themselves over wholly to working hard. Sometimes, up there on the stage, she felt as if she could conquer the world.

But one person who scared her was that damned Melvin. Everywhere she went, he seemed to be there. Working in the same small troupe, it was inevitable that she'd keep bumping into him. She could handle that, but it was the way she'd catch him looking at her, as if he knew something she didn't.

Rainey said it was 'only her imagination'. But there was something about him that made Bea's stomach roil with fear.

Suze kept him under control most of the time. While she was sleeping with him he had no need to stray – oh, the inclination was probably there all right, but Suze managed to keep him on a short leash, even if he did sometimes escape. Suze was no angel. Pretty in a tarty-looking way, she had a high old time with the men. Bea had also heard the stories of Melvin drinking in the bars, fraternizing with the local girls. He didn't seem to care much about Suze any more than he remembered he had a wife and three kids at home in Blighty. If indeed he did have a wife and three children! Bea shivered. There was so much gossip and speculation about Melvin. Rainey said it couldn't all be true.

'Wake up, I asked you a question!'

Jo looked at Ivy. 'What?'

Ivy began laughing. 'You were asleep then, weren't you? I asked if you know where we're going?'

Jo took a deep breath and allowed the rest of her thoughts to melt away. 'I do. It's to an Air Force base near Magrun, or some such name. It's a proper base.' She grinned at Ivy. 'You know how secretive the authorities are about giving out information. We'll be able to have a shower and wash our hair; proper bases have facilities, don't they?'

'Won't that be great!' Ivy said, a smile splitting her face from ear to ear.

'There might even be letters waiting for us.' She paused. 'I wonder if it's just us lot on the bill? Perhaps some American film stars have arrived as well. Wouldn't it be wonderful to meet Clark Gable or James Cagney?'

'Don't get too excited. It's probably us as usual.' Jo stared at her. 'Don't you ever worry that with the bombing and gunfire and everything, we might get killed?'

Ivy was looking at Jo as if she was mad. 'Don't be daft, I'm too busy wondering where we'll be sleeping, or if we can wash our clothes to worry about that.' She suddenly slapped at her arm. 'Damned mosquitos, I hate them, they get everywhere.'

'I thought mosquitos only flourished where there was water,' Bea said. She was fed up with travelling now, fed up with the constant smell of stale perspiration in the lorry. She was discontented with the others' quirks and habits that normally she could ignore, but now, because of their constant close proximity, had begun to get on her nerves. She took solace from the fact they probably felt the same about her.

'You try telling the mosquitos that,' said Ivy, examining the red mark on her arm that had already begun to itch.

Suddenly Blackie gave a shout. 'We've got a reception committee!'

Bea craned forward and sure enough ahead she could see men lining the sandy highway. Some were leaning against a wire fence and inside she could see huts – real buildings. There were aircraft, too many to count, lined up on a dusty concrete airfield. Bea felt her spirits rise.

'It's a proper camp,' said Rainey, her face wreathed in smiles as the trucks trundled towards the cheering men. Bea searched in her rucksack and immediately tried scraping out lipstick from the depleted tube and with a compact on her knees began applying the rich colour to her lips.

'Must keep up appearances for our audience,' said Bea. She pushed the lipstick into her knapsack and then craned forward again, looking through the dirty windscreen and listening to the men's cheers and watching their faces as they excitedly yelled and cheered the battered trucks.

Bea waved frantically and as soon as the vehicle slowed, jumped down from the back to be surrounded by uniformed men all talking at once. It felt so good to have her feet firmly on the ground again even if it was covered with sand.

'Please sing "Always In My Heart", Bea.' It wasn't just one request – the question rang in her ears as, with Rainey and Ivy, along with Jo and Blackie, she was escorted to a long low building.

Blackie was halted by a peak-capped, braid-wearing officer who instead of smiling had a serious look on his face. He and Blackie shook hands then the officer bent forward and said something very quietly to him.

The girls and Jo were jostled ahead towards the low building by another officer. Every so often the girls halted to exchange pleasantries with the men who stopped their progress, eager to see, touch and talk to them. Bea thought all the men looked tired and extremely weary. She wished she was dressed in something more glamorous than the creased khaki trousers, shirt and tie that she'd actually knotted properly today. She consoled herself that later when the show began the Bluebirds would be able to present themselves in their glitz and glitter and cheer the men with their singing.

Escorted into the canteen, Bea stared around her, looking for Blackie. He was nowhere to be seen. Normally a welcome to any camp would necessitate Blackie being present to make a short speech to everyone. This time it looked as if Jo would suffice to do the honours. Bea looked at Jo, who shrugged, waited until the rest of the troupe had joined them and when the cheers and stamping of feet had slowed, Jo announced to the men and officers present that they were delighted to be with them and hoped they'd enjoy the evening's show.

After their rapturous welcome, the Bluebirds and Blackie's Bombshells were swept from the limelight and shown into dormitories where they would later sleep, and then back to the canteen to be fed.

'Where is he?' Bea looked at Jo's worried face. Jo sipped at her welcome cup of tea and tried to make light of Blackie's disappearance.

'He'll be here when we're ready to go on stage,' she said. Bea knew her words held more assurance than Jo felt.

'Shall I go and look for him?' Bea asked.

Jo shook her head. 'Not yet,' she answered.

Tonight the men and women actually had separate dressing rooms! Usually the girls hid in corners of a tent or behind rails of clothing to escape the men's leering eyes. Bea hated being anywhere in the same space as Melvin.

'Here he comes,' Rainey exclaimed with relief when Blackie pushed open the swing door and came walking towards them. He didn't look right, Bea thought. He looked haunted, almost as white as the letters he carried.

'Sorry about the delay,' he said to Jo, kissing the top of her head. 'Bit of business to attend to.' Bea thought perhaps he'd had some sort of sneezing fit. The sand could affect people like that. Despite his paleness his eyes were red and swollen. He sat down heavily on a vacant chair and let out a long sigh.

'You're here now, that's all that matters,' said Jo, taking the handful of letters from him and standing up so she could distribute them to the eager entertainers.

Bea motioned towards the enamelled teapot but Blackie shook his head. 'There's no time for a proper practice,' he said. His eyes took on a faraway look as if he was thinking of something else before he blinked and said, 'But there's time for those who want to get showered before the programme starts, or perhaps relax with another cuppa.' He was on his feet again. 'I must go and check on the piano,' and then he was gone. Jo looked back at his empty chair and frowned.

Bea realized later as she stood watching the show from the side of the stage that there was whispering in the troupe about Blackie's behaviour.

The discordant notes jarred as Blackie played the piano, frequently making mistakes that were nothing to do with its tuning. Jo introduced the acts while Blackie watched the show without his usual enthusiasm. Then Jo was forced to sit through an excruciating and unexpected comment as Tiny Titch the comic, well into his dancing act, suddenly stopped and addressed the audience.

'I don't know what's wrong with our pianist tonight. He plays like he's in jail – behind a few bars and can't find the key!'

The audience laughed. Blackie didn't appear to have even heard the taunt.

Jo's face was stricken.

'It looks like we're going to have to carry Blackie tonight,' said Rainey, appearing at Bea's shoulder.

'Don't let his mistakes put us off,' said Ivy. 'These men deserve the very best we can do.'

The show continued. Bea had to admit Melvin the Magician and the Amazing Margo had the men spellbound as time and time again Suze held up items taken from the servicemen and though they were hidden from his sight, Melvin correctly named the objects. Even Bea had to admit he was a genius with card tricks. When the applause for his act died away, Jo stepped forward and announced the Bluebirds. Then she went back and sat below the stage. Her eyes met Bea's and seemed to be urging the girls to support Blackie. The Bluebirds went through their regular routine to great applause. Bea thought Jo looked a little more relaxed. Then Ivy and Rainey stepped back to allow Bea centre stage for 'Always In My Heart'. As Bea waited, the introduction, played of course by Blackie, faltered. Bea gave a wide, cheeky smile, put her hands on her hips and waited, then burst into the chorus, urging the men to accompany her. Blackie somehow caught up with the right notes. Her song and Blackie's playing was practically eclipsed by the men's voices. The audience loved it.

Afterwards the canteen rang joyously and tunelessly with everyone singing 'You Are My Sunshine'.

As the whole troupe jammed themselves back onto the stage for the final bow amidst foot-stamping and shouts, it was Jo who stood at the microphone begging for silence to make the final speech.

Bea saw Blackie rise from the piano and make his way through the cheering crowd, towards the kitchens. Without hesitation Bea slipped from the stage and followed him.

'Wait up!' Bea turned and saw Jo had also noticed Blackie's withdrawal from the canteen and had followed them. It was mere moments after that the heavy wooden door closed on Blackie. Bea and Jo pushed against the exit and when the door gave they tumbled out into the heat. They were in a yard where bins and boxes were lined up against a wall. Bea could just make out Blackie sitting hunched near a large packing case. He had his back to the two women but the shaking of his body and shoulders told Bea he was crying. She paused, unsure if he was aware of their presence. Then she put her hand on Jo's arm.

'You go to him, Jo,' she whispered. 'He needs you.'

As soon as Jo reached the sobbing man, Bea saw him look up and grab hold of her, hugging her tightly to him as though he couldn't bear to let her go. Much as Bea wanted to know what was causing Blackie's distress, this private moment belonged only to them.

Bea turned her back on the tragic couple, raised her eyes heavenwards and stared up into the starlit sky that reminded her of diamonds embedded in warm black velvet.

She was not so far away that she didn't hear Blackie's words.

'Jo, Madame Nellie and her husband Henry were killed in a Portsmouth bomb blast. I don't know what to do . . .'

Chapter Four

'I love you and I want to marry you as soon as possible . . .'

Rainey allowed the letter to fall on the single sheet that covered her as she rested on the bottom bunk. A sigh of happiness escaped her.

The queasiness that had bothered her all day had momentarily abated but she didn't feel up to getting dressed again and mixing with the rest of the troupe. The dance music was enticing, as was the sound of laughter coming from the canteen but she consoled herself with the thought that at least other people were enjoying themselves, despite the threat of annihilation by bombing hanging over them.

The show, despite the discordant piano, had been a sure-fire hit. Looking back, she wondered how, with her insides roiling, she had managed to stay on stage until the very end, when Blackie had suddenly rushed from the canteen followed by Bea and Jo.

She'd never known Blackie to be so detached from his music as he was tonight. It was all very upsetting and if he'd guessed the reason for her sickness it would only have made matters worse.

No one had come looking for her and with the rest of the troupe probably drinking unrationed spirits in the crowded canteen she doubted she would be missed.

Sweat ran between her breasts. She propped herself up on one elbow and sipped from the water glass she'd left on the table by the side of her bed.

Her mother, Blackie, Ivy and Bea would have something to say when they found out what was happening to her. And it wouldn't be anything complimentary!

She was about to throw everything away that had taken the Bluebirds four years of hard work to accomplish. She was dismissing Blackie's faith in them, Madame's guidance and her mother's dedication to a career Rainey had said she'd wanted above all else. Now, when everyone's dreams were becoming reality and a better life beckoned, it was she, Rainey, who was about to mess it all up.

She loved Charlie Smith and he loved her. Why torture herself when in her heart she felt deliriously happy about the future? She put the water glass back on her table, felt for Charlie's letter and pressed it to her lips.

Rainey's thoughts went back to that night after the show near Yenangyaung in Burma. The Japanese wanted control of the oil fields and the British were destroying them. A stinking pall of thick smoke hung over villages and the jungle.

One hundred and fourteen degrees Fahrenheit, Blackie had informed them before they'd ventured on stage in another makeshift theatre. The heat was like nothing she had experienced before. Burma and neighbouring India had at first seemed like a paradise with its temples, golden statues, pagodas and lush greenery that tantalized the senses. She'd loved the villages with their thatched houses on stilts and the bullock carts and the funny ancient bicycles with rickety seats at the sides to transport passengers.

Mules borrowed from locals had carried their props and provisions. The density of the jungle meant abandoning the vehicles at a hillside village. To Rainey it was temporarily living a life she never knew existed, until they reached the encampment and she was faced with the wonderful gratitude and eager, cheering voices from the war-torn and waiting servicemen.

No one had told her about the insects. Or the spiders

as big as her hand, lurking in their bedding or hiding in their shoes if they didn't frantically shake them out in the mornings. It was worse by the Irrawaddy River where the mosquitos and leeches feasted on any pale English skins that had been left unprotected. At night, eerie sounds from the jungle left the troupe sleepless.

She'd been so thankful to Blackie for allowing Charlie to accompany them as their official photographer.

Rainey had never slept with a man before. She'd considered herself the most sensible of the three Bluebirds. Ivy was the quiet, dreamy one and Bea, the most volatile. However, common sense flew away every time Rainey was in Charlie's proximity. She found it increasingly difficult to stop from doing what they both desperately desired, to make love. So many times he'd simply sighed and turned disconsolately away from her leaving both of them unfulfilled, frustrated and angry. And then one night it happened.

They'd gone for a walk, she to wind down after the show and he ostensibly to be alone with her; away from the everlasting chatter of the troupe. The strange sounds of the jungle warned them not to venture too far.

She'd felt the warmth of his breath as he'd leant across to kiss her. He'd put his hand on the back of her neck under her hair and pulled her face to his. His tongue met hers and played against her teeth until that one innocent kiss was as hot as the night about them.

Her mouth had wanted to devour him.

The musky smell of his maleness had overtaken her senses. She could feel him wanting her and his hardness excited her.

Rainey longed for him to be inside her. Charlie had whispered. 'You're incredibly beautiful. I've never wanted anyone the way I want to make love to you.' He began unfastening her buttons and this time she didn't stop him. The sensation of being completely at his mercy thrilled her to the core as the mutual exploration of their bodies began.

His kisses were as familiar to her as if she had been kissing him for years. They were lying on his lightweight jacket and he had moved her beneath him. He came into her gently, wrapping his arms around her, burying his head in her long hair, for he knew it was her first time. With the pulsing thrusts of passion she was transported into her own world of ecstasy. Afterwards, Rainey lay in Charlie's arms. She felt as if she had conquered the world. The smile on his face and the love in his eyes told her he felt the same.

That was the one and only time they'd made love. Even now remembering, a frisson of delight coursed through her. The troupe moved on and now Charlie was back in England.

News of the relentless bombing of the south of the country and the hit on his photography shop while customers and staff were inside necessitated his return by troop carrier. Of course, Charlie was devastated at leaving her. But Rainey knew he cared deeply for the people he employed. She also knew he would have no peace until he returned home.

From Burma and its dangers, the troupe had been airlifted to Libya, where Rainey discovered changes in her body that proved to her, without a doubt, she was pregnant. At first she couldn't believe what had happened at her one and only coupling with Charlie. She was also aware of the adverse effect her pregnancy would have on Blackie, on the Bluebirds and on their future. Then excitement took over. She wanted Charlie to be the first to know. Then she would shout it to the world and weather the storm that her news would cause.

'Get back, you little shit, and stop following me!' Melvin Hanratty turned, walked back a few paces across the stony beach and cuffed his younger brother around the ear. The force of it sent the ten-year-old sprawling. 'Where d'you think you're going anyway?'

The Portsmouth tide had just turned and it wouldn't be that long before the damp beach would again be covered by the murky sea. Already the water licked at the seaweed and debris above the shoreline.

Melvin watched as the scrawny boy scrabbled up, trying to gain a foothold on the uneven surface. He faced Melvin defiantly. 'I'm coming with you.'

'No, you're not.' Melvin glanced at fourteen-year-old Amy Jenks beside him, his eyes fixing on her tight, budding breasts beneath the thin pink jumper. 'Why don't you push off to the pictures, Markie?'

Whenever there was a lull in the raucous music from the nearby funfair and arcade, he could hear the splash of the rolling waves.

'I got no money.' There was blood oozing from Markie's elbow where the sharpness of a stone had cut into him. Something in Melvin's heart softened. He put his hand in his pocket and pulled out the pack of well-thumbed playing cards that he'd been using to teach himself sleight of hand. He transferred the cards to another pocket, dug deep and this time pulled out some coins.

'Take this and stop following me.'

Markie's face lit up.

That was ten years ago. That had been the last time Melvin had set eyes on his brother.

*

Now, he tipped the remaining whisky into his mouth, set the glass on the tabletop and looked around the crowded and noisy canteen for Bea. He didn't know what had prompted him to think about Markie. His brother could be anywhere now. Dead for all he knew.

He'd never gone home to the scruffy terraced house in Nelson Street where his father would, as usual, be drunk and half asleep and stinking in his collarless shirt and pee-stained trousers.

When he'd finished with Amy Jenks in the long grass near Clarence Pier, he'd sauntered into the arcade at the side of the funfair. At the rear, through the dirty curtains, Big Joe was sitting at his desk. He wasn't drinking. He liked to keep a clear head. Big Joe didn't do drugs either but he sold them. The noise from the machines that rarely paid out was background music.

White powder and brown leaves were bagged up on the table in front of him. With his slicked-back hair and pencil moustache Big Joe reminded Melvin of an old-time music hall star. The pomade he used liberally on his hair made the back room smell of oranges. But there the illusion ended for Big Joe was huge; he overflowed from his chair like he was ready to spill over the bare boards of that sleazy back room.

Big Joe said, 'Your old man still owes me.'

'I know,' said Melvin. 'What d'you think I'm here for?'

'All your errand-running ain't never goin' to make up for his gambling losses.'

'I can try, can't I?' Melvin had long ago realized a life with a drunk who sometimes had money and food in the cupboard was better for Markie than a life on his own where he'd get swept into the gutter to join the likes of the fat man in front of him.

Trouble was Melvin was tired of holding it all together.

'Any word from your ma?'

Melvin shook his head. 'If there was, I wouldn't tell you.'

'Clever mouth for a fifteen-year-old.' The fat man smiled showing his shark-like teeth.

Then he leaned forward as far as his rolls of fat would allow and pushed a couple of sugar-paper bags towards Melvin.

Melvin knew what was coming. He transferred his playing cards to his shirt's top pocket, picked up the bags that he knew contained either white powder or brown-green leaves and stuck them in his trouser pockets.

'I heard you're getting pretty good at making cards disappear?' A smile hooked the corner of Big Joe's mouth.

Melvin didn't answer.

'Make them bags disappear then.' Big Joe laughed, a

wheeze that made his chins quiver. 'The weed's for Tommy on the carousel. Get his money first. The snow is the hot chestnut vendor's. Again, money first, in case the bugger runs.'

Melvin turned to go. He knew the chestnut vendor would cut and mix the powder with Attapulgite, or fuller's earth, to expand the quantity of the drug, even though it was already impure. Did it matter to Melvin? It was none of his business what went on in the fairground. What mattered was he was helping to paying off his father's debt. Sometimes he even made a few coppers go a long way in providing food.

He was sick of clearing up after his father and sick of looking after his brother.

As he stuffed the bag of white powder in his pocket and followed it with the bag containing the fragrant mulch, he heard Big Joe say, 'Take your time. I'm sending someone to your house to get what your old man owes. You ain't never gonna work it off.'

The words dug themselves in his brain.

By the time the skinny carousel barker had paid him and Melvin's back pocket was full of his money, an idea was becoming a possibility.

He also pocketed the envelope of grubby notes for the powder from the hot chestnut man.

'You in a hurry? Want some nuts?' The luscious brown chestnuts in the pan over the fiery brazier were splitting in readiness to be eaten. The smell was heavenly but Melvin thought of the rat-infested shed where the nuts were stored.

Melvin didn't answer the man. Neither did he take the money back to Big Joe. He went instead to Portsmouth Harbour station and stepped out of the train two hours later at Waterloo in London to begin his new life. He could make playing cards disappear, why not himself?

Chapter Five

'What am I to do, Jo?'

Blackie felt like a little boy who needed guidance. His heart had a gaping hole in it at the loss of Madame Nellie Walker and Henry who had been substitutes for the parents he had never really known. Now they were dead, blown to pieces by that maniac, Hitler. He felt Jo's arms tighten about him.

'I'll have to go back to England. I've been assured a few strings can be pulled so I can leave almost immediately . . .' He paused. 'It'll mean breaking my contract . . .'

'It doesn't matter about that,' said Jo. 'Basil Dean will step up and put someone in your place.' She was running her fingers through his hair and the touch of her hand was a comfort to him. 'We've done so much travelling in such a short time, none of us know whether we're on our head or our heels.'

'But the girls?' Blackie pulled away, stood up and walked from the wooden crate he'd been sitting on back inside the camp kitchen where the generator gave a welcome light. Jo followed. He felt a sudden flush of gratitude that Bea had disappeared, leaving him alone with Jo. Now he'd managed to unleash his unhappiness he was comforted by Jo's presence. 'I'll need to arrange for another piano player, a saxophonist would be useful, or a small band so the Bombshells can go on with the tour . . .'

'Don't think about that now,' Jo broke in. 'I'm coming back with you, but I can't leave the girls here, and anyway, they will want to pay their respects to Madame and Henry.' He saw she was looking at him with deep concern. She'd loved Madame and Henry too, but he thought how perceptive she was not to offer him trite consolation. Someone needed to help him control his emotions and Blackie was glad it was Jo. She knew giving way to her own feelings wouldn't help him keep himself together. 'We both need a stiff drink,' Jo said, pulling out a canvas chair from a stack near a table and pushing him into it. 'Stay here. I won't be long.'

Blackie stared around at the kitchen equipment with unseeing eyes.

He remembered Madame taking him in when he was

a kid and Henry teaching him all he knew about theatre management. They'd hoped because of his looks to make him a star. After all, his parents had been headliners. As it turned out, he couldn't act, he couldn't dance, he couldn't sing. But Henry realized that Blackie had an uncanny knack for discovering talent.

It had all started with that peculiar sergeant sharing a foxhole with him in France. Alfie Bird had been Rainey's father, Jo's husband. Later, after Alfie had saved his life and, in the process, lost his own, Blackie was to discover the man was a wife beater, a thoroughly unsavoury character, but Alfie had been right about one thing: his daughter had a voice to rival Vera Lynn's.

Upon his medical discharge from the services, Blackie had tracked down Rainey, with Henry's help, from the photograph Alfie had pressed upon him in France.

At a pantomime in Gosport Blackie and Henry heard the three girls sing. Persuading the girls' parents to allow Blackie to represent them was relatively easy once Jo had promised to chaperone them. They had toured England, learning the craft of entertaining. They'd worked hard and conquered many a difficult audience, and now, almost four years later, not only did they have a recording contract with

Parlophone and the BBC but the offers kept coming in. ENSA had appealed to Blackie; he'd wanted to give something back to the brave boys who were fighting abroad. Yes, Blackie thought, he'd made a success of the Bluebirds, with their hard work and Jo's willingness to be a mother hen to them all. But he couldn't have attempted any of it without Madame and Henry's financial backing. And now Madame was gone; his mentor, his friend and, more importantly, his surrogate mother.

He heard a door open and hastily wiped his eyes. No one wants to see a grown man with tears on his cheeks, he thought. Jo pushed a glass into his hand.

'Drink this.' He did as she told him, feeling the heat of the alcohol roll down his throat. The charm bracelet jangled against her own glass as she sipped from it.

'You know I love you,' he said, surprising himself and her.

She smiled at him. He didn't often share his feelings. 'I fell for you the moment we first met, during that air-raid, sheltering beneath the stage at that hall where the girls were singing the Bluebird Song,' he said.

'It took you long enough to realize,' she said.

'Oh, no, I knew, but I thought that mechanic chappie Syd Kennedy had first claims on your affections . . .'

'You thought wrong then, didn't you,' she said. 'Syd

was and always will be a good friend, but nothing more.' She paused, setting down her glass. 'Why are we talking about Syd Kennedy when we should be thinking about the five of us going back to England? We should also explain to the girls and the rest of the company about what's happening.'

'I asked you what I should do and you've put into words every thought I lacked confidence to go ahead with.' He clasped her to him. He could almost hear her heart beating as one with his.

After a while he looked at his watch. 'I must start making plans. Get in touch with solicitors, make funeral arrangements and arrange with Basil Dean for more acts to come out.' He stared at her. 'If ever I lose you,' he said, 'I'll be the one who's lost.'

'Melvin's not married,' Jo said. It was difficult to be heard above the noise from the plane's engines. 'He puts that about to deter some of the women who think they have a claim on him.'

'Don't you think that's a weird thing to do?' said Bea. She narrowed her eyes.

'You wouldn't say that if you'd seen the women hanging about outside the venues back home in England, looking forward to meeting him,' said Jo. 'I try to discourage you seeing half of what goes on.'

Jo saw Bea shiver. 'He gives me the creeps,' she said.

'So you say. He's a clever bloke; belongs to the Magic Circle.'

'So what? That doesn't make me like him,' broke in Bea. 'He can belong to royalty for all I care! But is that why he wears that funny little badge with the rabbit on it?'

Jo nodded. She looked down the interior of the plane. Blackie had wandered off to chat to some air force personnel. She couldn't see him but she knew it would do him good to be away from chattering women and at least he wasn't sitting around moping about Madame.

'I shall miss Olive,' Ivy joined. 'But no doubt we'll meet up again in the future.' She and Olive had got on well together.

'I won't miss any of them,' said Bea. 'Especially not Mr and Mrs "Always Bickering" and that drunken comic . . .'

For a moment silence reigned. 'It's difficult to get on with people we don't know when we've been thrown together, even if it's in a good cause,' Jo said, ever the peacemaker. It was uncomfortable sitting on the wooden seating but Jo knew how fortunate they were to be in the troop transport bomber carrying them to London. Officials in Magrun had moved swiftly so Blackie could get back to England without delay.

Jo looked at Rainey asleep on the bench. A trickle of dribble had rolled from the corner of her daughter's mouth, but it didn't detract from her prettiness, simply made her look vulnerable. Lately, Rainey had seemed tired and withdrawn, though she was much happier now that she'd soon be seeing Charlie again.

Jo liked Charlie – he was a steady sort of chap. Meeting him had knocked her daughter for six. What you saw was what you got with Charlie Smith and it was clear he idolized Rainey. In a way their romance reminded Jo of the singlemindedness of herself at fifteen when she'd first met Rainey's father, Alfie. Like Rainey, she'd had very little experience of men but one look from the red-haired soldier in Kimbells, Southsea's ballroom, and Jo was like putty in his hands. But once she'd married him at sixteen he treated her like putty, slapping her around.

Charlie wasn't like Alfie; he wasn't much to look at but he was a kind man. He was the putty in Rainey's hands. Then Ivy's voice broke into Jo's thoughts.

'So the Bombshells are carrying on with the tour as soon as Basil Dean can send replacements?'

Jo nodded. 'George Formby's offered to step in, if he can, the boys love him. He always cheers them up and Betty Webb, the soprano, she's a dish . . .' She paused for a moment. 'Basil Dean's talking about Patricia Roc, the film star, and our Vera who's a favourite with the lads in uniform—'

'So we won't be missed, then,' Ivy said. 'I do feel guilty for wanting to get back home.' She pushed her fringe out of her eyes.

'I don't see why. The Bluebirds have given such a lot of themselves to the forces. The BBC and Parlophone are on Blackie's back for more recordings . . .'

Rainey opened her eyes, wiped her mouth and sat up. 'More work. Don't we ever get any time to ourselves?'

'And hello to you, daughter of mine!'

Rainey was rubbing the sleep from her eyes. She blinked at Jo.

'I thought all you ever wanted was to sing?' Jo asked.

'I've been singing and now I want . . .' Rainey shrugged. 'Something different.' She let out a yawn that turned into a huge sigh.

'When we get home we'll see what offers have come in,' said Jo. 'You're tired, Rainey, we're all tired and going home to a funeral for people we loved makes everything seem worse . . .'

Bea was staring hard at Rainey. 'I will never stop wanting to sing,' she said.

Jo should have felt happy by the determination in Bea's words. Instead she shivered. It felt like someone had just walked over her grave.

Chapter Six

Jo stood looking through the window of the solicitor's waiting room. Despite the sticky tape that criss-crossed the pane, put there to stop it shattering, she had an unhampered view of the opposite side of the street.

She felt as if she had been waiting for Blackie for hours. She could hear the faint click-clacking of a typewriter coming from somewhere in the thickly carpeted building. She glanced at the space where her empty cup had been and now regretted refusing the offer of a second cup of tea from the spikey secretary. She was also beginning to wish she had done as Blackie had asked and accompanied him into the solicitor's office to hear Madame's will being read.

The exposed skeleton of the house opposite had a metal bedstead hanging precariously over the edge of what remained of a bedroom floor. Pink roses climbed the strips of wallpaper blowing in the light wind. She felt as if she was intruding on the householder's privacy. Jo wondered if anyone had been in that bed when it was bombed by the Luftwaffe last night. She knew it had happened last night because the secretary had apologized for it and for the mess outside the offices as if it was her fault. Of course, any bodies would have been removed by the evening's rescue units. The proximity of death disturbed Jo, yet again.

Yesterday at Portsmouth's Kingston cemetery the remains of Madame and Henry had been buried together. The *News* had been present, taking photographs for posterity as the many notable people had arrived. Even now Jo was surprised by the resilience of Blackie, who had managed to hold himself together as each and every one of the mourners had shaken his hand. Later, refreshments and drinks had been provided by a favourite restaurant of Madame's near the King's Theatre.

Jo turned away from the window and the scene of destruction that had been someone's home, just as the heavy oak door was opened by the dark-suited solicitor. Blackie was shown back into the waiting room. Jo looked at Blackie expectantly. He appeared dazed.

'Have no hesitation in contacting me should you have a need.' The man was now shaking Blackie's hand. He smiled at Jo just as the dour secretary arrived to show them out onto Palmerston Road.

It wasn't until Jo was sat in the car beside Blackie that she asked in a small voice, 'Well?'

'I wish you'd been in there with me, Jo.' He put his hand over her fingers and squeezed. 'Madame left me everything, her business, her money.' He paused. 'I'm a wealthy man, Jo, an extremely wealthy man!'

Jo gasped, she wasn't sure what reply was necessary but before she had a chance to say anything he continued. 'The bomb completely destroyed the studio where they were working on a new Summer Show for the King's Theatre. I've asked that the land the studio stood on be sold, I couldn't bear to go on owning it knowing it was where their lives ended. The house in Southsea I'll keep and go on living there. Luckily Madame held much of the business correspondence at the house and also here with her solicitor. If it had been left at the studio and it had gone up in smoke there really would have been a terrible mess to sort out. I never realized Madame and Henry's true wealth, not that it ever came up, and nor did I know how many artists depended on her for their jobs.' Then he said softly, 'However, I'm now in a position to offer you marriage.'

Blackie, without letting go of her hand, twisted towards her. 'Jo, I love you. Will you do me the honour of becoming my wife?'

Jo felt her heart lurch heavenwards. Her whole world was changing. She looked into his ghost eyes and said, 'Of course. It's what I want more than anything! But we need to honour Madame by carrying on with her business. It was her and Henry's life's work. We'll work together, if you'll allow it, and marry after a short period of mourning.'

She got no further for his lips were upon hers and his arms were holding her tightly. Jo gave a silent prayer of thanks to Madame and Henry for their generosity and enthusiastically returned Blackie's kiss.

Chapter Seven

Charlie held Rainey against his naked chest between the white sheets in the dingy first-floor room above the Central Café. Every time either of them moved the bed creaked. Branches from the hawthorn tree growing in the backyard swept against the windowpane, its white mayflowers cheerfully ignoring the grey day.

'I won't always be living like this, my love,' he said. 'Young Eddie's got his men rebuilding my premises. Thank God it was my flat that the blast completely destroyed and no one was killed in the shop below.' He propped himself up on one elbow. 'I've told Eddie if there's more pressing work, and I'm sure there is, he's to get on with it. Bert's looking after me here just fine. And I've enough money put by to buy somewhere out of town if you'd rather. You've only to say the word and we'll get married.' He was dismayed to see a frown cross her face and pressed on. 'I know what you're worrying about. We'll do it together, tell your mother and Blackie about the baby and that we want to be wed.' She didn't reply, so he asked, 'That is what you want, isn't it?'

He watched Rainey splay her fingers over her stomach. There was as yet no outward sign of his child but he had little knowledge of the mechanics of the early months of pregnancy beyond Rainey's morning sickness. His heart contracted with pride and love for this beautiful woman who, incomprehensibly as it seemed, loved him.

Her hand came up and stroked his cheek. 'More than anything I want us to be together but that won't stop Mum and Blackie having a fit. Bea and Ivy are going to say I've let them all down.'

He moved so he was looking down at her. God how he loved this woman! 'I'm aware that all you've ever wanted since you were a kid has been to sing. So I feel like I'm stealing your hard-earned success away from you.'

'It took two of us to make this,' she said, as again her hand went to her stomach. 'I wanted you as much as you wanted me.'

'I know, my darling but . . .'

'But nothing,' She put her fingers across his mouth to stem his words. 'You do realize how happy I am, don't you?'

He kissed her fingers. He knew he was not going to be popular with Blackie. They were about to heap more problems onto a grieving man who already had more than enough to worry about. One thing he was sure of was that he would look after Rainey and the child he'd fathered until his dying day.

'Thank you, Bert, for allowing us to meet here.' Blackie sat on the edge of a Formica table. He'd taken off his jacket and it lay on a chair beside him.

'Think nothing of it, mate.' Bert said, wiping his freshly washed hands down his clean blue and white striped apron. He switched off the wireless on the shelf behind the counter and Bing Crosby stopped crooning. 'It's easier for everyone to meet here and I don't mind shutting up shop a bit earlier. I'm happy to help you, Blackie. When you got a business to look after it ain't always easy to trot about all over the place . . .'

Blackie knew he'd better interrupt his friend before he got on to the subject of walking sticks or King Tutankhamun, as he was quite likely to do.

'Thanks, Bert,' he said again, and stood up from the table to address everyone.

Ivy sat with Bea at a table in the centre of the room.

Maud, Bea's mother, stood at the counter where she'd been in conversation with Della. In the corner, snuggled tightly together, were Rainey and Charlie. Bert now stood with his hand proprietorially on Della's shoulder. Jo sat on the chair next to the one containing Blackie's jacket. The blackout curtains were drawn and the electric bulbs, minus the benefit of shades, gave a stark light.

Blackie could hear the patter of rain upon the big windows. After a spell of clear, dry, early June weather it would be welcomed by the gardeners, he thought. Quickly he brought his thoughts back to the people in the room.

'I'd first like to thank you for coming to Madame Nellie Walker's funeral. She and Henry were seldom apart before they died and it will be good to think they'll stay together . . .' He felt himself getting maudlin so he took a deep breath and changed tack. 'I expect word has got around that I've inherited Madame's considerable business.'

Bert clapped his big hands together and encouraged everyone else to show their appreciation of the man standing before them. Blackie waved a hand to silence him. What he had to say was hard enough without his friends giving him undeserved credit. Blackie gave a small throat-clearing cough.

'I didn't realize until going through Madame's books just

how many actors, singers . . . well . . .' Another small cough erupted. 'How many people she and Henry looked after; how many people depended on her for a living . . .' His eyes fell on Jo and he seemed to gain strength from her steady gaze. 'Jo and I have discussed this and so that no artists find themselves out of work . . .' He put out a hand and pulled Jo to her feet. Then, with his arm around her waist, he smiled again, first into her eyes then at his friends. 'I need to obtain new premises, possibly in Portsmouth, and work there full-time. The Bluebirds will tour, though not necessarily with ENSA, and I have also secured some very lucrative stage work for you.' Another pause. 'But I won't be able to accompany you like I did before.'

Blackie waited, thinking questions might be thrown at him, but as none came, he continued. 'I think the Bluebirds are ready to fly, to leave their nest. Jo will always be there for you. If necessary, she will chaperone but I don't feel that's needed now.'

Bert must have sensed his discomfort for he set to clapping his big, meaty hands together once more and that elicited a few more handclaps from his audience.

'And finally, to Jo and myself!' Blackie held up a hand to quell Bert's insistent handclapping. He began to speak and then the words poured from him like a tap being turned on.

'I've loved Jo from the moment I set eyes on her. She's stuck by my side through thick and thin.' He glanced at Rainey. 'And as we've talked things over with Rainey, who is happy for me to make an honest woman of her mother,' he paused, 'I've asked Jo to marry me and she's agreed!'

'Wonderful!' Ivy shouted. Her one word seemed to open the floodgate of congratulations so that everyone began talking and wishing them both well.

Blackie quelled the noise again. 'We've decided to wait six months before arranging our wedding, to give us time to get fully up to speed in the running of the business. We think Madame would have approved of our decision to look after the business first.' He looked at Jo and smiled. 'And naturally, when we do set a date, you're all invited!'

Cheers began again but quietened as Blackie added, 'I've tried to persuade Jo to come and live with me but she says that's not the way things are done. As soon as there's a ring on her finger, though . . .'

Bert began to chuckle, and it turned into a big throaty laugh that set people giggling. Blackie could feel the room full of goodwill directed towards him and Jo. He searched their smiling faces. Everyone seemed happy at the news he'd imparted. Everybody except for Rainey, who was frowning as she sat quietly whispering to Charlie, who looked as if he'd lost ten bob and found a penny. She'd seemed happy, no, more than happy – excited – when he'd spoken previously of his and Jo's proposed marriage. Surely she hadn't changed her mind? Then Rainey stood up. As her voice was heard the room went silent.

'So, you're in negotiations for the Bluebirds to tour again?'

Charlie was trying to pull Rainey back to sitting but she, determined to be heard, looked as if she was having none of it.

Why, oh, why did Blackie suddenly have the awful feeling his world was about to come tumbling down? Surely the three girls would be happy about his news of a tour?

'It's not finalized yet but I'm making plans for you to tour America in the show *Yokel Boy*!'

There was a breath-taking silence then clapping and whistling began. Blackie knew the girls were familiar with the hit song, 'Don't Sit Under The Apple Tree', that the Andrews Sisters and Glenn Miller had made famous and that it had come from the stage show of *Yokel Boy*.

'I thought that it would be the icing on the cake for you because that song is based on "Anywhere The Bluebird Goes".' He paused. 'You know, your Bluebird song, the folk tune you sang that made me decide you could be famous . . .'

He got no further for Rainey had pulled Charlie up

to stand beside her. One of the wooden chairs made a screeching noise as it slid across the floor.

'We have some news too,' Rainey said, brushing her auburn hair defiantly away from her face. She took a deep breath. 'Charlie and I are also getting married. Our baby is due at the end of December.'

Blackie's mouth fell open.

He looked down at Jo. The room was eerily quiet. Every bit of colour had leached from Jo's face.

'Not like this, Rainey my love,' Charlie whispered.

Rainey could hear the pain in his voice. Why oh why had she blurted out their secret in this awful way? Was it anger because the fantastic American tour, a pinnacle to their success as The Bluebirds, would either go ahead without her or more likely have to be cancelled because theatregoers would expect three girls on stage not two? There was no way she could travel to America, appear on Broadway, while heavily pregnant, was there? This could mean Bea and Ivy would miss out on the chance of a lifetime all because of her and her coming baby. Blackie had worked so hard to make the Bluebirds a success and because of her it was all going down the drain! The expression on her mother's face was one of absolute anguish. In that moment, Rainey knew Jo didn't deserve to find out about her pregnancy in this way. They'd been so close, shared so much together. Rainey's head felt like bursting because she'd hurt Jo. She should have confided in her, of course she should. Keeping her secret to herself, waiting only to tell Charlie had screwed her up inside until thoughtlessly, cruelly, she'd allowed herself to act totally out of character and blurt everything out in this crowded room.

Rainey fell back onto her chair, glad of Charlie's closeness. Would her mother or any of her dearest friends in this room ever forgive her for her outburst and its outcome?

Chapter Eight

'Jo, come back!'

Blackie wasn't quick enough to stop her. Her chair clattered over as it fell to the lino and Jo was out of the café in seconds. As the door slammed behind her, he grabbed his coat and followed her.

A dreadful silence now filled the room. Bea stood up and moved towards Rainey and Charlie. She saw Ivy, immobile, a strange and thoughtful look on her face. Rainey was now sitting back on her chair, her face hard, her green eyes glittering with tears.

Bea had suddenly become filled with a rage she couldn't contain.

'You selfish cow!' Bea spat out the words. 'Do you know what Blackie's trying to do for us? He's trying to make us worldwide stars! Do you know where being on the stage in America could lead for us?' Rainey jerked her head back as Bea put her face close to hers. Bea didn't wait for an answer. 'The sky's the limit over there! We could go into pictures!' Spittle flew from her mouth and landed on Rainey's cheek. Rainey's eyes were now wide open. For a split second Bea thought she saw fear sweep across Rainey's face but at that moment Charlie put an arm in front of Rainey to protect her and said calmly, 'Let me handle this, Bea . . .'

He got no further as Bea yelled, 'You're just as selfish as she is! For years we've dreamed of making something of ourselves and just when it's all possible you want to break us up . . .'

'I'm sorry you feel this way,' he said, 'you've every right but it's what Rainey and I want that matters to us . . .'

'*You* want! All Rainey's ever dreamed of is being able to sing . . .'

Rainey suddenly found her voice. 'Listen to me, Bea. More than being on a stage singing, I want Charlie. I want a family . . .'

Bea jabbed a finger at her. 'Love is blind, you stupid woman! You're blind!' She lunged forward and Charlie thrust out his arm, holding her away so she couldn't reach Rainey. Bea shouted into his face, 'You're trouble Charlie Smith!

That was Rainey's mother storming out and it's obvious she knew nothing about this! Do you know how hurtful to her that is?'

For a single second there was utter silence as Bea glared at Rainey, then she whirled on her high heels and pushed herself between the tables and chairs. Her footsteps clattered on the bare wood up the stairs. She opened one of the doors to a room reserved for overnight guests, banging it back against the wall.

'I think we all need a cup of tea,' Bert's loud voice came from below.

Bea hurled herself onto the bed and gave way to her tears. It was all over, it was all over. It was over.

Her dreams of escaping Gosport and being somebody had been shot down in flames because that stupid couple downstairs didn't care about anyone except themselves. Her tears came thick and fast. She'd never forgive Rainey, never.

After a while Bea sat up and stared around the sparsely furnished room. She'd not bothered to put the light on. The darkness was comforting. Rain hit against the glass and ran down the windowpanes in rivulets. The gnawing ache of unhappiness ate at her insides.

It was over, it was over. It was all over.

No one would want to engage two Bluebirds when there

should be three of them. Three Bluebirds was what the public wanted.

She slipped from the bed, closed the door and went and stood with her head pressed against the cold glass of the window and allowed the noise of the rain to soothe her.

The rage had left her. She felt like one of Monday's washed sheets squeezed through the wringer, leaving every bone in her body flat and weakened. Outside, the storm raged; the ghostly sound of the wind whistling around the tall, old building looking for ways to slide inside and cause even more havoc.

She had loved Rainey like a sister and Rainey had betrayed her, taking away her chance of stardom. Rainey couldn't appear on stage with her pregnancy proudly blooming. That wasn't what the public wanted to see. They paid their money to see desirable young women in glamorous dresses promising dreams to their audiences.

Bea kicked off her shoes, went to the bed and pulled back the counterpane. She climbed inside, breathing deeply of the sun-dried sheets and pillowcases, and cried herself to sleep. It was all over.

Chapter Nine

'Didn't your mother ever tell you the quickest way to catch pneumonia is to sit in the wind and rain on a wet seat without a coat?'

Blackie pulled his jacket from his shoulders and draped it around Jo's body. Then he sat down beside her on the wooden bench at the Ferry Gardens and slipped an arm around her shoulders, drawing her into him. A ferry boat was leaving the jetty bound for Portsmouth. The wind chased away the sound of waves but he could see the wash foaming behind the squat vessel as it left the pontoon.

He looked at her at the exact moment she turned her head towards him.

'I didn't know anything about it,' she said. 'She didn't confide in me. I thought Rainey and I were close.'

'It can all be sorted out,' Blackie said, sounding more

confident than he felt. At this moment he had absolutely no idea how Rainey could carry a baby and sing on stage, supposing she even wanted to go on being a Bluebird. Pregnant stars mostly kept out of the limelight so as not to offend the delicate senses of their enthusiastic admirers. Agents were paid vast sums of money to keep the public from finding out their favourite singers and stars were only human. 'I'm sure Rainey never meant to hurt you. This love for Charlie is overwhelming and new. It means everything to her . . .'

'How can you be so calm?' Jo's voice shrieked above the wind. 'My daughter is pregnant and she kept it from me. I can't stop her marrying even if I wanted to. She's over the age of consent. She'll destroy everything Bea and Ivy have worked so hard to achieve . . .'

Blackie had never witnessed Jo in such a state. She was the calm one, always the rock, the glue that managed to hold the five of them together. He thought of how she'd supported him upon hearing of the deaths of Madame and Henry. He didn't want to see her like this, yet in truth he had no idea what he could do to lessen her pain except be there for the woman he loved. He had to pretend he could fix things and then just possibly some idea would come to him.

Blackie cuddled her slight body into him so that her cries were muffled. He allowed her to sob for a few more moments, watching as the hard rain dripped and soaked into the material of his coat wrapped about her. Then he gently pushed her away, looked at her wet face and said, 'You've pulled me back from the brink. You're the reason I've now got the strength to sort this out . . .'

'I'm her mum and she didn't tell me . . . I can't trust Rainey . . .'

'Stop it. At this moment she's probably feeling as hurt as you. Jo, if you don't stand by her, who the hell will?'

He'd finally got through to her. Jo was frowning but she was looking at him and listening.

'Trust me,' he said, his voice softer now. 'I can sort out their careers. But we have to return to Bert's and you need to talk calmly to Rainey and Charlie.'

Her green eyes were wide open, staring into his. The rain beat a tattoo on the wooden seat. Tenderly Blackie used a finger to push back a sodden rat's tail of hair from her forehead.

Jo said, after a while, her eyes holding his, 'All right, I trust you.'

Blackie breathed a huge sigh of relief. 'Good, my darling. Nothing lasts forever; we'll simply take a step backwards, before we move on.' He wished he felt as confident as his words sounded.

*

Immediately Bea heard the door handle move she was awake.

'Come on, drink this, you'll feel better if you do.' Maud pushed open the door and came inside carrying a mug of steaming tea, which she set on the bedside table next to Bea. Then she sat herself down on the edge of the bed, which protested loudly. 'About time Bert invested in some new mattresses,' Maud sighed. 'Mind you, there's probably not a brand new mattress in the whole of Gosport . . .'

'Have you come to have a go at me, Mum, or talk about mattresses?'

Maud looked washed out but the smile she gave Bea was genuine.

Bea sighed. Her mother had brought in with her the smell of bacon frying. Bea realized she was hungry. She sat up and reached for the mug of tea. After taking a large mouthful and swallowing it, she said, 'I wasn't very nice, was I?'

Maud shook her head. 'I told everyone you were worn out after working in the sun and heat abroad. They're all aware of the dangers you girls have faced but it doesn't excuse your deplorable behaviour! Screaming at Rainey, especially with her being pregnant an' all . . .' She paused. 'Still. They all know how highly strung you are . . .'

'Mum, don't make excuses for me because I got up the

pole about Rainey and Charlie splitting up the Bluebirds.' Bea put her mug back on the table with a thump.

'You don't know that that will happen . . .' Maud covered Bea's hand with her own. Bea felt the soothing warmth of her mother's touch. But she pulled her hand away – she needed to make it clear to her mother just how upset she was.

'Blackie said he could get us work in America, but Rainey won't be able to cope with a baby and go on travelling. I don't think Charlie will want her to be away from him, or the baby, for long periods. Everything now will hinge on Rainey and the baby . . .' Bea had to swallow back tears that had risen.

'That's to be expected, you wouldn't want anything to happen to her or the little one, would you?'

Bea shook her head. 'Of course not. But . . .'

'But nothing, Bea!' Maud stared at her. 'You know what I think? I think there's a bit of jealousy going on because you've not experienced what it is to love someone.' Bea was about to say something but Maud hushed her words. 'I think you've forgotten how them two girls stood by you when you allowed yourself to be mauled over by that sailor in the yard of the Fox public house. You might have ended up in the family way because of that.' Maud gave a huge sigh that seemed to move her whole body. 'Look Bea, deep in my heart I know you only want what's best for Rainey and Ivy. But sometimes, just sometimes, what you wants for them isn't what they wants for themselves.' A smaller sigh followed before she added: 'Now, you sort your face out and come downstairs and act like you're pleased for Rainey.' Maud turned towards the door to leave.

Bea grabbed at her dress, pulling her back. 'Suppose Rainey won't accept my apology?'

Maud freed herself. 'You won't know until you come down and find out, will you?'

Bea heard her mother's footsteps clatter down the stairs.

'Blood's thicker than water, I always says,' said Bert to Ivy, who was idly flicking through an old copy of *Woman's Weekly*. He could tell by the way she turned the pages, deep in her own thoughts, that the magazine held no interest for her. So far Ivy hadn't made her thoughts known about the proposed tour, Rainey's pregnancy or the row that had followed. But that was Ivy, Bert thought, she was a deep one. He glanced at her again; he knew Ivy would say her piece when she was ready. With a fork he held the bacon above the frying pan and shook it gently, allowing the fat to drip back before he placed it onto a plate piled high with rashers. Della was buttering bread that had been cut by Ivy, and Blackie and Charlie were talking. Rainey was sitting next to Charlie.

Jo put down the towel she'd been drying her hair with and fiddled with Della's silky dressing gown that wouldn't stay belted about her body. Della had insisted upon their return to the café that Jo change into something dry. Blackie had divested himself of his sodden jacket and waistcoat and sat with his shirtsleeves rolled high on his muscular arms. Bert had wanted to lend him some dry clothing but Blackie had kindly refused.

'That wind's not going to drop. I think you'd all better stop here for what's left of the night,' Bert said. 'There's plenty of beds upstairs and if the weather changes and the Jerries come over, we can all go into the cellar. When Maud and Bea come down, I'll get Maud to phone Eddie and tell him where she and Bea are.'

He saw Jo had made her way to the empty chair next to Rainey and sat down. They weren't touching or looking at each other. It seemed to Bert that mother and daughter were enclosed in a bubble of icy silence. He hoped the closeness of the two would soon cause a thaw. He put the dish piled high with bacon on the hot plate to keep warm, left the cooking area and edged towards Rainey and Jo. Bert wouldn't have said he was eavesdropping, he just wanted to know everything was going to be all right between mother and daughter. As he neared the table next to theirs with the old biscuit tin ready to receive the overflowing ashtray of dog-ends and a cloth to wipe the table down, he heard Rainey say softly, 'I'm sorry Mum. I wanted Charlie to be the first to know about the baby. I didn't mean to keep anything from you.'

She paused and he could see Jo watching her protectively. 'It happened in Burma. It was the only time we were alone. I couldn't believe I could fall for a baby so quickly . . .' Jo tried to pull her daughter into her arms but Rainey held back. 'It was a mistake but now I want this baby so much and so does Charlie, but the girls are going to hate me for spoiling everything between us for the future . . .'

This time Jo did manage to pull Rainey into her arms. Bert heard her muffled sobs and instead of moving over to empty the ashtray on their table, he turned his back on them. He'd heard enough. Mother and daughter were reconciled and that was one worry out of the way. Back behind the counter he smiled at Della and emptied the cigarette rubbish into the waste bin. That was the good thing about mothers, they could usually forgive their kids anything. Rainey wasn't the first young woman to get wed with a baby on the way and she certainly wouldn't be the last. He had every faith in Blackie as well. Bert knew he wouldn't let the Bluebirds break up, not after they'd all worked so hard to get this far. Poor bugger, he thought, he'd not had it easy recently, and things were going to get worse before they got better, they usually did. But if anyone could fall into a cesspit and come up with a rose gripped between his teeth, it was Blackie; and with Jo beside him he could work miracles.

He looked at the tower of bacon sandwiches and kissed Della's cheek proudly. Bert laughed as her face reddened with pleasure. Perhaps he ought to think about putting his and Della's relationship on a more permanent footing. Then again, maybe two marriages in the future was enough at present.

The sound of a chair scraping the lino made him look up. Ivy was moving towards Rainey and Jo. Blackie was now shaking hands with Charlie; Bert couldn't hear the words they were exchanging but he could tell there was no animosity there, thank God for that, he thought. Ivy was saying something to Rainey. Jo got up from the chair next to Rainey and beckoned Ivy to take her place. Ivy had gone over to comfort Rainey. Just like Ivy that was, another regular little peacemaker. He realized Ivy wasn't frowning and she spoke little. It looked like she was keeping her thoughts, whatever they were about all that had happened, to herself. He glanced again at the pair of them and saw that Ivy's hand covered Rainey's. Surely it was going to be all right?

He poured boiling water into the big brown pot. Afterwards he reached up to the shelf and switched on the wireless. A crackling sound told him the station he liked best had stopped transmitting. He fiddled with the other knob and eventually found some dance music. A bit of music always calmed people down, he thought, that and something to eat. Yes, there was always something very comforting about fresh bacon sandwiches, he thought. Even the smell of them made people feel better. Bert put his hand on Della's shoulder.

'Della, love, go and shout up the stairs for Bea and Maud will you; it's about time all this silliness was put to bed. An' these sarnies need eating . . .'

Chapter Ten

The siren woke Bea. For a moment she struggled to remember where she was and why she'd gone to bed in her petticoat.

'Are we never to get any peace?' Her mother's voice was muffled by the bedclothes. Bea's memory returned. The row with Rainey, the look of displeasure from Charlie. Bea had the feeling that he hadn't really accepted her apology last night. Her thoughts were interrupted by Maud sitting up in the double bed, shaking her by the shoulder and saying, 'C'mon love, let's get downstairs with the others to the cellar.'

Within seconds Bea had hastily thrown on some clothes and grabbed both her mother's and her own handbag and gas masks and was opening the door ready to join Ivy who had her hand raised in readiness to knock.

'Good, you're both up,' said Ivy.

'I hope Bert's making a cuppa,' said Maud behind Bea, pulling on a cardigan.

'Don't worry, he keeps a primus stove down there and supplies,' Ivy said. She caught hold of Bea's arm and pulled her back from the stairway allowing Maud to go down first. 'You all right?'

Bea stared at her. 'Apart from feeling extremely stupid about my outburst?'

'Don't worry about it. I spoke to the pair of them, Rainey and Charlie, last night and both are ashamed they let their feelings for each other get the better of them.'

'It doesn't excuse me for my own selfishness in having a go at Rainey because we'll probably miss out on America and making our way to the very top.'

'We don't all want that, Bea.'

Ivy's words were said quietly. Bea halted, one hand on the banister rail, the other still holding the handbags and gas masks. She faced Ivy.

'What d'you mean by that?'

The reality of Ivy's words hit her.

'What do you mean by that?' she repeated. Her hand left the banister and gripped Ivy's arm.

'Ouch! Your nails are digging in . . .' Bea didn't let go.

'Ivy! What are you saying?'

Ivy looked Bea straight in the eyes. 'I want someone to love me the way Charlie loves Rainey.'

'You silly cow, you already got someone, my bleedin' brother!'

The noise of the engines had grown louder as planes drew closer. Bea heard a muffled bang. She breathed a sigh of relief. That bomb had definitely not landed in the town. Suddenly the nearby anti-aircraft guns opened fire with their loud rat-at-tat-tat reply, retaliating against the plane's bomb release.

'This war has made me realize life's too short to go without love,' Ivy said. 'I want a break from the everlasting living out of suitcases on the road from theatre to theatre.'

Bea clapped her hands over her ears as bombs began to fall; huge crashing sounds that caused the old building to shake. She dragged Ivy down the remaining stairs and with her shoulder pushed open the cellar door and both of them stumbled down the steps. The café walls shook once more and flakes of whitewash and dust fell about them.

'Bloody hell, that one's close!' said Della. 'Thank God you're both here.' She'd not bothered to dress but simply wrapped a silky black full-length gown about herself that had some kind of feathers around the neck. Bea noticed some of the feathers were no more than quills and that the gown, which had once upon a time been quite glamorous, was now mended in places. 'There's a single bed you can share over there,' she said, pointing to an iron bed covered with a candlewick spread.

Ivy was already climbing across the covers to make room for Bea. Bea's head was spinning with everything that was going on. Not just with the air raid that could annihilate them all at any moment but by Ivy's words. She wanted a break – a break? What on earth did Ivy mean by that? Did she really mean she wanted a break from appearing on stage?

The cellar was damp, mould practically covering one wall. Books, their pages swollen with moisture, bulged on a shelf fixed haphazardly to the wall. A paraffin stove gave off a smelly warmth and a thin light. There were no windows in the cellar, which Bert also used as a store. Several beds complete with pillows and blankets filled the room. Across another wall were stacks of boxes. Cutlery, mugs, and crockery had obviously resided there for years, without being opened, though mouse droppings at the ragged edges showed that at least something had got inside.

'I swear to you we constantly change the bedding,' said Della. She gave a small smile of apology for the state of the large room. Her dark curls bounced around her pretty face.

'Are we safe in here?' asked Charlie. He had his arm protectively about Rainey's shoulders.

'Probably not if it's a direct hit,' said Bert, busily lighting another primus stove. 'But safer than anywhere else outside and you'll be a lot better off down here than in the room you're renting off me.' He automatically ducked his head as an explosion rocked the wooden rafters above.

Bea guessed Bert being busy with a primus and a pan full of water meant he was making tea. Her panic suddenly subsided. Blackie and Jo were fully dressed, curled together on top of a single bed. Both had their eyes closed as though resigned to anything that might happen. Maud was now helping Della dust detritus from mugs and placing them on the table in the centre of the room.

Bea thought about Ivy's words. She wanted a break, she had said. Bea hoped that meant she would finally put Eddie out of his misery and confess that she cared about him. Bea's daft lump of a brother loved Ivy more than the silly girl could ever guess. Gracie needed a mother, not just her grandmother standing in for one. Would Ivy now step up to the mark?

And what of herself?

Was the fame and fortune she'd craved going to be denied her?

Next to her on the bed, Ivy gave a gentle sigh. Bea smiled – so like Ivy to fall asleep when bombs were raining down. Bea put her arm around Ivy's still form and leaned her head against Ivy's dark hair. She could smell the Amami shampoo Bert got off one of his customers in exchange for black-market butter.

Neither Ivy nor Rainey were impressionable girls any longer. They were young women who because of the war had had to grow up fast. All of them had money being deposited regularly in their bank accounts from record royalties and each had a tidy sum saved. She remembered what her mother had said to her last night. If Bea wanted to aim for the top, she had to do it under her own steam. Well, if necessary, she'd do exactly that!

She took a deep breath of Ivy's scented hair and sighed. Ivy surprised her by wriggling around and facing her. Bea's heart thumped wildly. She'd thought Ivy was asleep. She couldn't read Ivy's expression.

'What's happened to Rainey has made me take stock of things,' Ivy whispered.

Bea let out a deep breath. 'So, now you're going to say your piece, are you? Have you decided to have a go at me because I told Rainey just what I thought of her?'

Ivy frowned and shook her head. 'I understand how you

feel.' She paused. 'I also feel quite jealous of the love that Charlie and Rainey share. Four years ago we wanted so badly to sing on the stage. We worked hard and made that possible and I do love singing sultry numbers, but will that be all I'll ever do? Our careers need all of our time, all of our strength to get to the very top. And there's no room for anything else . . .' Bea could see the glisten of tears in her eyes.

'A career is what you want above all else, Bea, isn't it?'

Bea nodded at Ivy's words.

'I thought it was all I ever wanted,' said Ivy. 'I thought I had plenty of time to do everything I wanted in life. This war has opened my eyes, with its senseless death and destruction and its way of choosing an ending for us whether we want it or not. Rainey falling for Charlie and bringing a baby, a little piece of both of them, into this uncertain time has made me realize that if I want something more than singing my heart out, I too, need to think and take a chance before it's too late and that decision is taken away from me.'

Bea was about to speak but Ivy hadn't finished. 'I love your brother. I'm sure he loves me. We've been writing to each other but it's not what he writes on the paper, it's what he says between the lines. I also realize that like a lot of men he hasn't got the courage to come right out and say what's in his heart. He needs a push in the right direction and I can't do that if I'm hundreds of miles away from him.'

'So you'd give up show business for Eddie?'

'There's no reason to think it would come to that. What I want is Eddie and little Gracie and I mean to get what I want.'

Chapter Eleven

'I'm glad you stayed at the café last night. I got a real jolt of fear when that explosion's blast reached this place and caused damage. I honestly thought ol' Adolf was easing up on us. Number twenty-two copped the bomb full on,' said Eddie. 'What's broken windows, a few dislodged roof slates and a shattered fence compared to coming home from the Criterion picture house to find your home gone?' Eddie knocked another nail in the wood then shook the fence to make sure it was secure enough. He swept his blond hair back from where it had fallen over his forehead. 'The main thing is the Denbys are safe and no one got hurt. They were fortunate that relatives have taken them in.'

Maud, hanging out nappies on the washing line, said, 'It was a George Formby picture they saw, wasn't it?'

'What's that got to do with anything, Mum?' Eddie turned to her.

She stared at him. 'Well, you could say George saved the day again, didn't he?'

Eddie shook his head and gave her a funny look. 'It was night, Mum, it happened at night!' Still he had to admit Maud was quick off the mark there with George Formby always causing chaos in his pictures then ending up by sorting everything out and being the hero. Maud never meant any harm by her gentle light-hearted look at last night's tragedy. Everyone knew if you didn't keep up a sense of humour in this Godforsaken war it would drive you mad.

'Bugger!' Maud seldom swore. 'I forgot to wipe the line after all the dust and grime in the air. Now I got black lines on the terry nappies.'

'I don't suppose Gracie will kick up a fuss!'

Maud smiled at him. Earlier he'd listened avidly as his mother told him about the happenings in the café last night. He'd not said much, though, it wasn't his way.

When all was said and done, Rainey had made her choice. She might not have wanted to bring a baby into the world as it was now, with Hitler trying to rule everyone, but she and Charlie loved each other and there was no doubt they'd make smashing parents.

Babies bring their love with them, he firmly believed that. Look how Gracie had enriched his life. He couldn't imagine her not being with him now.

Rainey had talent. Being a mother and a wife wouldn't take that talent away, would it? Why couldn't she have everything? Surely there would come a time when if she wanted to sing again, she could?

Bea was different. She was driven with ambition to be the best. She'd allow no one to get in her way.

He let out a big sigh. Maud was checking Gracie was still asleep in her pram. He'd put the hood up and left the pram in the shade but the end of June was warm. He saw Maud replace the piece of curtain netting he'd fixed in place to stop that ginger tom from up the road having a crafty sleep in the pram.

His mother had said Ivy seemed happy enough that the Bluebirds would take a bit of time out. Well, they needed a break, didn't they? A rest would do them all no end of good. And if Ivy wasn't gallivanting all over the place he'd really like it if they could spend some time together. He wondered how she'd react if he told her he loved her and wanted to look after her? He'd never ever want her to do anything she didn't want to, though. He loved Ivy so much, all he wanted was her happiness.

*

Bea walked with Rainey and Ivy past the Dockyard gates, eager to find Blackie's new premises in Queen Street. In spite of the constant bombing of Portsmouth and Gosport, Blackie had been extremely lucky to purchase both a small warehouse and the tall Georgian house opposite that had so far escaped Hitler's ministrations. Even more luckily for him, with paint and building materials being in such short supply, both premises had needed little more than elbow grease to get them clean and habitable. Being near the ferry and the Harbour train station meant easy access for clients and the street backed on to the beach. Not that much of the sea or beaches along the foreshore were accessible. Barbed wire now kept the public away and building work was changing the face of the shoreline. There were no mudlarks, children diving for pennies thrown by people into the dark muck. Sometimes, just sometimes, the kids came up victorious with a coin clutched in their fingers. Bea could smell the mud stank of decay.

South Parade Pier had been closed to the public. Bea remembered when the Bluebirds had sung their hearts out in the revues performed there. A stab of sadness made her realize everything was changing, both in her life and about her.

Forces vehicles often lined roads near the beaches in Portsmouth, Gosport, Stokes Bay and surrounding areas.

'Do you know what all this is about?' Bea asked Rainey staring at the men working near the shoreline. 'It looks like landing stages are being built.'

'Nobody seems to know what's going on. It's all very secretive,' Rainey said. 'I thought you were asking why Blackie wants to see us.' Rainey was wearing her favourite grey slacks and a short-sleeved fluffy pink jumper. There was now a tiny roundness about her stomach, Bea noted.

'Well, that as well. It's all right for you two, doing what you want and taking things easy but I'm fed up . . .' Bea had on her favourite black high heels and a shoulder-padded dress patterned with tiny flowers. She knew she looked good and that men were taking second glances at her. She quite liked it that they sometimes whistled at her as she walked by, but she was always thinking *you can look but you can't touch*.

'I wonder what Blackie's new premises are like,' Ivy asked, interrupting Bea's thoughts. 'At least we can get here easy enough; it's only across the ferry from Bert's café. Jo's with Blackie almost constantly now; has she said anything to you about how the business is going, Rainey?'

Rainey shook her head. 'Not really, except they've had to make changes. Some of the acts have broken up, some of the actors have joined the services . . .'

Weeks had passed and there'd been no further information

about America, the show *Yokel Boy* or work being offered to the Bluebird girls. Bea had enjoyed the break but she missed being in the limelight. Ivy had taken to spending more time than ever with Gracie and Maud, only so she could be there when Eddie came home from work. She'd begun dressing for ease and the comfort to roll around on the floor playing with Gracie. Bea loved to see how Gracie happily clung to Ivy and thrust out her arms to be picked up whenever she saw her. Today Ivy wore a tweed-style flared skirt and a square-shouldered blouse from which washing definitely hadn't removed baby-sick stains from one shoulder. Bea was beginning to find it hard to remember how beautiful Ivy had looked in the magnificent frocks that Madame had provided for her, frocks that now hung in a spare cupboard in Jo's house in Albert Street. It seemed to her that instead of being three girls with one thought in their heads, that of stardom, Rainey and Ivy, in such a short while, had turned their backs on a life that Bea desired more than anything. She quickly dismissed those thoughts and looked about her.

This side of the ferry was even more battle-scarred than the Gosport side. Like in Gosport, brick dust covered buildings and the smell of cordite hung in the air. Bricks and rubble were piled within the bomb sites between pubs and shops. A woman came out and shook a coir mat, glared at them and went back inside the doorway of the Admiral Nelson pub. As the door slammed, Bea said, 'I suppose she thinks that makes the place a bit cleaner for the customers.'

Rainey said, 'It's called keeping up appearances.'

Bea allowed her eyes to scan Queen Street. As in Gosport, every other building down the long High Street was a pub.

'There it is!' Bea pointed to a tall terraced house with long thin windows. The front door was shiny black. 'Looks like it could have been newly painted. Where's the hall for the acts to practise?'

'Across the road.' Ivy had stopped and was staring at a building on the opposite corner.

Like the house, the warehouse's large doors were shiny black. Bea said, 'I think we should ring the house bell.' She'd noticed a large businesslike brass button on the wall by the entrance.

Just then a sash window clattered up and a voice shouted, 'Yoo-hoo! I'll be down directly!' Jo's face beamed at them. The window slid down again. The girls waited outside the door for Jo to reappear.

Bea said to Rainey, 'I hope it's just us your mother greets like that!'

'Bless her,' Ivy said. 'She's been waiting for us to arrive, hasn't she? She wants to show us how well they're doing working together and how they've smartened up the place.'

Jo's smile was a mile wide as she opened the door and urged the three young women inside. 'Welcome to the premises of Blackie Wilson and Associates,' she said, proudly stepping aside so they could enter and she could close the door. Framed pictures of Blackie's clients adorned the walls. He'd brought in some of the photographs of the established stars whose signed photos had decorated the walls of Madame's house in Southsea.

'It's got a lovely calm feel to it,' Bea said, looking beyond the wide hallway to carpeted stairs that curved upwards.

Jo said, 'Yes, it has. It's a long, thin house, quite roomy, ideal for Blackie's needs, except there's not enough space for a band plus singers or acts with quite a few people in them to practise here. So Blackie's rigged up the hall across the road with microphones, a proper stage and seating so that's where he can assess the acts' worth . . .' She paused. 'Eddie's been able to help with reclaimed stuff from bombed properties. It's been nice to see so much of him now that he and you,' she winked at Ivy, 'spend time together.'

Rainey and Ivy began talking at once and Jo said she'd

give them a proper guided tour later. A door opened off the passage and Blackie stood there smiling at them.

'Welcome,' he said. Bea thought he looked tired. That possibly a few more lines hovered around his beautiful odd-coloured eyes. He ushered them into a large room where a log fire burned brightly.

As if reading her thoughts Blackie said, 'I know it's July and the weather is good but this place has been boarded up since the beginning of the war, when the owners left for the country, and we're trying to dispel the damp that's got in. Welcome to the waiting room.'

The carpeted room contained upholstered sofas and chairs. Bea noticed new copies of *The Stage* on a small table. The tall windows were framed with dark red velvet curtains which Ivy was touching, rubbing the material between her fingers.

'Nice,' she announced. 'Good quality.'

'They were already here,' Jo said. 'As was a great deal of the furniture. The previous owners were happy to include it in the sale. Everything's been cleaned but I still fancy I smell moisture in the air . . .'

'It'll soon go,' Ivy said. Blackie opened a further door and to what was obviously his office.

'Come along in,' he said, 'and sit down.'

This room was all varnish and dark wood, and Bea liked the feel of it straight away. Businesslike, she thought. A large desk separated a leather-covered chair one side of it from four high-backed chairs on the other. Bookshelves adorned one wall. The windows of this room were also graced by velvet curtains but this time no fire burned in the black grate that had a large mantelpiece above it, again adorned with actors' photographs. She stared. The central photo in a silver frame was of her, Rainey and Ivy taken quite a while ago, in their Air Force costumes. She remembered that day: it was before their travels, taken by Charlie in Bert's café. She swallowed away the lump that had mysteriously formed in her throat. Blackie exchanged a broad smile with her. Bea suddenly had the feeling that he, at least, was on her wavelength.

Bea thought she'd hurry along the proceedings. She wanted to know if there was work for her. She sat down on one of the chairs and crossed her legs, setting her handbag on the floor beside her. With the three girls and Jo sitting down, Blackie began talking.

'Thank you for coming. I'll be as brief as I can. You've all three, in the past couple of months, decided which paths you'd like to follow.' He paused and looked at his watch. 'Well, I hope you have,' he added. In front of him on the wide table was a pad, ink, and some handwritten notes on top of typewritten pages. Bea was about to speak but he waved her into silence by saying, 'Let me speak first, then I'll answer any questions you might have.' He took a breath. 'Bea, I'd also like you to stay behind when Rainey and Ivy leave.'

Bea frowned but Blackie was smiling at her so she didn't think it was anything worth worrying about.

'When I took you on none of you signed a contract. Therefore, legally you can opt out of being a Bluebird at any time. I trusted you, and you trusted me to do what I thought was best for you. However, you've all signed contracts with the record company, Parlophone, and with the British Broadcasting Company. You must uphold those contracts.'

A short silence followed. Bea saw Ivy press her lips to a thin line. Rainey sat immobile. Blackie suddenly smiled. 'There are three more records you must *all* make, and two broadcasts.' He got up from his comfortable chair and went round to stand in front of Rainey. 'I understand your condition and whilst I'm happy for you, those two con-tracts must be met, preferably before the baby's birth. I've arranged dates for the recordings which I hope will meet with your approval. The records will then be released at agreed dates after the birth of your baby. All right?' Rainey stared at Blackie. He was offering her an agreeable way out if only she would comply with his wishes. Rainey would be out of the limelight, have her baby, but still be heard on the wireless and she could go back to stage work if she so desired at a later date.

'Fine,' said Rainey, 'if that's agreeable with Ivy and Bea, I'd like to get it all over and done with well before my baby comes.'

Bea saw Ivy digest this news then nod. She opened her mouth to speak but Blackie continued. 'Both of you,' he nodded to Ivy and Rainey, 'want a break. I foresee you,' he looked towards Rainey, 'being out of the public eye for . . .' He paused and tapped his fingers on the wooden tabletop, 'maybe a year. That's a lot of time in show business. The fickle public might forget about you.' He looked at Ivy. 'When you all decide you'd like to return to the stage – if you do – I'll do my best to advertise and get you reinstated.' He looked at each of them in turn. Only Rainey and Ivy nodded.

'I'm not happy.' said Bea. Just then the doorbell rang sharply. Jo slid from the windowsill and went to open the outside door. 'I know who that is,' she said. As she passed Bea, the scent of lily of the valley wafted over her.

Bea said to Blackie, 'We all understand Rainey can't be on stage looking like a barrage balloon and Ivy wants time to think. But I don't. I want to be out there in front of an audience. What's happening about *Yokel Boy?*'

She heard sighs from Rainey and Ivy. Blackie stared at her before saying, '*Yokel Boy* has been put on hold. The war has caused problems with backers. They're businessmen, after all, and unwilling to commit . . .' He looked at his watch again. 'But I've something in mind for you, never fear.'

Blackie stood up. 'Rainey and Ivy, thank you for your cooperation. You must see that I've tried to work out what's best for all concerned while still giving you two the option to carry on working perhaps in the future. If that's what you want?' Both girls were nodding. Of course, it was what they wanted, thought Bea. Rainey would get married and have her baby, and Ivy already spent so much time with Eddie and Gracie at the house in Alma Street that sometimes Bea felt like an intruder there instead of a sister and daughter. Time off and getting paid for it, as money from royalties would be going into all their bank accounts, was a very good deal. But there was nothing in that for her, she thought angrily.

Blackie said, 'Could you two leave me alone with Bea, please? Jo will give you tea.'

Muttering to each other, Ivy and Rainey left Blackie's office. As the door opened and they filed out, Bea heard a male voice. Blackie's office door closed on them but Bea could still faintly hear voices coming from the waiting room.

Blackie was now looking out of the window with his hands clenched together behind his back. 'You're a different kettle of fish, Bea, and I'll get straight to the point.' He turned from the window and stared at her. 'Parlophone would like you to record for them.'

'So you've already said, we have a contract.'

'No. This is to be a different, new solo contract. They'd like you to record "Always In My Heart" under your own name of Bea Herron.'

Bea gasped. She put her hand over her mouth and stared at him. She couldn't believe what she was hearing. Her heart was thundering against her ribcage. Then she dropped her hand.

'You mean . . . A solo career?'

Blackie nodded.

Bea looked towards the closed door. 'But Ivy and Rainey?'

'They both have what they wanted. Some time off. You, on the other hand, want to work. I've had an idea that will put you in the spotlight, if you'll agree . . .'

Bea went to him and threw her arms about him. He smelled of lemon cologne, she thought. 'Anything, anything!'

'You need to be on stage in the public eye. You'll need to tour . . .' Bea could feel her excitement growing. 'I have a partner for you.'

Bea gasped. 'A partner? But I sing alone.'

'Yes, that's part of the deal. But you've always appeared on stage with Ivy and Rainey. The partner I have in mind for you has lost the very able actress he worked with. So rather than have two good acts doing nothing I've decided to put you together. You'll get to sing on stage. His act will incorporate new ideas, some never attempted before, that will have the audience spellbound. You'll bring the absolute glamour that has stopped him from becoming a top star . . .'

'Right,' said Bea. 'But you're saying I can't have a solo singing career without accepting your offer to work with this other artist?'

'You've got it in one, Bea. But, and here's the big but, you'll be headliners, the both of you. And I can promise you gowns that will knock the audience for six!' He stood looking at her. Bea knew he expected her to ask questions so she asked the only one she wanted an answer to, for both she and Blackie knew she would do anything to be top of the bill.

'Who do you want me to partner?' She held her breath.

'He's outside now. A well-established, good-looking star with a terrific new routine, and he's as ready to sign a contract as I'm sure you are, Bea . . .' Blackie went to the door to the waiting room, opened it and said, 'You can come inside now, Mel.'

Bea gripped the desktop to stop her legs from giving way as Melvin Hanratty entered the office.

Chapter Twelve

The sound of the waves slicing apart as the boat cut through the murky waters dividing Portsmouth from Gosport helped sooth Bea's troubled mind. Sitting on the wooden slatted seat in the sunshine had a calming effect that was exactly what she needed. A light wind ruffled her long hair. She should be happy, even delirious that she was going to be a top-liner in her own right. Yet happiness eluded her.

Of course, she'd recognized him straight away, Melvin Hanratty. He'd shaved off that thin moustache and looked even more handsome than before. She shivered in the late June sun, remembering she'd had little to say to him after the introductions had been made by Blackie.

'C'mon,' said Rainey, who sat next to her. 'Tell us what happened when Melvin went into Blackie's office.'

American destroyers were moored outside the dockyard

and tankers waiting in the channel of water made it more difficult for the squat vessel to weave its way to the Gosport pontoon.

Bea looked at her friend. Pregnancy suited her. Her face glowed and her hair shone and for a moment Bea allowed her anger to rise to the surface. She wouldn't be in this predicament of having to work with a man she couldn't stand if it wasn't for Rainey. The next second she felt ashamed of herself. Rainey had a perfect right to live her life the way she wanted, didn't she? And as for herself, she'd been given a chance most talented singers would kill for.

'Melvin has a new act and I'm to accompany him to top venues. The act will include me singing and Blackie's secured a separate deal with Parlophone for me to make solo records.'

Rainey stared at her for a moment then threw her arms around her. 'That's wonderful!' she said. 'I've been so worried knowing how this baby has put an end to us gadding about for a bit.' Rainey put her hands over her stomach as if to reassure the tiny baby within. Bea had noticed her doing this a lot lately.

'If I'm going to make it to the top like Vera Lynn, I want to do it on my own,' Bea said. 'But I'll be working in the public eye at the same time as my records will be heard on the wireless . . .'

'Why do I sense you have misgivings?' Ivy interrupted.

'Well, you know I can't stand Melvin,' Bea said. In truth, Bea was scared. Scared she was striking out without Ivy and Rainey. Scared she had to work with Melvin. Part of her wanted to beg her two friends to carry on singing as the Bluebirds. Tell them that somehow they'd surmount the difficulties Rainey's baby would no doubt bring, and also allow Ivy to spend some quality time with Eddie and Gracie. Alas, the time to suggest that was well past.

Bea knew she was extremely lucky that Blackie was willing to risk time and money on her. A solo singing career would be wonderful. But working with Melvin scared her to death. 'I mean it, he scares me,' she said to Rainey.

'That's all in your mind, Bea,' Rainey said. 'He's just a bloke, like any other bloke,' she picked up one of Bea's hands and squeezed it. 'You'll be working with Melvin, not marrying him!'

Bea nodded. She didn't want Rainey to know the depth of her dislike for the man because it was something she didn't understand herself. 'If I make a name for myself singing, I can always give up working with him,' she said. The idea took hold and she realized the truth in it. If her solo singing career took off, she'd be booked in her own right to sing to audiences and she wouldn't need Melvin and his act. Bea smiled at Rainey and squeezed her fingers in return. She wouldn't say anything else about not wanting to work with Melvin. Rainey felt bad enough about the split she'd caused in the Bluebirds; she didn't need to be reminded of it all the time.

'Well I think it's all worked out for the best,' said Ivy.

The boat bumped against the jetty and Bea watched as a rope was thrown by one of the deckhands to land over a bollard, ready to pull the ferry ashore. Soon they'd be walking up to the Ferry Gardens where summer flowers blossomed in the day's warmth. Ivy had said she thought it was great, the deal that had been offered to her. So why did Bea sense that that wasn't really what Ivy thought, at all? Ivy went on. 'Let's go and tell my mum and Bert what's going on. I don't know about you two, but I could do with another cup of tea.'

It didn't take long to walk up Mumby Road to the café and immediately Bea pushed open the door the noise of voices, the sound of the wireless, and the dance music coming from it, plus the smell of cigarette smoke and fat, engulfed her.

'Sit yourselves down and I'll be with you in a moment,'

said Bert. 'Della, pour our girls some tea.' Della looked up from the bread she was buttering and a big smile crept over her face. As soon as his customers had been served Bert came from behind the counter and stood at their table surveying them. Della put a tray of teas on the table. 'Well,' he asked, 'did the meeting go as you all wanted?' Bea never got a chance to speak for both Ivy and Rainey began telling him everything. After a while, she saw Bert was staring at her. Then he asked, 'Have you dates and venues for shows with your new partner?'

Ivy and Rainey went quiet.

Bea said, 'Blackie wants us to practise and perfect the new act but we do have a start date in September at the Portsmouth Coliseum. I can't believe such a lot has happened in a few months . . .'

'How are you getting there, to Portsmouth, love?' Bert frowned and looked concerned. 'The nights will be drawing in soon.'

'He said that's up to me. I can either hire a car to fetch me from Alma Street or go across the ferry. The Coliseum is fairly near to his offices. Blackie said I could sleep there if I didn't want to come back across the water in the dark but I'd be alone in that big cold place as he'd be returning to his house in Southsea. Blackie also said I could stay at his place in Southsea, but he couldn't guarantee he would be able to pick me up.' She shook her head. 'If Jo, who's about to marry him, can't mess up her reputation by living with him, I hardly think it right I go back to his house to sleep, do you?'

Bert nodded sagely, then asked, as he used a cloth to wipe a tea-stain from the Formica tabletop where a spill had fallen, 'And are you all able to get to London for the recordings at the BBC and Parlophone Records?'

'That's not a problem. Blackie needs to be there for those too, so he said he'd arrange transport for that.'

'Fair enough,' said Bert. 'You can't expect him to be at your beck and call now he's running his own business.'

'So it looks like things for you are turning out for the best, after all?' Della said, patting her dark curls. Bea saw the black look she gave her daughter. In that instant Bea realized Della wasn't particularly happy about Ivy putting her career on hold.

'I know,' said Bert, 'why don't you move out of Alma Street and come and stay here at the café? We're two minutes from the ferry so you won't need to either get a taxi or walk all the way home late at night. That would be all right, wouldn't it, Della, my love?'

Della grinned at Bea. 'It will certainly take away the worry of you getting home safely. I'll bet when I mention it to your mum she'll bite my hand off in gratitude!'

'You'd do that for me?' Bea looked at the two of them.

Bert put a meaty arm around Bea's shoulders. 'I don't like to think of you traipsing about in the dark,' he said. 'Of course, it'll all depend on how long you and that Melvin are appearing at Portsmouth. You might get sent further afield and then you'll go into digs, won't you?'

Bea nodded. To her it was beginning to sound as if there were a few more good possibilities for her and Melvin's theatre work together. 'That would be really nice,' she said, suddenly kissing Bert on his grizzled cheek. 'I think Mum will agree it'll be safer for me to live here what with the bombing and everything.'

Della laughed, 'You've made him blush,' she said. Bea stepped back and looked and sure enough the back of Bert's neck had turned scarlet and the colour was creeping over his face.

Ivy suddenly piped up. 'Maybe I'll be able to stay over at your house, Bea? Your bedroom'll be going spare and it would be nice to see more of Gracie and Eddie.'

'Does that mean you're hoping to hear wedding bells soon, Ivy?' Bert could never resist a quip. Ivy's face turned scarlet. She was just about to take a mouthful of tea and she spluttered it all down herself.

Bea began to laugh. Bert with a straight face said, 'Nothing would please me and Della more than to see you married to Eddie, Ivy love.'

Chapter Thirteen

Melvin slammed the door to his room in the cheap lodging house and fell onto the unwashed and unmade bed. He reached for the bottle of gin he'd persuaded the barmaid of the Rose and Crown to sell him. He grimaced as he swallowed a mouthful neat. It wasn't what he usually drank, but beggars couldn't be choosers. Anyway, he thought, gin did the trick, didn't it?

He stared around the room. Thin curtains that didn't meet in the middle hung at the window. A single wardrobe held his everyday wear and the expensive suits he used for stage work. His top hat and tails were hung inside a large bag to keep the dust off them. A small sink, the tap corroded by hard water, a mirror hanging above the sink from string, no chair. Yes, it was definitely time to climb back up the ladder of success. He'd let himself go since he'd returned from Africa. He took another mouthful of gin.

Yes, gin did the trick and he did the tricks!

Thank Christ he'd managed to persuade Blackie to give him a new contract. The authorities would soon be knocking at his door, or writing him letters when they found him, asking him to enlist, and he didn't want that. So far he'd escaped that net by working with ENSA. The promise of more touring would get them off his back again. He smiled, thinking how delightful it would be travelling with the delectable Bea.

Blackie was aware he'd not worked since returning from Libya. Mel knew Blackie was nobody's fool but the man only had hearsay to account for what might have happened that night in the desert.

Margo, or to use her real name, Sue, had been seeing a stupid airman. She'd omitted to tell him she was also sleeping with Melvin. The poor idiot must have really cared about her for on that last evening Melvin only had time to zip up his trousers before the first punch landed. He'd fought back, of course he had, all the while thinking why the hell was he bothering over a tart like Sue.

Earlier that night he'd been sitting out on the dunes, minding his own business, after crawling beneath the unguarded fence. He'd been thinking about the new act when a very drunk Sue, in an ugly mood because of a row with the airman, tracked him down and started giving him the old come-on. Why she couldn't wait until later and simply wander into his tent as she usually did he never had fathomed. He'd guessed that Sue, filled with drink, had wanted to prove to herself she could make any man want her. Being offered it on a plate? He would have been stupid to have turned it down, so he hadn't. Enter angry airman boyfriend.

Sue had tried to intervene. Somehow she'd received a punch from him that had felled her. That stopped the fight straight away. The silly cow lay there and it was the airman who noticed the blood first; leaking from the back of her head in the moonlight, red all over the yellow sand.

'She's dead!' the airman said. She'd struck the edge of a cemented-in fence post with such force that she had snuffed it.

Mel saw his career finished, him swinging from the noose when her body was discovered. The stupid airman had been crying, blubbering like a baby as they dug with their hands a hole deep enough to hide her body from prying eyes and desert predators who might dig her up again.

At one time Mel had had to slap the bloke to knock some sense into him. 'You're trained to kill. What's the bloody matter with you?'

The man had whimpered, 'She wasn't much more than a kid.'

After a while the bloke had quietened and seen sense. The plan was that before the ENSA truck rolled out in the morning to go on to the next camp, Mel would pretend to go looking for Sue. The airman was to say nothing, beyond that she'd stormed off after their stupid argument earlier in the bar. He'd be in the clear because there were witnesses to that part of the story. As it turned out, the stupid airman never got a chance say anything to anyone, for, at some point during what remained of the night, the blasted love-sick fool had run off into the desert.

That was the truth.

The lie was that people thought Sue had run off with the airman. Mel soon found, though, that his act didn't work without her. His card tricks were brilliant but the glamour was missing. He'd had to return to England.

In the dead of night he wondered about the airman. Had he died in the desert? Perhaps, unable to reconcile himself to Sue's demise, he'd taken a pistol and shot himself. Who knew? Who cared? Not Mel. As for Sue, she wasn't worth thinking about.

His worry was money. His savings were almost non-existent now. Horses were his downfall, and drink. But he knew he was strong enough to stop both when he wanted, if he wanted. And he'd eventually pay the blasted bookie.

He'd already proved himself by devising the new act, quite different from the memory game. A 'surprise' meeting with Blackie in a Portsmouth pub that Mel had cunningly engineered had resulted in Blackie bemoaning the fate of his beloved Bluebirds. It had been Blackie who'd suggested, after a few well-aimed hints, that Bea could be Mel's ideal partner. Her rise to fame, briefly halted because of circumstances beyond her control, would take an upward swing with his new act. And who knows, perhaps in the future he might be able to melt the Ice Queen's heart.

Though Mel was back in Portsmouth he had no intention of looking for his brother or raking over any old coals from his past. His name had been on billboards in many cities and Markie had never bothered seeking him out.

'Bea and Mel, Beauty and Magic.' It had a nice ring to it. But first he had to clean up his own act. No more betting. Cut down on the drink. A meeting had been arranged in the near future for Bea and himself to show Blackie how they could and would conquer the theatre-goers.

He sat up on the bed, took an extra-large swig of gin straight from the bottle, then got up, went over to the small sink and tipped the rest of the booze away.

'Start as you mean to go on, Mel,' he told himself. Besides, there had only been a mouthful left in the bottle.

'I'll have you back living in this flat in next to no time,' Eddie ran his fingers over the polished slice of oak timber he'd salvaged from a bombed boatyard. It was now a focal point as the mantelpiece in the living accommodation over Charlie's refurbished shop in Stoke Road.

'You've done a smashing job,' said Charlie. 'I'll never be able to thank you enough.'

'Money, mate,' laughed Eddie, 'just pay the bill.' Charlie laughed with him this time.

'I'll write a cheque here and now.' Charlie fumbled in his inside jacket pocket for his chequebook and set it on the old table Eddie had been using as a repository for his paint pots, brushes and tools. He found his fountain pen in his top pocket and after unscrewing it, began to write.

'That's a good-looking pen,' said Eddie. 'Real silver, isn't it?' He'd never owned anything half as nice.

'Picked it up abroad,' said Charlie. 'I've not seen one like it in this country.'

'Well, don't you leave it lying around, you might find it grows legs and walks.' Eddie grinned as Charlie wrote out the cheque. "I'll come back in a couple of days and put the finishing touches to the nursery.' Eddie looked towards the door of the small room Charlie had specified to be painted in soft neutral colours, if he could get hold of the paint.

Charlie handed him the completed cheque. Eddie looked at it, nodded amiably back at Charlie and after folding it, put it in his top pocket.

'I get fed up down Bert's at night,' Charlie said. 'Oh, it's different when Rainey's there with me, but Della won't allow her to stay overnight. She reckons the café isn't a knocking shop and she's not having customers think they can do what they want in Bert's place. Talk about locking the stable door when the horse has bolted, you'd think as Rainey's already pregnant, Della would bend the rules a bit, but no, no overnights for us. So I'll be more than happy to move in here and spend some time putting the finishing touches to this flat. You made a damn fine job of the shop below.' He screwed on the lid of the pen and replaced it in his top pocket.

'Fair enough,' said Eddie. In Charlie's position he'd feel the same. 'Second time you been bombed. So third time lucky, you'll never have to worry about a hit again. I hear your employees are ready to return to work?'

'Yes, for once everything seems to be going swimmingly,' Charlie said, running his fingers through his salt and pepper hair. 'Did I mention we've got a date for the wedding?'

Eddie shook his head. 'I've not heard a peep about this from the girls . . .'

'No, it's just got sorted today. Only a few months ago we were in Africa, now we're getting married. Eighth of July is the earliest I could get but it'll be a small affair, family only, a few bevvies afterwards. Rainey doesn't want people gossiping about the bump but I'm over the moon about everything. Mind you, I had to take the first date I could beg from the Registrar, people seem to be getting married left, right and centre. I suppose they want to be wed before the men go away to fight.'

'Congratulations, mate.' Eddie slapped him on the back.

Charlie looked sheepish at Eddie's show of affection. 'We'll have a big celebration when the baby's born, though. I don't mind telling you I'm ashamed at taking Rainey away from her big chance of fame.' He paused like he wanted to say something more but didn't know how to, so instead he said, 'Cary Grant is marrying that heiress Barbara Hutton on the same date, so if it's good enough for him, it's good enough for me.'

'How d'you know that? I thought their wedding was supposed to be a secret.'

'Like all secrets, it got out,' Charlie said with a smile. 'I read it in one of those film magazines Della buys.

They're calling Cary Grant's wedding at Lake Arrowhead in California "cash and Cary" because Barbara Hutton's got millions of pounds.' He began to laugh. 'I haven't got the looks of Cary Grant but I'm going to love my Rainey like no one's ever loved a woman before, and it'll last until the day I die.' Eddie liked Charlie – he wasn't afraid to say out loud how he felt about Rainey. It was refreshing because most men didn't want to share their feelings. He looked around the large room, he certainly wouldn't mind living in a place like this.

'Are you going to stay here in this flat for a while, then buy elsewhere, Charlie?'

'Rainey doesn't want to move away. No big house for her, she'd rather stay in Gosport, so we'll be making this our home. She's near her mum and friends here. She doesn't even want to go on a honeymoon for a few days. Says she'd rather come home to this flat. Just as well, really, as I need to get working again to earn money. Rainey says she's got money coming in but I don't want anything to do with money of hers. In fact, I've already seen a solicitor about leaving whatever I've got to Rainey and the little one.'

Blimey, thought Eddie, Charlie doesn't say much but when he does he runs like a tap! He was surprised by Charlie's next question, though.

'When you getting married?'

Eddie was staring at him. Finally, he took a deep breath and said, 'I'm scared to ask Ivy; I know she's already taking time out from the stage to spend with me and Gracie. I've tried telling her she should put herself and her career first because it makes me feel bad that if she's not in the public eye she'll soon be forgotten about.'

Charlie was moving about the living room, admiring Eddie's workmanship. Eddie thought Charlie hadn't been listening to him, so he was surprised when Charlie spoke again.

'How d'you think I felt when Rainey told me she was pregnant?' He ran his hand over the painted surface of the wall. 'Part of me was delirious with happiness, the rest of me hated myself for being the man who broke up the Bluebirds!'

'Rainey's always had a mind of her own,' said Eddie. 'If she wants something, she'll move heaven and earth to get it. She got what she wanted, being up there on a stage, now she wants you and a home. There's a bloody war on, mate, we could get killed any minute, so enjoy the fact that a beautiful woman wants you and your baby. You wouldn't stand in her way if she decided to eventually return to the stage, would you?'

'No, no, of course not.' Charlie smiled at him, then he said, 'Thanks for the advice, Eddie, I value it.' He took another look around the room. 'You've made a really good job of this place, I'm sure we'll be very happy here.' Then he faced Eddie. 'Dunno about you, but I fancy a drink after all this baring of souls. How about a pint in the Vine, Eddie, before you drive home and I toddle off back to Bert's?'

Chapter Fourteen

Bea sat on the bus staring at the rain running down the window. The air inside the double decker was warm, stank of cigarette smoke and was very damp because of the wet-clothed passengers. Sitting on the seat in front was her grandfather Solomon with Gertie tucked in by his side. Bea smiled indulgently at the pair of them. The move a couple of years ago from the family home in Alma Street to Lavinia Boarding House had done Solomon a power of good. He was never without someone to talk to or to play draughts with and he definitely had a twinkle in his eye when Gertie was around.

'Aren't you warm in that suit, Gert?' Bea asked. The suspiciously dark-haired elderly woman looked back at Bea. Her dangling jet earrings danced about as she allowed her painted lips to part in a smile.

'I always wears this black wool suit when I goes to see Helen Duncan. I figure if I looks the same she might possibly remember me.'

'I just wondered if you weren't a bit hot, it being summer?'

'July and a bloody downpour, good weather this is, eh? I should have put me raincoat over the top. You was very wise to wear your mackintosh.' Gertie laughed showing her small white false teeth. 'It should be a good night. Are you excited?'

Eddie, sitting on the seat opposite holding Ivy's hand, answered for Bea. 'My sister gets excited about anything . . .'

'Shut up, you! Better than always having my nose in a book like you!'

Solomon turned, looked across at Eddie and said, 'Why do you two always have to argue about everything? Two grown-ups acting like a couple of kids . . .'

'Sorry, Grandad,' said Eddie. His tongue-in-cheek look towards Bea told her he wasn't sorry at all.

'I hope you're not going to play up when we get to the hall at Copnor.'

'No, Grandad,' said Bea dutifully. Then she added, 'They say Helen Duncan's a witch!'

Gertie twisted round to face Bea, her eyes narrowed. Bea gave her a half smile. 'Sorry,' she said. 'I know you set great store by her.'

Gertie turned back again, staring resolutely ahead. Bea sighed. She hadn't meant to hurt Gertie. Gertie had, after all, lost her son who'd been in the navy and she followed Helen Duncan, going to as many séances and meetings as she could, hoping to hear news of her beloved boy. Bea knew Gertie didn't believe all the rubbish that had been in the newspapers about Helen Duncan being a fraud. After all, if the medium had known HMS *Barham* had sunk when no one else had heard a thing about it, Helen had to be in touch with the 'other side', didn't she?

Bea thought she should learn when to keep her mouth shut and her thoughts to herself. After all, Gertie had invited her to the evening out to Copnor to see the great woman in action. Gertie had told her she was fed up with Bea saying she wished she knew what was ahead for her now she was embarking on a solo singing career. Eddie had been invited because he had a van to pick everyone up and take them to the ferry to catch a boat to Portsmouth. Lately, except for work, where Eddie went, Ivy went too, their hands locked tightly together like they were frightened of losing each other. Bea sniffed, she knew she shouldn't tease Eddie but she couldn't help it. It was really quite sweet to see him being so obviously in love with Ivy. And Ivy? She was always looking at Eddie with those big brown cow eyes of hers. Bea was roused from her thoughts by Gertie.

'It's the next stop,' Gertie said, peering through the dirty and wet window of the bus. She turned to Bea. 'Usually she holds séances in the flat above the chemist's shop but due to popular demand she's meeting people in a nearby hall.' She held fast to Solomon's shoulder as she got up from her seat. The bus slowed and stopped to let people off. Bea was the last to step down from the vehicle and onto the pavement. She had a sinking feeling inside her stomach and wasn't looking forward to being out in the rain again.

When they reached the hall, there were plenty of people milling about and sheltering from the rain. There was a smell of incense in the room, a bit like the scent in church, she thought.

'We'll have to sit at the front,' said Ivy. 'I wonder why everyone's crowded at the back?'

'That's because if you're in the front row she might pick on you with a message and while people come hoping for exactly that, most people are also very shy,' said Gertie. She pushed Solomon ahead of her and he sat down and promptly allowed his legs to stretch out in front of him.

'Anyway, there's more leg room here,' Solomon said.

Bea was sandwiched between Eddie and Gertie. Gertie

had already eased off her tight shoes to allow her bunions to breathe. Bea saw Ivy was staring around the large room, her hand still clutching Eddie's. Heavy brown paper was taped over the windows that were set high in the walls, not that the electric light was that bright. Bare bulbs hung down, dimly illuminating the room that also housed row upon row of mismatched, occupied chairs. Bea suddenly realized they hadn't paid to enter the hall.

'We haven't paid to come in,' Bea whispered to Gertie.

'Another thing that proves Helen isn't a cheat,' she answered, squeezing Bea's hand. 'Helen says this isn't a business so she can't charge and things only happen if her spirit guide, Albert Stewart, a Scot who was sent to Australia many, many years ago, comes to talk to her . . .'

'Spirit guide?'

'Yes, he's a sort of channel for the dead.'

At that moment Bea felt a tickle of cold air brush across her face and she shivered. It was, she thought, almost as if someone had walked across her grave.

'You all right, love?' Gertie leaned forward and looked into Bea's face.

Bea nodded. 'Yes, I'm all right,' she answered.

Gertie started talking again. 'Sometimes, though, Helen has another spirit guide, a little girl called Peggy. She's very mischievous. Helen has to call her to order because she dances and sings . . .'

Bea felt her neck go cold. Why on earth had she wanted to come here tonight? Another thought struck her, 'Who pays for this hall, then?'

'Why, Helen of course. It's all free because she likes to pass on her gift to as many people as she can . . .'

'Surely she can't afford —'

Gertie interrupted her. 'What usually happens is that we all leave an offering in the big dish on the table outside the door on our way out. That helps Helen. She's so generous you know, wouldn't dream of making people pay.' Her explanation ended there as Solomon suddenly had a coughing fit.

'Oh, Grandad,' said Bea, foraging in her handbag, extracting a handkerchief and passing it across Gertie to him. Gertie immediately took another handkerchief from her sleeve and waited for his coughing attack to ease a little. Solomon coughed phlegm into Bea's clean white linen. When his rasping breathing had quietened, he leaned across Gertie and said in a tired, strangled voice, 'Thanks love. I won't offer to return the hanky . . .'

'No, Grandad,' she said with a sad smile. 'I certainly don't want it back!'

She watched him stuff the offending article in his pocket and take Gertie's clean one.

'Damned gas,' said Gertie. Solomon had been gassed during World War One. Since living at Lavinia House he'd been relatively free from bad turns. He also suffered from the effects of shell shock. Luckily, since Gertie had taken to being his companion, she knew how to care for him when a bad episode occurred.

There was a stage in front of them and curtains were pulled across at the back. Bea saw a movement behind the thick material. Rain was hammering on the roof and against the windows.

'Good thing it's wet,' Bea said. 'Hopefully the bad weather'll keep the German planes away.' She thought of the scene of destruction that had been their first sight of Portsmouth Hard tonight. There'd been gaps between the pubs lining the road near where the gates of the dockyard stood. Hitler had given the south of England a right old bashing, she thought. She sniffed; the hall now smelled of wet clothes and stale sweat. To Bea it seemed as if the air inside the room was thick with the heat of expectant bodies. Some of the dim lights then went out but it wasn't completely dark. Gertie squeezed her hand.

'She'll be out in a minute,' Gertie whispered.

The audience hushed. A woman parted the curtains at

the rear and stepped forward to the centre of the stage. Bea hadn't known what to expect but it certainly wasn't the dumpy middle-aged woman standing before them who began to speak.

'Thank you all for coming. My name is Helen Duncan and I am a spirit medium. As you can see, I'm no wonderful film star. But I am privileged to be the vessel through which, with the aid of my spirit guides, the dead choose to speak. I say choose because I can't summon your passed-over relatives. They have to want to speak to you through me. Sometimes they choose to stay quiet. I have no control over what may or may not happen . . .'

Bea could hear the Scottish burr in the woman's voice. She looked just like anyone's mum, thought Bea. Suddenly Helen's head fell forward onto her chest. There were gasps from the audience and fidgeting as Helen stood completely still. After about ten seconds, the woman raised her head and said in a clear voice:

'Thank you, Albert. Albert, my guide, has a woman at his side. She's doubled up in pain. She has grey hair. Her stomach . . .' She paused and put her hand to her ear as though trying to listen carefully. 'What's that Albert? Her name is Lily. Is it Lily or Laura? You're very faint, Albert. Can anyone take this?'

Suddenly a voice from the back of the hall shouted, 'It's my gran!'

There was movement as a young woman with bleached hair and very dark roots stood up and again shouted, excitedly. 'Laura, my gran!' Bea noticed the blonde was very thin, almost skeletal, and she was dressed in clothing that didn't fit her. Bea could see the woman's hands, clutching the back of the seat in front of her, were red and raw, her fingernails bitten. At her side were two hollow-eyed, skinny children.

'My gran died two months ago. She was caught by shrapnel as she tried to get to the air raid shelter. Our house went up in smoke . . .'

Helen held up her hand and the woman fell silent.

'A message for her blonde granddaughter? Is that what she's saying, Albert?' Helen looked at the young woman.

'Albert says she's sorry things are so difficult for you at the moment. But you're not to give up hope. You will rise above these bad times. Oh! Oh! Albert, you say Laura's fading . . . Yes, I know so many people want to speak to their loved ones, Albert . . .'

Helen put her hand across her forehead, then took it away and seemed to stare at the audience without seeing them. The silence was broken by the blonde saying, 'Thank you,

Helen, you don't know what my grandmother's words mean to me. I was ready to give up but now—'

Helen interrupted her by saying in an agitated voice, 'Albert, Albert, what are you on about? You have someone who wants to say thank you? A World War One soldier who died in France? His name is John, Joe, James, I can't hear you very well, Albert.' Helen shook her head and began walking down the couple of steps that led to the auditorium. She walked slowly along the first row and Bea's heart was beating fast as she stood in front of Solomon and said, 'Albert tells me the message is for you. Your name please?'

'Solomon,' he said, looking wary.

'Yes,' said Helen. 'This man is saying you tried to pull him to safety in France. Because of this you were gassed.' Her words stopped. She put her hand on Solomon's shoulder and said. 'Will you take this, Solomon?' Solomon looked as if he'd been slapped in the face. He opened his mouth to say something but nothing came out so he nodded his head. 'Albert says he thanks you for trying. Albert, Albert what have you got there? A dog, oh, a Golden Retriever?' Helen walked back onto the stage and asked, 'Who has lost a golden Retriever? Who will take this?'

'I will,' came two voices in unison.

'Albert's telling the dog to get down because he's excited, he's jumping up,' said Helen.

Bea twisted in her seat and saw two people had put up their hands. One a young man, said, 'My Mickey ran away when the bomb hit next door . . .'

'No, this is a Retriever who has passed, Albert says. He has a leather collar; an old dog with a grey muzzle?' The young man who had called out put down his hand and sat down. The second man, elderly, kept his arm in the air.

'I'd like to think it was my dog but my boy was too old to jump anywhere. He died in my arms . . .'

Bea could see the old man was near to tears.

Helen said, 'On the other side there is no pain. The dog has heard your voice and is trying to tell you in his own way he remembers you with fondest love . . .'

The old man stared at Helen then sat down and put his head in his hands and sobbed. A young woman sitting next to him put her arm around him. The old man looked up. 'He was my best mate, was my dog.' Bea saw him stare at Helen. 'Thank you,' he said quietly.

Helen shook her head. Then she looked down at her feet encased in their sturdy black shoes.

'I am only a channel,' she said, her voice full of humility. After a few seconds she began again, tossing out names that

Albert had come up with. Bea could feel the excitement in the hall. The soberness at the beginning of the evening had disappeared and now expectation was at a height with so many of the people claiming the names of the dead. So eager were they to be reunited with their loved ones.

Bea saw Eddie look at his watch. She sensed he was fed up. But he caught her eye and motioned her to look at Solomon who sat very still. His eyes were open but it was as if he was in a world of his own; he certainly wasn't watching or listening to what was going on about him in the hall. Bea wondered if he was still thinking about the message Helen had given him. Bea smiled back at Eddie and he tapped his watch. She looked at her own wrist-watch and saw they'd been sitting in the hall for an hour and a half. The time had simply flown by. Bea glanced at Ivy, then at Gertie, but both were totally involved in the goings on about them.

Bea didn't see Helen get down again from the stage but when the woman bent over her and said in a low voice, 'My dear, Albert is telling me there is an unhappy spirit wanting to get in touch with you,' Bea's heart began thumping inside her chest.

'Who?' she asked, her throat went suddenly dry. The smell of incense was much sharper now, she thought.

'A young woman with a name beginning with the letter M. No, Albert says it's an S.' Helen's forehead creased, then she continued, 'This woman hasn't been on the other side for long, and Albert says it's very important you do not . . .' Her voice faded, then came back loudly, 'Do not trust this man. His handsome face disguises a cold heart. I can't hear the name . . . Albert, don't go!'

Bea stared into Helen's face, her eyes were closed, her breath warm against Bea's cheek.

Bea was filled with a sudden fear. She gave a small cough then said, 'No! I don't know this person. No! No!'

But Helen had already stepped away from her and was standing fully upright in front of the stage steps. Bea stared. Helen blinked. Suddenly she looked as if she was emerging from a deep sleep. She stared at Bea and looked confused.

'What on earth am I doing off the stage?' she asked, and without giving Bea a chance to say another word, turned and climbed the couple of stairs back onto the stage, where she faced the audience.

Bea was shaking. Gertie lifted one of Bea's hands and rubbed it as though trying to get some warmth back into her. 'Alright, love?' she asked. Bea nodded. She knew she couldn't really tell anyone how she felt, which was scared stiff!

'I'm not quite sure what is happening now,' Helen said. 'Albert seems to have disappeared and I have the beginnings of an almighty headache.' She put her hand to her forehead and Bea saw she suddenly looked exactly what she was: a middle-aged frumpy woman.

Someone, a woman, called out from the audience. Helen turned to her.

'I'm sorry, I can't answer any questions. I speak through my guide and have no recollection of what's gone on in this hall tonight. I repeat, I am a mere vessel. I must go now. I'm very tired. Have a safe journey home everyone . . .'

And then the hall erupted with cheers, whistles and loud clapping as Helen Duncan walked to the back of the stage, slid open the centre curtain and stepped out of sight.

Bea, still shaking, looked along the line of chairs to where Ivy sat. Her face was a blank and told Bea nothing of what she felt.

People began to move around in the hall. The scrape of chairs sounded on the bare wooden floor. Voices were no longer hushed but loudly exclaiming about what had happened during the evening. Bea could see a man standing at the door shaking hands with people as they left.

'Who's that?' she asked Gertie. Even to herself her voice sounded shaky. The words Helen Duncan had spoken had upset her. But until she'd worked everything out in her head about what had happened on this very strange evening, she was determined not to let the others know how she felt.

'C'mon Solomon, time to get going,' said Gertie, helping Grandad to his feet. He was very quiet.

'You all right?' Eddie came over and offered him his arm.

'Bit shook up, Eddie, to tell the truth. No one, only I, knew what had happened that time in France.' Eddie stared at Bea. Bea not feeling right herself, shrugged apologetically.

It took a while, standing behind the crowd, to get out of the hall as everyone was delving into their pockets and purses to put money in the large earthenware bowl.

Bea ignored the bowl and walked on. She didn't see why she should voluntarily give money for something that had upset her. She turned her eyes away from the man who seemed, nevertheless, to stare right through her.

'I think that might be her old man,' said Gertie. 'Anyway, he always helps out.' She took a pound note from her handbag and put it in the bowl. Bea gasped at the amount.

Gertie said, 'That's from all of us. A very interesting evening, thank you, so much.' Bea knew Gertie was sad that Helen hadn't had a message from her son.

As Eddie passed the bowl he put in a handful of coins. The man nodded his head and gave a small smile.

'Goodnight,' he murmured.

Solomon said nothing. Unsteady on his feet, Bea held on to his arm as they walked from the hall towards the bus stop. It wasn't until they were sat below deck in the cabin of the ferry boat surrounded by cigarette smoke and smelly bodies that Solomon spoke again.

Chapter Fifteen

'I do think that woman is a witch!'

Solomon stared into Bea's eyes. They were fortunate to have found seats. It was standing room only for most of the passengers who were crushed together in the downstairs cabin. The rain and wind buffeted the small boat making it roll and heave in the sea. 'She had something to say to both of us, didn't she girl?'

'I'm taking no notice of her, Grandad. It's all a lot of eye-wash,' said Bea with a certainty she didn't feel.

'Well, no one but me has ever known the truth of how I got gassed. But that woman's words brought it all back to me, the shame of what I did.'

The noise in the cabin made it almost impossible for Bea to hear Solomon's voice. She knew there was little chance of them being overheard by anyone else so she moved closer so she could whisper in his ear.

'If you want to talk, Grandad . . .'

'Yes, I do!' He was angry now, Bea noticed. Solomon was a very private gentleman. If he felt anything at all about Helen Duncan's words he would be feeling as she did, as if somehow she had been stripped naked in public. Her Grandad grabbed hold of her hand and said, 'Bea, you're the one most like me in this family and I know you'll not speak about what I'm telling you, but if I don't get it off my conscience now, I never will. When I've finished talking I don't ever want to think or talk about it again.'

Bea snuggled against him on the wooden bench, her ear close to his mouth so she'd not miss a word.

'I was gassed by this Blue Cross stuff the Germans were shelling us with. It caused your eyes and throat to burn something terrible. Sickness? I never seen nor felt nothing like it.' He paused. 'But I'm getting ahead of meself. We were told to wear our respirators at all times. The Germans had the upper hand with their planes continually swooping over us at low heights, machine-gunning us and dropping canisters and flares to guide their artillery. We were told to withdraw to a place called Henin where the Germans had possession of a hill overlooking the place. Don't ask me why we was sent to Henin, it beggars belief. Like sending lambs to slaughter but we had to do as we were told.

'The shelling in the valley wasn't so bad at first but it lay under a haze of yellow gas. The valley was full of broken guns and dead gunners. It was like something out of a ghostly horror story, all deathly still one minute then it would begin again, gunfire and sharp bangs, and it looked horrible through our gas masks. When night fell there was little protection in the trench when the buggers came at us again. I saw men hurled into the air by a shell and fall like a splattered tomato back in the trench. There was a young lad next to me who was old beyond his years at what had already happened to him. He was trembling all over. His name was James and he'd signed up telling the authorities he was older than the fourteen years he really was. He said his brother had gone down at sea and he wanted to murder the bloody Huns what did it. Well, the Germans kept up their attack all night. They lost a lot of men as well. Everywhere we looked there was bloody broken bodies. The cries of them wounded is something I hear every night in my sleep.'

Bea saw his old eyes were filled with tears but she didn't say anything. She wanted him to carry on.

'Two wounded Germans were crawling towards our trench. Suddenly the young lad next to me gave a blood-curdling cry and climbed up and ran towards them, firing his weapon. He hadn't got but a few yards when he went down. The two Germans had already copped it from our boys. The lad was lying there. I could see he was still alive. He was about six feet away from me, his gas mask was off and I could hear him calling for his mum.

'I could hardly see my hand in front of my face through my mask, so I ripped it off and slithered over the top towards the lad. He was lying quite still, crying, when I wriggled up to him. One of his arms looked as if a dog had ripped it to pieces.

'You're all right, lad, I've got you,' I said. He looked at me so gratefully. Suddenly I began to cough, my throat felt like it was on fire. Then darkness swallowed me up.

'When I came to, lying on the ground, I was coughing up all manner of stuff. I could hardly breathe and there wasn't a bone in my body that didn't hurt. I dunno what was happening because I couldn't see. I thought I'd gone blind. I was told I was in a recovery tent. Then I remembered the boy. "James?" I managed to croak.

'Don't you worry about anyone else except yourself,' this voice said in English. I could just about make out a bloke bending over me. 'We're going to try to get you home.'

I said the boy's name again and that doctor looked at me, then shook his head. I knew then that if I'd obeyed orders and kept my gas mask on I might have been able to save that lad.' He paused. 'And meself. My lungs was on fire. You'll have heard Maud tell you what I was like when I came home to Blighty. The slightest noise had me cowering under the table, sweating like a pig. The only place I felt safe was the lavvy at the bottom of the garden because it was a small space. I was a nightmare for your mum and gran to look after. All that shell shock and them nightmares. And still they come.'

He wiped his hand across his eyes.

'I don't understand why you blame yourself Grandad,' she said. 'You were brave, you tried to save that lad . . .'

'I disobeyed orders and took off my gas mask, and now I'm paying for it,' he said. 'I should have listened to my betters. If I had I wouldn't be this husk of a bloke, would I? I might have saved James.' He paused, then he stared hard at her. 'I don't ever want you saying anything about this, Bea.'

'Wild horses wouldn't drag it from me,' she said.

'How d'you think that witch knew my secret?'

Bea shook her head. 'Maybe Helen Duncan was waiting to come on stage and looked through a slit in the curtain. She saw your coughing fit and put two and two together.

Half the men who survived the Great War suffer like you. It was a lucky guess, Grandad, nothing more. I bet you had one or two good men trying to keep you from harm. If they looked out for you, she'd be right in guessing you'd look out for someone too.'

He thought for a moment, 'Was what she said a lucky guess for you an' all?'

Bea shook her head. 'The silly woman told me not to trust someone. The warning is supposed to come from a woman with the name beginning M or an S. I've never heard anything so daft in all my life! She's no witch, she's a trickster, Grandad!' Bea said the words with force, but did she honestly believe them?

Just then Bea felt the bump of the ferry against the bollards lining Gosport's wooden jetty.

'Need a hand getting up, Grandad?' Eddie now stood next to Solomon so he could use him as a lever to pull himself upright.

'Thanks lad,' Solomon said. The cabin full of people began to move towards the stairs. Bea sighed as they made their way off the ferry boat, up the slippery wooden slope from the jetty towards the Ferry Gardens.

Eddie had left his van on the piece of waste ground opposite Bert's café.

Bea, in readiness for her daily excursions to and fro across the ferry to practise at Blackie's place and later the Coliseum was already installed at the café. Her room at Alma Street had quickly been taken over by Ivy. Bea wasn't looking forward to the questions about the evening that Bert and Della would ask as soon as they were inside. All she wanted to do was go to her room, to bed, and to think about the bombshell Helen Duncan had dropped on her. It was one thing to say to Grandad that she didn't believe a word of what the woman had said but in the darkness of her room she knew she would think very deeply about 'messages from the other side'. She also wanted to think about how best she could ease Solomon's conscience and perhaps put an end to him thinking he deserved all he'd received from the Great War. Bea knew Solomon would never speak to anyone else about his confession to her tonight. He'd said he never wanted to talk about it again. She hoped he'd remember she would always be there for him.

Ivy pushed open the door to the café and before long Bert and Della joined them all at a table with mugs of hot, dark tea to listen to Gertie and Eddie regale them with what had gone on in the hall at Copnor.

Inside it was warm and cosy. The incessant rain had kept customers away and now Bea could see Bert was itching to get rid of his friends. Bea asked, 'No Charlie or Rainey tonight?'

Della chipped in with, 'Oh, no, they're finishing off odds and ends at the flat. It's looking really lovely now. Are you all ready for the wedding, love?'

In only a few days Rainey would be married to the man she had given up her career for. Bea no longer felt angry about Rainey's decision that a home and family meant more to her than success on the stage. After all, it was what Rainey had wanted and the Bluebirds were still being heard on the wireless, thanks to previous Parlophone and BBC recordings. What Bea missed most of all was the camaraderie that had existed between the three of them.

Bea held open the door with the blackout curtain pulled around so Gertie, Solomon, Ivy and Eddie could make a run for it to Eddie's van. As Solomon squeezed by her he whispered, 'Nothing to fear from the dead, Bea, unless like me you allow them to haunt you.' He gave her a clumsy kiss on the cheek as he added, 'It's the living we have to worry about.'

Bea shouted her goodbyes into the rain then fastened the door.

'Slip the bolt across, love; we're not taking any more customers tonight.' Bert at her shoulder smelled comfortingly of soap and bacon fat. 'Now don't you run off up them stairs, me and Della's got something we want to say to you.' Della looked particularly glamorous tonight in a tight black skirt and frilled white blouse. She'd recently cut her dark hair and looked even more like Hedy Lamarr, especially in the café's dull light.

'Sit down for a while,' Della said as Bert moved away. 'Bert needs to get something upstairs.'

Bea pulled out a chair from beneath a table and sat down. The last thing she wanted was to stay up half the night chatting to Bert and Della, but she could hardly refuse their request while staying with them, could she? The wireless played dance music and for the first time that evening she began to relax.

In no time at all Bert was downstairs again.

He had what looked like a tiny umbrella in his hand. Her first thought was he might be going to talk to her about his collection of walking sticks, except what he held was too short for a cane.

'Bert and me have talked about this and it will make us feel easier if you agree . . .'

'Agree? To what?' Bert set the small umbrella in front of her on the table. It was about a quarter of the size of a normal brolly, thinner, had a curved handle, and seemed to be made of a black, satiny material. 'You want me to go out in the rain and try this out?' Bea went to touch the object.

She was startled when Della slapped her hand away and said, 'Easy!'

Bert laughed, showing his uneven white teeth. Then he said. 'Della doesn't want you to touch the wrong button by mistake.'

Bea frowned. She saw there were two large buttons close together on the handle near a twisted black cord designed, no doubt, to go around someone's wrist.

'It's very short for an umbrella. Does one of these buttons automatically open it out?' She looked at Bert questioningly.

'Why don't you press one?' Della had an impish smile on her blood-red lips.

With the cord around her wrist, Bea found she could easily hold on to the object, with her thumb within easy reach of both buttons. The small thing was extremely light.

'Go on,' said Della.

Bea squeezed the first button. The black cover shot away revealing itself to be a silk-covered metal sheath, which now hung from the handle. The metal casing concealed a thin knife. Its blade glittered in the light. If the cord hadn't been around Bea's wrist she would have dropped the vicious-looking thing.

'Oh!' the cry escaped her throat. Quickly she wriggled her wrist free from the cord and stared at the lethal weapon now lying on the Formica table.

To her horror Bert and Della were both trying hard to stifle their laughter!

'That's not funny,' she said crossly. 'That thing could do a great deal of damage!'

'That's exactly what it's designed to do.' Bert picked up the object and pressed the second button. Within seconds the sheath sprang back and the blade was concealed once more. 'There's a third button on the base of the handle that allows the silk on the sheath to billow out on tiny wires so it can be used as a little sunshade.' He smiled, 'No good in downpours like tonight, though.'

'It's for you!' said Della, and Bea felt her mouth drop open.

'You can't be serious?'

'He's serious all right, girl,' said Della. 'He picked it up in a box of odds and sods at an auction at Sloane Stanley hall. He's spent a long time cleaning it up. Bert's worried about you coming home from the Coliseum in the dark . . .'

Bert said, 'There'll be times when you'll have to walk alone in the blackout past Victoria Park and down Queen Street . . .'

'I'll get a taxi . . .'

'Not when there's a raid on, you won't, Bea. Taxis won't be running. You might not find a shelter. And if you don't get on the ferry in time you'll be stranded over the water.'

What Bert was saying certainly made sense to Bea. After all, everyone took cover when the bombs fell, except for the ferry boats. They always ran, but stopped at midnight. Bea glanced back at the object on the table. 'It looks just like a baby umbrella.'

Bert let out a belly laugh. 'Pick it up and press the other button this time.'

Della released her wrist so Bea did as she was told. Lo and behold the shade ballooned out. Bea laughed too. 'It's magic,' she said. 'And you thought of me when you saw this?' Her question was directed to Bert although it was Della who answered.

'You three girls are like our own kids,' she said.

'I don't want anything to happen to you,' Bert added. 'I know you think this is the best chance you have of appearing on stage again, and if that's what you want, I'd like to feel I've helped to make you safe. It's a dangerous world out there, love.'

'Thank you both for caring about me,' she said humbly.

Later, in bed, Bea thought about the peculiar gift Bert

had pressed on her. At first she had been appalled that he thought she could actually use such a terrifying thing on anybody. She didn't know whether it was against the law to carry concealed weapons but she'd known many chorus girls who hid sharp objects in their bags. Some even had police whistles, to ward off unwanted advances from men.

She picked up the slender umbrella from the table next to her bed. She slipped it over her wrist. Then she took it off again. She knew she could never actually hurt anyone. But the comfort having it with her when she walked alone through the dark streets would be immeasurable.

Chapter Sixteen

Rainey flopped down onto the sofa, sighed deeply and looked around her at the newly decorated flat. 'It's so lovely in here. I can't believe in a couple of days this is going to be my – our home.' She laughed as she corrected herself. She thought the Utility furniture that Charlie, with Bert's help, had managed to obtain gave it a sophisticated look. The whole place smelled of polish. It was only waiting for her to move in and put her final stamp all over it.

Her hands cupped her stomach. She was getting quite a little bulge there now and Charlie was so proud that he was to become a father. She thought of earlier this evening when he had driven to Albert Street and picked her up in his car. Upon leaving the house she had pulled a long shawl from the coat hook near the front door.

'Why not take a cardigan?' he'd asked. She was wearing

a beloved cotton dress with a sweetheart neckline. It was tight about her waist and she knew in a few weeks' time it definitely wouldn't fit her.

'If it gets chilly this will cover more of me,' she'd replied. He'd walked towards her, gently run his hand over her burgeoning stomach and said, 'Exactly. But I don't want you to hide my baby growing inside you. I want the whole of Gosport, no, the world, to know how proud I am to be your child's father.'

Rainey had looked at him then, wondering why she was allowed to have this much happiness. 'That would definitely set the gossips gossiping,' she'd replied.

If she'd had her way, she would have moved into the flat with him as soon as it had become habitable. But Jo, for respectability's sake, had begged her to stay at home until after they were married.

'You know what people are like in Gosport,' said her mother. 'With a little luck we can pretend the baby's premature but you'll be seen as a wanton hussy if you cohabit before a ring's on your finger. And don't forget to tell him you won't be seeing him the day before the wedding. That's bad luck, that is.'

So tomorrow Bea and Ivy would be visiting her at Albert Street to wish her happiness and also to help her decide whether she would wear make-up to the Register Office. She wanted to look as glamorous as possible for Charlie but she also thought it might be better to keep make-up to a minimum. She rather fancied the 'pure and chaste' look, except she wasn't either pure or chaste, was she?

'I'm glad we're not having a big wedding,' Rainey said. 'I know it's supposed to be the most special day of her life, a woman's wedding day, but I already have everything I've ever wanted to make me happy. I'm quite content to let Blackie and Mum push the boat out when they get married.' She hadn't even wanted a wedding dress, feeling it was a little hypocritical to wear white, but Charlie had magically produced a length of parachute silk from a 'friend' and Maud had run up a gorgeous two-piece costume on the sewing machine at Lavinia House.

Charlie sat down beside her on the sofa.

'A big wedding, a small wedding, all I care about is that we can be together. I hate it that I have to take you home. I promised your mother I'd make sure you're safely back at Albert Street before it gets dark; you're safer in the shelter there.' An Anderson shelter had been delivered to Charlie's photography shop and was in the process of being erected at the bottom of the long garden near his dark room. His priority had always been to marry Rainey and provide her with a home, even before reopening the shop. I'm taking the photographs myself. I can't trust anyone else to make a better job of capturing the woman I love in print. We'll be able to look at the photos in years to come and see our wedding day really was the happiest day of our lives.'

Charlie bent across and brushed his lips across her eyelids, little butterfly kisses that Rainey knew would lead to bigger, more serious kisses. Even the lemony smell of his cologne, if she wasn't already sitting down, would have made her faint with desire. She stood up and, taking him by his hand, led him towards the bedroom.

'If I'm not seeing you tomorrow I need to leave you something to remember me by until I meet you at the Register Office,' Rainey said. 'Then we can come back here as husband and wife and carry on where we left off tonight!'

Chapter Seventeen

'What did you think of Helen Duncan?'

Ivy opened her eyes to see Eddie standing by her bed with a cup of tea in his hand. It took her a second or two to gather her thoughts together. He'd obviously been thinking about their visit the other day to the medium. With his fair hair sticking up ridiculously at the crown like a schoolboy's, she could see he'd not been up long. The smell of his musky maleness wafted over her and made her heart beat faster.

'Good morning to you, too,' she said, wriggling to a sitting position. He put the tea on a chair next to her bed, then sat down on the counterpane beside her. He pulled his dressing gown over his knees to hide his worn pyjamas and then asked, 'Well?'

Ivy's thoughts sped back to last night when, very tired, she'd gone almost straight upstairs to bed. But first she'd visited the front room where Solomon used to sleep before he'd moved to Lavinia House, and which was now Eddie's room, and there taken a peep at Gracie in her cot. The little girl had kicked off her sheet and was lying frog-like, flat on her back. Her white cotton nightdress had risen above her chubby knees and Ivy had had to stop herself from leaning over and kissing those star-like hands in case she wakened her.

Now she could hear the wireless downstairs churning out happy dance music and she guessed Maud, too, was already up. She remembered Eddie's question and answered, 'I thought we'd exhausted that subject at Bert's. However, people will believe what they want to believe,' she said, reaching for the cup. 'Because of the war there are many wives and mothers with unanswered questions about their missing loved ones. I think if they can gain comfort from what she tells them, how can that be a bad thing?' Before Eddie had a chance to say anything she carried on. 'But a lot of the stuff that came out of her mouth could be perceived to be the truth by many of the people in that room. I wouldn't call her a fraud but what she said could apply to almost everyone or anyone.'

He looked thoughtful. 'She upset Grandad,' he said, running a hand through his wayward hair.

'Bea was talking to him on the boat coming home. She's good at sorting people out, probably because so many people have tried to sort her out.' Ivy didn't want to get into a detailed discussion about the merits of the spiritualist. She licked her lips. The tea was good and strong, just the way she liked it, not quite as good as Bert made it but Eddie was getting better at it. She also liked the way Eddie always brought her a cup of tea if he had time in the mornings. 'Anyway, maybe that woman helped Solomon come to terms with something that happened when he was in the services. He doesn't like to talk about the First World War, does he?'

'Nor would you, if you was invalided out with shell shock and had your lungs spoiled with poisonous gas.'

Ivy was well aware Eddie had witnessed far more of Solomon's awful episodes than she had. 'I agree but sometimes facing things is better than keeping them bottled up.' She took another swallow of tea.

'A bit like you realizing that it's not Gracie's fault she came into being by my one mistake?'

Ivy, wondering what had warranted this very probing question, allowed herself the luxury of the last swallow of tea before she answered. Eddie, seeing the cup was empty, took it from her and replaced it with a small clatter on its saucer.

'I knew as soon as I held Gracie in my arms that day down the café that I loved her and wanted to do the very best I could for her,' Ivy said. 'So put that in your pipe and smoke it.'

He was looking at her. 'Even though she's not your child?'

'I love her like she is mine . . .' Ivy paused. She knew what she was going to say next would either bind her and Eddie closer or split them worlds apart. 'You don't know how many times I've wished she belonged to me. I felt you had betrayed me by fathering a child by Sunshine.' She paused. 'Oh, I know you'd never actually put into words that you cared for me but I *always*,' she stressed the word, 'always thought you cared.'

It seemed to her to be forever that he stared deep into her eyes, into her soul even. He asked, 'Why did you jump at the chance to swap addresses with our Bea when Bert offered her a room at the café?'

'I thought that was pretty obvious . . .'

'Because of me?' he asked hesitantly.

'Not just you. Gracie as well.'

She could see he was thinking about her words. 'You do know I love you,' he said finally.

'And I've loved you since I was a kid.'

She gave him a shy smile.

'Perhaps that was the trouble. It's taken me a long time to realize you've grown up. I've always thought of you, like Bea, a kid. It's taken me a long time to get it into my thick head you're a woman with a mind of her own.'

She went to speak but he put a finger across her mouth, hushing her words.

'If I said all these weddings were giving me ideas, Ivy, what would you say?'

She moved his finger away and held on to his hand. 'Are you asking me, Eddie Herron, to be your wife?' Ivy's heart was now beating so fast she was sure he could hear it. She had waited forever to hear him suggest marriage to her.

'I suppose I am,' he said. A shy smile began to form on his lips.

'Ask me then?'

He gave a small strangled cough and when his voice had cleared he asked, 'Ivy Sparrow, will you marry me?'

Ivy looked at the large hand that she now held tightly. It was calloused and rough, but it was warm, strong and dependable. She knew now he loved her. She could feel he loved her. A few months ago she would have melted into his arms like ice cream on a hot day. But so much had happened in those last few months that had changed her life and the way she thought and felt about those changes.

'No,' Ivy said.

She gripped his hand lest he wrench it away. She needed to explain her answer, to make him understand how much she loved him and maybe then he would come around to her way of thinking. She saw the confusion in his eyes. She'd expected him to pull away from her, but it was not so; if anything she felt more pressure in his fingertips as he held on to her. In a very small voice, he said, 'Well!' Then he blew air out of his cheeks. 'Can I ask why your answer is a "no"?'

Just then Maud yelled up the stairs, 'Ain't either of you ever coming down?'

Ivy didn't answer but Eddie turned his face towards the door and as he did so his hand slid away from Ivy's. 'In a minute, Mum,' he shouted.

'I'll give Gracie her bath, then,' came back Maud's voice.

Ivy fully expected Eddie to leave her and go downstairs. Instead he looked at her, his eyes very bright. She had hurt him by her refusal and that was something she really hadn't intended to happen.

Her words came out awkwardly, in a rush. 'I'll live with you, though!'

'You already do,' he said swiftly.

'No, I'll live with you properly, like my mum and Bert live together.'

A frown passed across his forehead. 'I wouldn't ask you to do that! Whatever would people think? And why would you even suggest such a thing?'

Ivy took a deep breath. 'All my life I've wanted to sing. The Bluebirds gave me that chance. With Rainey marrying and expecting her baby, the Bluebirds will be out of the public eye for so long that we'll be forgotten. Oh, yes, the records will help, but the public can be fickle. Your Bea is the one with the guts not to let her dreams die. She's striking out on her own while she's got the chance.' Ivy paused. 'Ever since I first met you I've wanted you. Why can't I have both? You and a career?'

There was no expression on his face as he took in her words. For a long while Eddie was silent. So silent that from downstairs Ivy could hear Maud talking and chuckling as she bathed Gracie in her little enamel bath on the kitchen table.

'People in the public eye do get married, you know.' His voice was quiet.

'As Blackie's always said, not when they're just starting out. The public like to think stars could be accessible, available.' She frowned and looked at him beseechingly. 'Tell me you understand?'

'I do understand. But what about the gossip? Won't that damage your reputation, living in sin with a man?'

'I'm living with you now, Eddie Herron. There's no gossip, is there? Is it such a sin?'

'No, but that's because we're living together but we're not, you know . . .' Ivy saw a rosy glow begin to cover his neck and flow upwards to his face. '*Living together.*'

'So?' Ivy said. 'Are you going to be the one to go out in the street and shout it from the rooftops if we share a bed?'

Eddie, her tall, strong, blond man, looked suddenly petrified. The blush that had risen from his neck now furiously covered his face. Inwardly Ivy smiled. Of the three Bluebird girls she was considered the quiet, shy one. However, she fully realized that if you wanted something, you had to go after it.

Eddie shook his head. Then he found his voice. 'We're not the only two living here . . .' Ivy knew then she had got what she wanted and he was considering every word she'd spoken. Of course, one day she'd allow the love of her life to put a ring on her finger but for now she'd be a mum to Gracie, a wife to Eddie and get her career back on track.

'No, we're not the only ones living in this house. Downstairs is your mother who loves you and Gracie to bits. Do you not realize that when you're not around me and your mum talk about things, all sorts of things?'

She wanted to laugh as more confusion showed in his eyes. She also knew he'd be mortified if he ever found out it had been his mother who had come up with the idea. One day, she knew, they'd tell him, but for now the time just wasn't right.

Chapter Eighteen

Eddie was banging on the door next to the photographic shop. It was his job to make sure Charlie was ready for his big day tomorrow and he'd taken the day off work to do it. He stepped back and looked at the shop window and the shelves waiting for stock. Eddie thought he and his men had made a pretty good job of renovating both the shop and the flat what with the strict regulations on purchasing new goods. Reclaiming materials from bomb-damaged premises and obtaining fire-damaged stock meant he'd been able to finish this job in record time.

'Come on, mate,' he said, giving the door another thump.

'You looking for me?'

Eddie spun around at Charlie's words. 'No wonder you ain't answering the door if you're out here.' His face broke into a smile at all the flowers in Charlie's arms. 'Cor, what are you, Charlie Boy, a walking flower shop?'

'Put your hand in my top pocket and get the key out. If I try to do it, I'll drop this lot.'

Eddie slipped his fingers in Charlie's jacket pocket and pulled out the key.

'Don't you smell nice?' he said opening the door. 'I don't know if it's you or the blooms. Hang about, I'll take some of them off you.'

Once they were inside with the steps in front of them, Charlie said, 'Kick the door shut. I'm going to leave this lot here on the stairs until I decide where I'm going to put them.'

Eddie watched as he carefully bent forward and released the blooms onto the uncarpeted wooden steps. Inside, their heavy scent was cloying. 'Smells like a tart's boudoir in here,' Eddie said. He didn't know a lot about flowers, but he recognized lilies, geraniums, London Pride, roses, lily of the valley, wilting poppies and spays of mauve lilac. He didn't know what a tart's boudoir smelled like either but it seemed the right thing to say. 'Where did you get this lot, over the allotments?' Since the government had advised people to 'Dig for Victory', gardens were filled with vegetables. Flowers were an extravagance and expensive to buy.

'That's right,' said Charlie. 'I wanted to fill the place with flowers for when I bring my bride back tomorrow. So I've been over the allotments buying whatever I could.'

Eddie was quite overcome. He slapped his hand on Charlie's shoulder.

'Rainey's going to love that,' he said. He looked at the lilac dubiously. 'Not sure about this, though, mate.'

'What? What do you mean?' Charlie bent down and picked up a spray of the sweet-smelling, cone-shaped mauve flowers.

'We got a lilac bush at the bottom of the garden but Mum won't have it brought into the house, says it's unlucky!'

Charlie sniffed at the lilac's tiny star-shaped blossoms. 'Don't talk daft. That's old wives' tales, that is. How can anything so pretty be unlucky?' He shook his head. 'You'd believe anything, you would. I wouldn't mind betting you swallowed all that claptrap that Helen Duncan spouted the other night. Your Bea told Rainey that the woman made Solomon get up the pole. Then she wouldn't tell her what about . . .' He didn't finish but began walking up to the flat and Eddie followed him. At the top of the stairs he turned a key in the lock and he and Eddie walked into the newly furnished flat. 'I'll put the kettle on,' said Charlie.

'You've got it nice in here,' Eddie took a walk around the

large living room. It had been an empty place the last time he'd looked it over for any final bits and bobs that needed to be done. 'Yes, very comfortable. What else did our Bea say about Grandad?'

Eddie had a special relationship with his grandad and he prided himself on looking out for him; he even went up to Lavinia House and played draughts with him when he had a spare moment. Eddie had been a bit put out to see him and his sister talking for so long on the ferry, especially as he couldn't hear a word above the crowd chattering, the rain hitting the roof and the drone of the boat's engines. But although he'd asked Bea about their conversation on the boat, Bea's exact reply was to tap her nose and say, 'Mind your own beeswax!'

Eddie stood in the doorway to the kitchen watching Charlie fuss about with the kettle and waited for his reply.

Charlie lit the gas, turned to him and said, 'That was all she said, "Solomon got upset". Nothing else, you know what Bea's like, she keeps her mouth shut like a clam.' Eddie knew exactly what she was like. Charlie added, 'She's not round Albert Street today fussing about my bride, is she?'

'No, she's gone to Portsmouth. It's the first rehearsal with that bloke she's not keen on. I'll say something, though,

when our Bea puts her mind to it she can be a go-getter . . .'
He suddenly stopped speaking, realizing he was getting into
deep water talking about Bea; after all, the Bluebirds would
still be on stage if it wasn't for Rainey's pregnancy.

'Messed everything up, didn't I?'

Eddie looked at the five-foot-two bloke putting out mugs.
He didn't look like he could plant a seed in a flower pot,
let alone get a woman as gorgeous as Rainey Bird in the
family way.

He didn't answer, so Charlie added, 'Don't think I don't
feel bad about the girls splitting up. He turned and faced
Eddie. 'I hate myself and I blame myself.'

'Shut up, mate. Don't let's go there again.' Eddie wasn't
too happy talking about personal stuff. He suddenly remembered the flowers on the stairs and how this little man was
romantic enough to show his love for his beloved by putting
flowers everywhere for her to see when he brought her back
here after the wedding. Charlie was a good bloke, Eddie
thought, a really good bloke.

Eddie cleared his throat. 'You know why I'm here today,
don't you?'

Charlie said, 'To make sure I've got everything in hand
for tomorrow?' He poured the tea into the mugs, shoved
one on the small table in front of Eddie and foraged in his

trouser pocket, taking out his silver pen. Eddie noticed a scrap of paper with a list on it near Charlie's mug of tea.

'Still got that spiffing pen, then?'

Charlie handed it to him. 'You can put more ticks on my list if you want. But I'll have my pen back after. Tell you what,' he chuckled, 'I'll leave the bloody pen to you in my will, if you like!'

Eddie laughed as he read the long list. 'I'll just call out the most important items. Have you put out your best suit?'

Charlie nodded. Eddie put a tick on the paper.

'Ring?' Charlie nodded again. Another tick was added.

'Is there anything you haven't done in readiness for the big day?' Eddie asked.

'Actually, I'm right up to the mark. The only thing that's amiss is the General Post Office haven't been able to install a telephone yet, but that's all in hand. I've done all the menial jobs. And while old Hitler was pelting us with his bombs last night, I shined my shoes and put a love note under Rainey's pillow . . .'

'I don't need to know about that, you daft bloke!' Eddie stared at Charlie, took a mouthful of tea and said, 'Well there's something you didn't get done and that's get your hair cut.' He put a hand to his head and felt his own hair. 'I could do with a trim an' all.'

He drank down the rest of his tea and then passed the pen back to Charlie. 'You make a good cuppa,' he said. 'Why don't we bring them bloody flowers up and put them in the sink in some water, then go to Tommy's for a haircut? Then pop along to the Vine for a couple of pints? It's your last day as a free man and I promised to be back home early so Mum can get her hair done.'

'I think that's a good idea,' Charlie said. He went quiet. 'I really am sorry about messing things up,' he said.

'Aw! Shut up, you can buy the first pint,' Eddie said.

Coming back up the stairs with his arms full of flowers, Eddie thought that Rainey had done all right for herself with this funny little bloke with his camera shop and his loving ways. They'd make a good couple. Then he thought about Ivy and him. If it hadn't been for Charlie and Rainey, he wouldn't be in a loving relationship with her, would he? He knew he'd never hurt Ivy, he loved her too much. He wasn't the romantic sort like Charlie but he'd do everything he could to help her have the success she wanted and deserved. After all, he smiled to himself, remembering last night, him and Ivy were as good as married now, weren't they?

He'd been sat in the armchair and had just picked up Agatha Christie's novel *Five Little Pigs*. Gracie was fast asleep upstairs;

she'd been a Tartar when he'd bathed her earlier while Ivy, in the scullery, washed up the pots from the meal they'd eaten. The smell of liver and onions still hung in the air.

'I'm off now,' Maud had called from the passage. 'Don't worry about me, I'll probably be late. You know how Rene Simpson gabbles on and on about the church jumble sale . . .' She'd pulled the front door closed as she'd left and he'd heard the jingle-jangle of the key hanging on string behind the letter box.

'That leaves you and me, a sleeping child and an empty house,' Ivy said mysteriously. She'd taken the book from his hand and sat herself on the arm of the chair.

He could tell she was nervous. He put his arms around her. Her slight body was warm. She smelled of honeysuckle. Her dark eyes were fixed on him and he knew just how much courage she'd dredged up from inside her heart to approach him like this.

She lifted a hand and trailed it through his hair. 'You never think of blokes having such soft hair,' she said. 'Yours is just as silky as Gracie's.'

He could almost feel her heartbeat thumping as hard as his own.

'I like you touching me,' he said. He had to be very gentle with her. This was Ivy, his Ivy, the woman he loved.

Virginal Ivy who had cared about him for as long as he could remember. She had come to him of her own free will and he knew the daring, the bravery it had taken her.

Eddie reached for her hand and pressed it to his lips. He thought of the talk they'd had that morning. How she'd refused to marry him, saying instead she wanted to live with him and to love him. She wasn't a girl any longer but a woman who wanted to make choices for herself. Eddie let go of her hand and pulled her onto his lap.

'I'm not going to touch you unless you want me to, but I love you,' he said. 'And if I do touch you, I'll stop whenever you say so. I'm very attracted to you, Ivy, love. I'm only a simple man and I can't help my reactions.' He could feel his hardness against the soft swell of her buttocks.

'There's nothing simple about you. You're hard-working, funny, dependable and I want you, as much, if not more than you want me.'

He tucked an errant strand of dark hair behind her ear and kissed her. A light kiss that took her by surprise but he could see it delighted her all the same. Her lips parted and she whispered, 'I liked that.' Eddie suddenly thought of other women he'd made love to. There'd been quite a few including some already wed and dissatisfied with their lot. But this was Ivy, his Ivy, and for the first time ever she actually wanted him to touch her in a sexual way.

'Good, shall I do it again?'

She gave a tiny nod.

And nothing else mattered at that moment except that he wanted to kiss her, to touch her, to give her unbearable pleasure and to hear her cry out his name. More than he wanted his own pleasure, he wanted hers.

He'd said softly, 'Let me take you upstairs to bed.'

And now, remembering . . .

It had been the most memorable night of his life.

Chapter Nineteen

'He's got your music and I'll be over later in the morning to sit through what you've put together, so far.' Blackie pulled Bea quickly back onto the kerb as a lad on a bicycle almost ran her down. The morning had only just started and there was warmth in the air promising a scorching day. It matched the smell of burning still hanging about, a legacy from the previous night's bombing raid. Rubble and broken chimney pots cluttered the road and pavements, waiting to be cleared.

'Thanks,' said Bea. She was shaking. She picked up her handbag that she'd dropped in the confusion. Hidden inside was her gift from Bert. He'd got on her nerves so much this morning before she'd left the café that she'd taken the little umbrella with her to shut him up.

'You're a bag of nerves, woman,' Blackie said. Bea saw

him look back at Jo standing on the doorstep just as Jo raised her eyes heavenwards and shook her head. Bea hadn't seen much of Jo lately because she and Blackie were working so hard to build up the business.

Later today, Jo, Rainey, Blackie, Maud, Ivy, Della and Eddie, would all be meeting at Jo's house to check over plans for tomorrow. Of course, Charlie wouldn't be there as it was unlucky for him to see the bride the day before the wedding. Bert, too, would be absent. He had to open the café. But he was closing the next day in honour of Charlie and Rainey, pleased as punch that he'd been asked to accompany the bride to the Register Office.

'Be careful,' shouted Jo, and waved them forwards across the street that was now clear of traffic.

'I wish you'd stay to watch us.'

'I'm up to my eyes in work, Bea. I've been through Mel's script with him and it all looks pretty good . . .'

'Who's going to play the piano for me?'

'That's covered, Mel's playing.' Every time Bea heard Melvin's name a tiny piece of ice dug deeper into her heart.

'I didn't know he could play.'

'The bloke's a lot more talented than you give him credit for. Who do you think played for Blackie's Bombshells when we first left them in the desert?'

Bea felt herself duly ticked off.

'Sorry,' she muttered. Blackie's mention of the desert made her think of Melvin's previous assistant. 'What happened to Amazing Margo?' she asked. In her head she was thinking Sleazy Sue. Blackie stopped on the pavement outside the door they were about to enter and said, 'Bit of a mystery there, the girl apparently ran off with some airman, left poor Mel right in the lurch. He couldn't go on without his stooge so he took over running the show for me and playing the piano until they were all due back in England. He took it bad, Bea, so don't mention any of it.'

Bea looked into his eyes and smiled.

'That's such a shame,' she said, not caring at all. 'I'm not doing none of that fake memory work. You did make that clear, didn't you?'

Blackie nodded. 'He's got a good act worked out. You assist him –'

'And I'm not wearing one of them skimpy all in one black or flesh-coloured body-suits . . .'

'No, Bea. You'll be in frocks all the time. I might add Jo's been in contact with the seamstress who worked for Madame, luckily she still had your measurements, and I can tell you our contacts have done you proud with materials for outfits that'll knock even your eyes out.' He stared at her. 'You do have those same measurements?'

'More or less,' Bea grinned. She put her hands on her hips and posed cheekily, 'Well, what d'you think?'

She knew she looked good in her yellow sundress with the nipped-in waist and flared skirt. Maud had brought it home from the church hall before it went in the jumble sale and altered it to fit every curve. Bea had borrowed a dab of California Poppy from Della and been given a very bright red lipstick that some customer in the café had left behind. Della said the colour was too tarty for her but Bea was welcome to it. Bea was thankful for everyone rallying round but thought it stupid that for the first time in her life she had money to pay for new things but because of the war they weren't available.

Blackie, well used to Bea and her antics, pushed her through the door of the hall. She could hear a piano playing 'You Made Me Love You'. It was one of the songs she was to sing.

Blackie put out his arm and she halted. 'Listen, Bea. Mel's come up with a mix of magic and it's a showcase for you and your voice.' She opened her mouth to speak but he ignored her and carried on. 'He'll use you as his assistant for card tricks – he's a genius with the cards. You'll sing one song,

Vera Lynn's, "Yours", and win the audience's hearts, then he's going to make you disappear on stage . . .'

'What! Nobody told me he'll be getting rid of me like that! What's the sense in that?'

'Stop!' Blackie's voice had risen. He sighed then took a deep breath.

'The big finale is you come down from the back of the hall singing your second song! That's "You Made Me Love You".'

There was a moment of silence, then. 'How the hell is he going to make me disappear?'

'All will be revealed in due course, Bea. Trust me, he's a clever bloke!'

Bea narrowed her eyes. 'Is that it for me? My bit is over with?'

'No, you'll greet him again on stage and then you'll get the audience singing, "You Are My Sunshine". You'll get down amongst them, like you're very, very, good at doing. The crowd is going to love you.' He suddenly expelled a deep breath of air, like he was glad he'd told her what was going on.

Bea grudgingly admitted, 'They're good songs.'

'Thank God for that,' he said. 'Now I've good news for you. Parlophone would also like you to record under your own name, as we discussed, both "You Made Me Love You" and "Yours" on the flip side. Jo's got the London dates.'

Bea looked into his eyes. 'Really?' It was all beginning to feel like a dream, she thought.

'Really, Bea.'

She nearly knocked him over throwing herself at him. Blackie untangled her from his person and pushed her into the room where the tinkling notes were coming from. The music stopped at their entrance and Mel got up from the piano and walked towards them. He brought with him a few pieces of paper he had picked up from the top of the piano.

'Welcome,' he said. 'It's lovely to see you again, Bea.' He didn't bend towards her for a brief kiss on the cheek, neither did he stretch out an arm for a handshake. But Bea couldn't help but notice the strong scent of sandalwood. It almost overpowered her California Poppy.

She gave him a sort of smile. She didn't trust the man but she knew she'd never allow one person in any audience to know that. Melvin handed a sheet of paper to both Bea and Blackie, keeping one for himself.

'Amended notes,' he said. 'This is what I propose we attempt today.'

'You do know I'm not staying to watch, but I'll almost certainly return later,'

Blackie reminded him.

Mel nodded. Bea realized how much more good-looking he was without his moustache. She had to admit he oozed a certain charm.

'You do realize I'm the headliner, here?' She rattled the sheet of paper he'd given her.

'Of course, Bea. That's why I prefer we work to a schedule and if there's anything on here,' he waved his sheet at her in turn, 'you aren't happy about I'll be glad to change it.' He turned to Blackie. 'Bea's costumes have been delivered; they're hanging up.'

Blackie, obviously eager to leave, was already backing towards the door. 'Right, as I've said, I'll be over with Jo later, and she'll want to check on those. Don't forget I'm only across the street if you need anything,' he announced to the air as he disappeared, leaving Bea alone with Melvin Hanratty.

Bea sat down on a chair near the stage. Her insides were churning with . . . with what, she wondered? Fear? Not exactly, for she knew Melvin Hanratty wanted and needed this big break as much as she did. So, he was hardly likely to do anything to jeopardize the chance given them by Blackie, was he?

Mel disappeared into the back room and now she could hear the pop of the gas and then the chink of teacups. Bea took a deep breath. In the last five minutes since seeing Marvo the so-called Magician, her moods had fluctuated like nobody's business. She knew she should try to calm herself. She was supposed to be a professional, wasn't she? Not some scared rabbit.

She looked down at her handbag by her feet and remembered the umbrella. If he started anything she could always kill him with it, couldn't she? Oh, for goodness' sake, she told herself, pull yourself together!

Bea took another deep breath and began to read from the handwritten page. 'Mel comes on first after the Master of Ceremonies' introductions. The large black cabinet should already be on stage plus other effects on table. Mel then gives a little bit of nonsense about the audience not really wanting to watch him but would rather listen to Bea sing. Bea comes on stage in tight black dress . . .'

At this point Bea wondered why 'tight black dress' was specified. She carried on reading. 'Bea sings to great applause.' (She liked that bit.)

'Banter with the audience about Mel not liking her song, audience participation. Mel asks if he should get rid of her. He will, whatever the audience reaction. First trick, sword through Bea, sword comes out of her back. Mock faint by Bea, audience horrified. Mel pulls out sword, Bea reacts with audience. Of course, she's not hurt. Her bubbly personality makes everyone happy.' (Bea liked this bit as well.)

'Mel begins card tricks. Bea interrupts. Mel carries on, more interruptions.

'Mel makes a bargain with Bea that if she steps into the cabinet and stays quiet while he gets on with his card tricks, she can sing again which is what she and the audience wants. Bea again interacts with audience. He leads her to cabinet on stage – empty of course. Mel makes big show of proving it's empty. Bea enters. Cabinet closed and padlocked. Mel does card tricks. Then tells audience it's about time for Bea to sing again. He opens cabinet. It's empty.

'Silence. From back of audience Bea's voice is heard. She comes walking down the aisle wearing a gorgeous silver dress and steps up on to the stage where she charms the audience into singing along with her. "You Are My Sunshine". Curtain.'

'Well!' The word came involuntarily from Bea. This could work, she thought.

This could really work. The act was making the most of what both she and Mel had to offer. Though how she could have a sword stuck through her and live remained to be seen, and how she would get out of a locked box she had no idea. Mel must have researched the tricks well enough, she was sure of that. For tricks they would be, she knew. The magic was all in people's heads.

At that moment Mel came back into the room again and stood in front of her. He had a mug of tea in each hand and a worried look on his handsome face. Another waft of sandalwood competed with her California Poppy.

'Well?' he said. 'What do you think?' He looked at the piece of paper, knowing she'd perused it. Bea gave him the biggest smile.

Chapter Twenty

Bea watched the sun disappearing behind Nelson's ship, the *Victory*. It had been moored near Portsmouth's Dockyard for as long as she could remember. The ferry boat on which she was travelling would soon reach Gosport's pontoon. Tonight she'd be free to enjoy the last preparations for tomorrow's wedding of Rainey and Charlie.

The mucky seawater stank of brine as the chunky boat ploughed through the waves. At least it was a change from the ever-present stench of burning that hung over Gosport like a malevolent cloud.

She wondered if everyone was still speaking to each other, for no matter how loving a friendship was, weddings and funerals brought out the very worst in people. She'd missed being part of the preparation of the bride today, but it couldn't be helped. That first meeting with Mel and Blackie had been important.

She and Mel would be opening at the Coliseum in September so they'd have to work like devils to make sure every part of the act was as good as it could possibly be. Earlier she'd seen the worry in Mel's eyes as she'd finished reading the makeshift script he'd written.

'I'm sure it'll work,' she'd said. 'But I need to ask a lot of questions.'

'That's to be expected,' he'd replied.

She'd begun drinking the tea he'd made while he sat down a few chairs away.

'You have a wonderful stage presence that gets the audience eating out of your hand. I've tried to make the most of that by casting you as the "goody" and me as the so-called "baddy". At the end we come together. Then we are one with the audience by the final song.'

'I see that. It's a sort of story within a story, but what if we have an audience that just doesn't want to interact? Everything will be as flat as a pancake. The act will sink.'

'Oh, ye of little faith,' he'd said with a grin. 'There are no bad audiences, only bad acts. I've watched you a hundred times and if you can't get an audience going, no one can.'

She'd preened a bit at those words. But already she was thinking about other matters.

'Why "tight black dress"?'

He'd smiled at her, showing small, very white teeth. For a fleeting moment she thought the smile gave him a wolf-like apearance.

'Finish your tea and I'll show you how the trick works.'

Hurriedly she gulped down her drink and as he got up she handed him her empty mug and followed him out to the room that doubled as a store room and kitchen. She noticed there was a passage off it for the lavatory.

'Oh!' The word escaped her as her eyes lit on two dresses on wooden hangers hung over the slightly open door of a huge black lacquered cabinet. The silver dress gleamed. The black sequined dress glittered in the sunlight dancing through a window.

'That's the first dress you'll wear, the black one. Blackie and Jo are hoping you'll try both on today so the seamstress can make any necessary alterations.'

'I'm not trying it on while you're around,' she snapped.

He'd sighed. 'Take it into the lavatory and bolt yourself in then,' he'd said. 'But it is necessary there's a fitting very soon because you and I have to practise the art of deception while you're wearing it.'

She'd glared at him while she'd tried to work out what he meant. Then she'd taken down the black dress and stared hard at it. It was beautifully made and designed to fit her like a second skin. At her knees it fishtailed out. In her mind's eye she could see herself wearing her favourite black high-heeled shoes and maybe an ostrich feather as a hair ornament. Very classy, she thought. The dress wouldn't leave much to anyone's imagination but she would certainly look glamorous.

As her hand ran over the sequins, she felt a wide tape sewn in at the dress's waistline. Automatically she guessed it was a sort of tie-up corset to make her waist appear smaller. She stared hard but could find no strings that would allow the material to be pulled tight. Then she noticed the cleverly designed black waist buckle. But it wasn't really a buckle, it was more like a disguised vertical slit. Bea had blinked. She really had to look very carefully and up close to realize the buckle was simply an illusion.

Mel had laughed, then, at her peering closely at the sequins. 'Would you like to see the sword I'm going to stick right through you?'

She'd turned to him in horror but he was delving into a long box. Then in his hand he held a shining, full-size sword with a handle fashioned with sparkling red glass stones.

He made a few dramatic air slashes like a swordsman. Bea thought he'd looked as dashing as Errol Flynn.

'That looks fearsome!' Then realizing what she had said and what the sword was for, Bea had cried, 'You're not sticking that in me!'

'Do me a favour and go and slip that dress on.'

She hadn't moved so he'd added, 'If you want to see how the sword trick works, go and change your clothes! The lavatory is along there,' and he'd pointed to the passage. She grabbed the dress along with her bag and when she was in the cubicle she bolted the door. When she emerged, Bea wanted to look in a mirror as she felt the dress, comfortable as it was with its pre-shaped bustline, when zipped up really did pull her in at the waist. She'd examined the inside of the dress and discovered a wide, heavy Petersham lining that went halfway around the waistline and ended in the small of her back where another almost invisible vertical opening was situated.

Putting her clothes on a small table after she'd emerged from the lavatory, she walked into the room where the stage was. Mel was sitting in a chair rereading the notes he'd made.

'What d'you think?'

She didn't really need to ask, she could see by the smile on his face and the excitement in his eyes that she looked exactly as he had envisioned. He led her over to a corner and pulled a blanket off a large oval, free-standing mirror.

'What do *you* think?' he asked, repeating her words.

Bea couldn't answer. It had been a long time since she'd been dressed in anything so beautiful. She was still admiring herself when Mel picked up the sharp-looking sword. Fear swept through her. Either he didn't notice her apprehension or he was ignoring it for he stepped right in front of her and poked her in the stomach. 'Keep quite still,' he demanded. She couldn't believe it when she saw the blade tip disappear.

Bea cried out, 'Oh!'

It was then he began laughing again. 'Keep still for God's sake! Look,' Mel said. 'The sword is made of two lengths of German flexible steel tape, stuck together, so you see only the two shining silver sides. It's strong enough to stand out erect, yet it's quite bendable. Now I want you to stand up straight before me. Allow your hands to rest on your stomach as if you are protecting yourself.' He positioned her hands so that her fingers were splayed out. Deftly he reinserted the pointed end of the 'blade' vertically into her make-believe belt buckle. 'Don't move,' he advised.

Bea felt the sword slide and move around her waist within the Petersham lining. She looked into the mirror and it appeared as though she really had part of the sword embedded in her stomach.

'Not far enough yet,' he said. 'Stay still and keep watching.'

'It tickles!' Bea said.

She was side-on to the mirror and suddenly the blade appeared, sticking out at the back of her waist. She remembered the other vertical slit in the back of the dress. This time she gasped. It looked just like he had stuck the sword right through her! For there it was, sword handle to the hilt at her front, blade poking out of her back.

He let go of the sword and smiled at her.

'My God, that's good,' she said. 'It looks just like the real thing.'

'Hold still while I pull it out.' Gently he began to slide the length of bendy metal from her waistband. 'You and I have a lot of acting work to do on this . . .'

'No one will guess that's not a real sword from down in the audience,' she said.

'That's exactly what I'm banking on.'

And in that moment Bea began to believe that she could work with him.

And a moment later she realized working with him was going to be hell on earth. For as he pulled gently on the sword, he used his other hand to hold her waist and she felt his fingers move with just a little too much familiarity up to her breast. Her heart suddenly turned to ice. She moved abruptly so his hand had to slide away. He said nothing. And she didn't want to talk about what had just happened.

The mock sword back in its box, Mel said, as if nothing out of the ordinary had just happened between them, 'If you're happy with the dress, go and change and we'll talk about your disappearing trick.'

'I'm happy,' she said as calmly as she could. That was an untruth, for she wanted more than anything to get out of that room and be with other people. 'I'm also thirsty. Perhaps we could talk about everything over a drink in the pub, there's enough of them on Queen Street. It must be nearly dinner time now ...' She knew she was rambling. She'd meant simply a lemonade or orange juice for she'd weaned herself from alcohol long ago when it had become her crutch. Already she'd spent too much time alone with Melvin Hanratty. She thought of his fingers on her waist ... Her first instinct had been to slap his hand away and scream at him.

Ever since that business in the dark yard at the back of the Fox she'd kept away from situations where she was likely to be pawed. This was different, though. She was supposed to work with the man. She'd read the proposal for the act and liked it. She thought she and Mel could really make a success of this. But she wasn't about to become another Margo and sleep with him, definitely not. God! She was going to have to be an exceptional actress to keep herself sane and the audience happy and him away from her, wasn't she?

'No,' Mel's voice was sharp. 'No alcohol. I need to keep my wits about me. So do you. Besides, I'm teetotal. I've already thought about food. Blackie's bringing over sand-wiches whenever he deigns to get here.'

'Fine,' said Bea. 'Is there anything stopping you putting the kettle on again now?'

He gave her a smirk and touched his forelock as though she was his superior.

But he walked away from her. In the safety of the locked lavatory Bea changed back into the clothes she'd worn that morning. She fingered the black dress again. She realized she would probably be wearing it when she was put in the box. The silver dress she should also ensure fitted her. That one would be for the finale when she appeared at the back of the auditorium, an escapee! How was that going to work, she wondered?

She was pleased there was to be no shenanigans with her holding up articles from the people in the audience and him, blindfolded, telling them what the articles were, making the audience believe he really could read minds.

She wondered if his last assistant, Margo, Suze, or whatever her name was, was happy with her new man. She must have fallen in love with that airman to have run off like that. Bea shivered. She could remember ENSA, Burma, Libya, and Melvin staring up at her, a glass in his hand, while she sang on stage. But he'd told her today he was teetotal? Make allowances, she told herself – maybe, like herself, he had given up alcohol. Or possibly he couldn't help himself and he lied about everything.

Thinking about lies made her ask, as soon as she was back in the room with him, 'It's rumoured you're married with children, is that true?'

He turned and looked at her. 'I am when a woman becomes so troublesome she thinks she has some sort of claim on me.'

'You're despicable,' she said.

'No,' he answered, with a smile, 'I want what I want, when I want it. Then I get bored.'

Bea shook her head. 'Like I said, you're despicable.'

'You won't be saying that when your ice queen act melts . . .'

'In your dreams, Mel!'

He was standing by the sink. The kettle began whistling and Mel began the ritual of tea-making. Bea sat at the table. She thought it was time to get the conversation back on a safer footing. 'So, how does the disappearing trick work?'

He turned. 'Before I explain, you must promise not to tell anyone how my tricks are done. Magicians never reveal their secrets because the tricks may be stolen and used by other people. Promise me, whatever you learn from me stays between us?'

She nodded. 'Will you be letting Blackie in on your secrets?'

'Not at all.' He looked thoughtful. 'He'll know what I'm doing but not how it's done. We all have secrets we'd rather keep to ourselves, don't we?' His eyes met hers.

'If you say so. Now before we have tea why don't you explain the box trick?'

He ushered her towards the large shiny box and opened its door, moving her dresses to hang from the dado rail. 'You will see there is no floor . . .' He waved an arm inside. 'It is empty.' She noted the box was on castors for easy movement, which meant there was a gap of a few inches at the bottom of the cabinet.

'If I stand inside people will see my feet,' she said.

'Get down and look. There's a mirror a third of the way along the bottom, reflecting the front castors. The audience will assume there is a bottom to the cabinet because they can see four little wheels. You must stand behind the sliver of mirror. You will be standing on the actual floor of the stage, but the audience won't realize that.'

'Shall I pop inside?' She gave him a small smile.

'If you want, but I can't make you disappear as the box isn't set over the stage trapdoor. That will drop you beneath the stage, enabling you to move along and emerge through the door at the back of the stage. The audience, of course, will be unaware of this going on. They will believe you are in the cabinet, because I will padlock the door.' Bea took in his words. She stared at the inside of the cabinet. It was roomy enough for her to stand upright.

Mel was talking again. 'In the meantime I've done my tricks and opened the box, you've vanished and will come down from the back of the auditorium singing your little heart out to the applause you deserve.' He raised an eyebrow. 'Just one thing, do remember to stand at the back of the box. We don't want the audience to watch you going down beneath the stage.'

Bea couldn't help herself, 'That's so simple!'

'Most of the greatest tricks are, dear girl,' he said.

'Remember, you can fool some of the people all of the time, all of the people some of the time, but you can't fool all of the people, all of the time.' He gave her a smile that lit up his handsome face and added, 'That's why presentation is of the utmost importance. Simplicity works. We can do this, Bea! We're "showmen", you and I.'

Just then Bea heard voices and Blackie and Jo appeared carrying plates.

'We've got food but it's only paste and lettuce sandwiches,' said Jo. 'I hope you've got the kettle on.'

And now the ferry bumped against the buoys hanging from Gosport's pontoon. In a few minutes she would be safely in Bert's café, enjoying perhaps one of his famous bacon sandwiches. Tomorrow was Rainey's wedding day.

As she walked up Mumby Road, swinging her handbag, Bea thought of the silk dress, courtesy of some of Rainey's parachute silk, dyed pale yellow and hanging on the back of her bedroom door that she would wear to the Register Office to wish her friend every happiness.

She thought about Blackie's genuine smiles after she'd sung to the piano accompaniment by Mel, the songs she would sing not only for the show at the Coliseum but her Parlophone record under her own name. She'd tried on the silver dress, giggling with Jo as she undressed, and which was a perfect fit. Then she'd shown it to Blackie and Mel and saw by the looks on their faces that they approved. And so her first day of rehearsals was over.

Bea would need to assess how she felt about working with Mel. But the contract was signed, there was no going back. There was still heat left in the day. Bea looked at the flowering purple loosestrife growing on the bombsite opposite the café. She could hear a bee buzzing. Life goes on, she thought. Then the warning siren cut through the air, sharp, shrill. The buzzing sound wasn't a friendly bee but Hitler's planes.

Chapter Twenty-One

Charlie sat alone on the sofa listening to the wireless. He liked the jazzy music issuing from it because it made him feel less lonely. Tomorrow he wouldn't be alone, his beloved Rainey would be here with him and they'd be a married couple, expecting their first child. They'd be so tightly bound together no one could ever prise them apart. He took a sip of the gin the middle-aged barmaid in the Vine had produced from under the counter when he'd asked for a bottle of whisky. Not that he minded gin, it was alcohol. It had been his companion since Eddie had left earlier to go home to his mum and baby Gracie.

He put the glass down on the floor at his feet, sat back and surveyed the room. He thought the colourful display of flowers made the room bright and cheerful, and it was possibly their pollen that was causing the intense sleepiness that was stealing over him. Or was it the alcohol? Not that it mattered. In a moment he was off to bed to get an early night for tomorrow. He had saved some of the deep-red roses aside from the arrangement and they now stood in a jug of water in the kitchen. Tomorrow before he left the flat he would crush the blooms and spread the petals across the freshly made bed where later he and Rainey would make love. Red roses for love, he smiled to himself. With a bit of difficulty he took his silver pen from his pocket and put a shaky tick by, 'put new sheets and pillowcases out ready to remake bed in morning.'

He looked at the list and felt proud that he had accomplished all his jobs. He slipped the pen back in his pocket, picked up the glass and saw it was empty. Perhaps one more little drink, then bed? Charlie gave himself a mental pat on the back. Tomorrow was all sorted out. The car containing Eddie would be here early and together they'd ride to Fareham. Panic suddenly hit him. The ring! He peered at the paper. Ah! It was ticked off. That meant Rainey's wedding ring was in the breast pocket of his suit which was hanging up. The gold band was all ready for him to slip on her finger. He breathed a sigh of relief.

His lovely bride would arrive looking as beautiful as ever. The pampering by her friends today could never make her any more gorgeous than she already was. He listened carefully to the wireless. The Andrews Sisters were now warbling away about the Boogie Woogie Bugle Boy. He had just decided a tiny smidgeon of gin would be perfectly in order when Moaning Minnie began her mournful cry.

'Damn that noise!' His voice seemed to echo in the emptiness. Charlie heaved himself up from the depths of the sofa, his empty glass rolling away as his unsteady foot kicked against it, and made his way to the window that looked out over Stoke Road. Careful not to expose a single chink of light through the blackout curtains he looked high across the night sky.

'You're early tonight, you buggers,' he said. As if on cue the first planes emerged from behind the roofs of the shops opposite, the noise of their engines barely audible at first but growing louder the nearer they flew. There seemed to be more of them tonight, he thought.

His mind went back to last week when he had stood in Gosport High Street near the ferry, watching with the crowd as a cordon of English Spitfires flew above the channel.

He remembered the people cheering, waving at the small fighter planes that reminded him of silver wasps with their own exceptional sting. Watching them made him feel so proud of the young flyers risking their lives to save their country.

And now the drone of the aircraft was ever nearer, overhead. He realized he hadn't yet seen or heard the sounds of falling or exploding bombs. No doubt the pilots were aiming for Portsmouth Dockyard just across the water.

He saw the first black dots begin to fall from the bombers. Then the awful thudding noises as they hit targets and exploded. Smoke billowed into the newly glowing sky. The bombs seemed now to scream as they fell towards the town centre. Charlie put a hand against the wall to support himself. Had the building really shaken? There was a sudden familiar tension in his stomach that he fought to suppress. He shrank back as a deafening blast ripped into Stoke Road and he saw pieces of the shop roof opposite fly high into the air. The wall he was holding began disintegrating, falling, splitting in on itself and his feet seemed no longer to be standing on anything solid. He was flying. No, he was falling and it was the walls of the flat that were flying and the furniture that was hurtling, pinning him, crushing him . . .

'I think it's very disrespectful for Charlie to keep us waiting like this.' Maud's voice was strident, raised so she could be heard above the noise of the train that had pulled into Fareham station directly behind the Register Office where they waited. A screech of brakes and a cloud of steam burst forth showering smuts over the small crowd of people standing below in the street.

'We've got a quarter of an hour before the wedding is supposed to take place so stop worrying, Mum.' Bea touched the cream silk flower that kept sliding about in her golden hair. She knew she should have used a hair grip to secure it.

'Bert won't bring the bride late, he's a stickler for time is my Bert.' Della shrugged her shoulders in the fox fur slung around her neck. Bea wondered why on earth she'd worn the evil-eyed thing over her red dress. It was ten in the morning and already warm. Della would be complaining about the heat soon.

'The taxi took Eddie in plenty of time to pick Charlie up, well before we left home,' insisted Maud.

'Eddie said when he left him last night Charlie had done everything he needed to do except have a bath and a drink and go to bed early,' said Ivy.

'Well,' said Maud, 'how hard can it be to get up at a reasonable hour on your wedding day to wait for my Eddie and the taxi?'

Bea had to bite her tongue. Whenever Maud got on her high horse there was no bringing her down. It wasn't as if little Gracie was there to take her mind off the groom's lateness because a neighbour had kindly offered to mind the small girl.

Bea saw Jo look at Blackie. She knew Jo was a little put out that her own daughter hadn't asked Blackie to bring her to the Register Office but Blackie and Jo had been so involved with Blackie's business lately that they'd not spent much time in Gosport at all. Bea thought they made a good-looking couple; Jo in a dark-grey costume and a little hat with a veil, and Blackie in a dark suit.

'There's a taxi!' shouted Della.

'It's not Charlie, it's Rainey.' Maud put her hand to her forehead almost knocking the hat that looked like an upside-down mushroom off her head. The black cab drew up slowly outside the steps of the Register Office. Rainey's smiling face could be seen, along with Bert looking most uncomfortable in a navy-blue suit. The taxi stopped.

'Carry on up to the park then come back again,' Jo yelled in at the window wound down by a worried Bert.

'The groom's not here yet!' Maud's voice was extra shrill as she shouted at the taxi driver. Rainey caught Bea's eye with a questioning look. Bea shrugged. Rainey gave a half smile and settled back in the seat and the taxi slid off again.

'It's a shame there's no telephone in the flat or his shop yet,' whined Maud.

'We could have phoned him from the call box on the train station.'

'He'll be on his way,' said Blackie. 'Shall I walk up the road a little way and see if there's a traffic hold-up?'

'Better not,' said Bea. 'If you get lost, Mum'll have a heart attack! Besides, Rainey's got here from Gosport all right, hasn't she?'

Blackie looked at his watch then took hold of Jo's hand. 'Look, love, I know we weren't going into the Register Office until the bride arrived but I think it would be as well to know what time the next wedding is planned, don't you? We don't want to keep anybody waiting.'

'Thank goodness someone's got a bit of sense about them,' said Maud.

'Stoke Road got hit last night,' said the taxi driver. 'The streets aren't cleared properly yet.'

'Oh, yes,' Eddie said. It was an awful thing to sound so blasé about streets that got bombed when your own home had been left standing. It wasn't that Eddie didn't care – he was simply thankful Alma Street was all right. He stared out of the window. He'd got used to seeing piles of rubbish everywhere. He put his fingers inside his collar and tried to pull it away from his neck. Damn thing was strangling him.

The first thing he'd do, when Charlie and Rainey had tied the knot and they got out of the Register Office would be to pull his tie and collar off and stick them in his pocket. 'What streets would those be?' He enquired of the driver.

'The little houses next to the Vine pub. They're gone.'

'Oh, my God!' Eddie said. 'They've been there donkey's years. The pub's all right, is it?' Eddie thought about him and Charlie drinking in the bar yesterday. A smile lifted his lips.

'Oh, yes. And the fish and chip shop's still there. That photographer's shop got it again though . . .'

Ice froze around Eddie's heart. 'Say that again,' he said, leaning forward the better to hear the taxi driver.

'The chip shop's fine—'

'No!' Eddie grabbed the driver's shoulder, pulling him back against the seat. 'The photographer's . . .' His voice was a shout.

'Don't do that mate, you'll make me swerve. An accident on this road is the last thing I need . . .'

'Sorry,' Eddie said. His head was whirling; surely the driver had got it all wrong. He craned his neck, looking about him and beyond the driver's front windscreen. The taxi was travelling along the main road towards Elmhurst Road, which was the taxi's destination. Elmhurst straggled like a long snake from Stoke Road to the allotments.

Eddie spotted shop windows in the process of being boarded up with odds and ends of wood. People were standing about dejectedly, some in little groups, some simply watching the proceedings. Broken bricks, glass and tiles decorated the pavements.

'Here we are, corner of Elmhurst Road, Guvnor, just like you asked. As instructed I'll wait until you fetch your mate. Mind where you step . . .'

Eddie had already tuned the driver's voice out. His eyes searched the huge crater. The door he had knocked on yesterday when Charlie had come up behind him with his arms full of flowers was lying across the road propped against a tree. A few wooden steps led to nowhere, looking ghostly, hanging drunkenly to what little remained of the shop's wall. The crater, a huge hole, ran the length of the shop and beyond, encompassing a space where three cottages had once been. The Vine stood alone, apparently unscathed. A woman was sitting on the kerb staring about her, unseeing.

Strewn about was broken furniture, planks of wood and slates, and the stink of wet, burnt rubbish was everywhere. Eddie threw open the door of the taxi, got out and began pacing up and down the road, stumbling over wrecked household items. He saw a broken rocking horse straining against the remains of a wire fence. Two terry towelling nappies swung gently on a high line that still held a hand-made bag of pegs.

Charlie! He had to find Charlie, Eddie thought, he must have been taken somewhere. Where were the people and kids from these houses? Hospital? He didn't want to think of them lying covered up on the ground but it crept into his mind and he thrust the thought aside. A man in a flat cap with a mongrel dog on a piece of string was walking towards him along the opposite side of the road. Eddie ran over to him.

'The bloke who owned the shop, lived in the flat, over there,' he pointed back towards the crater. 'Do you know where he is?' The little brown dog sat down at the man's feet.

'Weren't nobody got out of that shop, mate, nor the houses. The rescue and fire people was there all night . . .' Eddie saw the man needed a shave.

He couldn't believe this scruffy little man was telling the truth. 'But it's my mate's wedding day . . .' Eddie grabbed hold of the man's jacket lapels, bunching them in his fist. The dog leapt up and began barking, showing his teeth. But before Eddie could say anything else, he was yanked backwards away from his assault on the stranger. The taxi driver had his arms pinned tightly about Eddie's body.

'Hang about, mate. You leave him alone.' Eddie stopped

trying to struggle as the driver's words sank into his brain. The man, highly affronted and not just a little scared, but still holding tightly to the dog's makeshift lead, said, 'If you've lost someone over that side of the road, best get down the cop shop, they'll know!' He dusted himself down.

Eddie looked at him. The animal was still growling but now it was more like a low rumble.

'That's enough, Bess.' All the same, the man stepped further away from Eddie, and dragged the dog with him.

'Thanks mate,' said the driver to the man. 'We'll do just that.'

Eddie ran his hands through his hair. 'Sorry,' he mumbled. 'I don't know what came over me.'

'Let's get you back in the car.' Eddie allowed himself to be led across the road to the taxi. 'I'll take you down to the police station,' the driver said.

'I'd appreciate that,' Eddie said softly. He could feel tears pricking the backs of his eyelids. He was about to climb back into the car when he noticed something glitter in the brick dust at the kerb. He bent down and flicked away the dirt from the thin object. It was Charlie's silver pen.

Chapter Twenty-Two

'We'd better be getting back home to Albert Street,' said Jo to Bert. 'You've been an absolute brick to everyone today. I don't know how I'm ever going to repay you . . .'

'Repay me? What are you talking about? We're all mates here, Jo. But can you do one thing for me, love? Leave Rainey upstairs with Bea. You've got to get back to work sooner or later, and then she'll be left on her own. Far better she's here with all the hustle and bustle . . .'

'She needs me. I'm taking a bit of time off, Bert, to stay with her . . .'

He put his hand on her shoulder; she was like family to him. All these people sitting around in his premises with handkerchiefs mopping wet eyes because of the dreadful demise of Charlie were his family.

He knew Jo was wrestling with her conscience. Rainey

couldn't control her grief. Neither should she be left alone. 'Then you stay here as well. There's plenty of room. Spend as much time together as you need.'

Bert couldn't blame Rainey for not wanting to return to the house in Albert Street. She'd left there in a taxi, with him, that morning, deliriously happy with hopes for the future. Jo had understood that when Rainey had begged him to bring her to the café, it was because she couldn't bear to go back to her home where all her wedding paraphernalia was lying around wreathed in memories of her husband-to-be, the father of her unborn child. It was not because she was rejecting her mother.

Earlier, a kind policeman had informed Jo that the body in the mortuary, or what was left of it, had been identified as Charlie Smith by Eddie Herron. Bert looked across at Eddie. His face was without colour; Ivy sat next to him, her hand clasped in his.

'You saw how she fled up them stairs to the safety of Bea's room. Rainey'll be all right here with Bea, love,' he said. 'And she'll be even better with her mum around as well.'

'Thanks, Bert,' she said. 'I don't know what any of us would do if you weren't around dispensing sensible wisdom. I'll take you up on your kind offer. I think you're right, my girl needs somewhere neutral she can think and begin to heal.' She gave Bert a smile that made him feel ten foot tall before she added, 'Rainey and I will need a few things from home . . .'

Blackie now stood at Jo's shoulder. 'What's happening?' he asked.

Bert thought he'd aged ten years since this morning. 'You take Jo home,' he said, 'she needs to pack a few things as well as a bit of tender loving care from you.'

'Please, Blackie, I'd like to leave now and I'd like it if you'd stay with me tonight,' Jo said.

'What about the neighbours?' Blackie gave her a small smile. Bert knew he wasn't being flippant, merely trying to lighten the heavy atmosphere a little.

'Bugger them, for once,' she replied. 'I need you. Tomorrow morning I'll be here before the dawn chorus starts, Bert. That's time enough to start getting things back to normal, if they ever will be.' Bert saw her look into Blackie's ghost eyes; he lifted a hand and gently smoothed back stray hairs that had fallen across Jo's forehead. It was a blessing, thought Bert, that Jo and Blackie had each other and a strong love between them.

'Go on, get off home,' Bert said. It had been a long day. He'd shut the place for the wedding, never dreaming the café would then be used as a place of mourning. Not that he really minded. He loved these people. He'd invited them back, cooked for them, made pot after pot of tea for them, and then sent round to the Fox for beer and strong drink.

'Mind you, you can all bed down here for the night, I got plenty of room,' he added.

Blackie shook his head. 'No, mate. You've done enough. If Jo and I make a move, the others might follow.' His words were drowned out by a lusty cry from Gracie. Maud had earlier fetched her from the neighbour, wanting everyone, including the toddler, to be together.

'You lot got no homes to go to?' Bea stood on the bottom stair. Bert hadn't heard her come down. She looked creased and rumpled, her face strained. Over her arm was Rainey's wedding dress.

'How's my Rainey?' Jo asked.

'Asleep.' Bea gave out a long sigh before passing the dress to Jo. 'I've finally impressed on her that she needs to keep calm for the baby's sake. Will you take this with you? She don't need a reminder as soon as she opens her eyes. I've got stuff she can wear.'

'Thank you, love,' Jo said. 'For everything.' She wrapped her arms around Bea and held her tightly until Blackie untangled them. 'I'll be back in a few hours.'

Bea shook her head. 'That's good because Rainey's a mess. It's to be expected.' She wiped her hand across her forehead. 'I came down to say goodnight, I'm turning in.' She looked towards Blackie. 'Can you make my apologies to Mel? He's given me a list of instructions as long as my arm about things to remember for the act. Tell him I'm a quick learner.' Blackie nodded.

Eddie was now at his sister's side. 'We'll be off as well,' he said. 'If them German buggers decide to fly over again tonight I'd rather be down the shelter. No offence,' he said to Bert.

'None taken.'

Bert saw Gracie had been sick on Eddie's shirt. Already it had taken on that stale smell. Ivy stood at his side with the child in her arms. Gracie was waving her silver rattle and teething ring. Every so often it went in her mouth then reappeared covered with long gobbets of dribble that she wiped in Ivy's dark hair.

Eddie shook Bert's hand. Bert pumped it up and down like he was trying to extract water from it.

'You done good today, Eddie, lad,' he said.

Maud said, 'I must get word to Solomon. Tomorrow is soon enough for bad news.' Bert had heard the old man hadn't been too well lately. The summer heat didn't agree with him so he and Gertie had apologized and begged off the wedding because of all the standing about. Bert knew what it was like, the aftermath of gas and shell shock, because he suffered too, didn't he? You could be perfectly well one minute, then be rubbish for days.

Della was now at his shoulder. She slipped her hand in his. Bert smiled down at her. Whatever would he do if anything happened to her?

Chapter Twenty-Three

'Remember when I used to creep into bed with you?'

Jo smiled at Rainey's words. Her heart was breaking looking at the swollen face of her daughter. She guessed that Rainey had slept little and instead had tried to cry away her grief.

'Yeah, I never knew you were there until I woke in the mornings.' Jo smoothed down the crumpled white sheet she'd just climbed beneath then put her arms around her daughter. Her clothes lay rumpled over the back of a chair.

Blackie had just dropped her off at Bert's café and he was now driving back to Portsmouth and to work.

Jo had been given a quick cuddle by Bea as the two women passed each other in the passageway. Bea, too, looked drawn and pale, thought Jo.

'I'm glad you're here, Rainey's a wreck.' Bea had said. 'I'm getting her a cuppa and something to eat that she probably won't want.' She looked at her wristwatch and added, 'Bert's been up for ages, as usual.'

Jo had smelled the aroma of fat frying and had heard the wireless playing softly.

'Rainey says she doesn't want to get out of bed today,' Bea smoothed back her white-gold curls from her face. Suddenly she leaned forward and enveloped Jo in another hug, this time much tighter. 'Oh, Jo, I've laid next to her all night and never in my life have I heard anyone break their heart like Rainey has.' Bea's body began to shake with her own fresh sobs. 'I don't know what to do. Crying like that, can't be good for the baby.'

Jo could almost feel Bea's heart beating like a bird trapped in a cage. 'You're a damned good friend to her, Bea, and for that I'm grateful.' She paused. 'Go and get yourself something to eat and drink, you'll feel better then. I'm going to try something I used to do with her when she was a child and upset about something.' She pushed Bea away from her and stared into her blue eyes. 'She doesn't have to get out of bed if she doesn't want to. She needs to grieve for Charlie . . .'

And now Rainey, folded into her mother's arms said, 'You used to come into my bed and cuddle me when I was a kid . . .'

'You'll always be my baby girl just as that child you're carrying will be your baby no matter how old it gets.' Jo put her head on the pillow and pulled Rainey down with her. She stared into Rainey's green eyes, just like she used to do when Rainey had woken after a bad dream and Jo climbed into bed to soothe her. 'Talk to me, love,' she said.

'Oh, Mum, why did Charlie have to die?'

Jo stroked her hair. 'No one can answer that, love. But you must be thankful he loved you, for he did, you know, with all his heart. Some people never experience love like that in the whole of their lifetimes . . .'

'I loved him too, Mum . . .'

'I know you did and it'll be up to you to keep his memory alive for his child. I had an idea. Why don't you start a box of memories that you can delve into when you feel you want to be especially close to him?'

'What do you mean?' Rainey sniffed. Jo was glad she'd stopped crying. Jo had read about this idea in one of Della's magazines.

'You could collect small treasures, articles that hold special meaning for you and which you'd like to share with your child.' Jo jiggled her gold bracelet containing charms that Blackie had presented her with so she'd never forget the different countries they'd visited together while travelling with ENSA. 'A bit like this bracelet reminds me of travels with my Blackie.'

Rainey extricated herself from Jo arms and pulled a grubby handkerchief from beneath her pillow and blew her nose noisily.

Jo laughed. 'You've got to feel better after that!'

Rainey gave her a watery smile after pushing the hand-kerchief back beneath the pillow.

'Photographs?'

'If you like, Rainey love. But not only photos of him so your child can see what Dad looked like, photos of you,' she paused. 'I've got a brilliant one Charlie took of you all, the very first day you met . . .'

Jo noted the faraway look in Rainey's eyes. 'The one in our Bluebirds uniforms? Taken here at the café?'

Jo nodded. She could practically feel the happiness the memory of that very first photograph session evoked, even though it had started badly.

'I remember Charlie was cross because he had to wait for you and me to arrive, the bus was late because of an air raid. Charlie said, "It's your time and your money you're wasting"!'

Jo smiled. 'You gave him such a disapproving look!'

'I wondered who he thought he was, talking to us like

that. Afterwards I realized his abrupt manner hid a shy man who had kindness in his veins instead of blood.'

Jo smiled at her. 'See? You can share that with your son or daughter.'

'I think that's a brilliant idea, Mum. A box full of memories.' Rainey grew silent. Jo thought she was about to start crying again when she said. 'I'm really, really sorry I upset you by not sharing the secret of our baby with you. Those words coming from my mouth wasn't the way I wanted to tell –'

Jo interrupted. 'That's all water under the bridge now. Of course, Charlie had to be the first person to know of your news. And we all say things we'd rather we hadn't in the heat of the moment. It's over and done with now. Think of the many other happy things to remember about Charlie. The things he did to please you. He was a good man . . .'

'I know, but what if I forget what his face looks like? The sound of his voice? What if I forget some of that past with Charlie?'

'That's where your memory box comes in. The past is never dead.' Jo enclosed Rainey in her arms again. 'Memories keep it alive, love.'

*

'Jo not here today?' Mel was surprised that the office door had been opened by Blackie. Wasn't that usually Jo's job?

'Come to pick up the key for over the road, have you?' Blackie removed the key to the auditorium from his desk drawer and handed it to Mel. Before he let it drop into his palm, he added, 'Of course, you don't know, do you?'

'What?' Mel frowned. Blackie was staring intently at him.

'Jo's daughter's fiancé was killed in an air raid the night before their wedding. Naturally she's in a state.' Mel knew Jo's daughter as the flame-haired Bluebird, the one who had been seeing that photographer chap who'd accompanied them abroad touring for ENSA.

'That's a bit nasty, isn't it?' That also accounted for Blackie looking a bit worse for wear, he thought.

'Jo and her daughter are sorting out the funeral and Bea's helping. Not sure when she'll be back. Ivy'll be with them.'

Mel was aware his wasn't the only act that was practised in the auditorium; it was regularly used by other performers. He handed the key back to Blackie and shook his head.

'I'm very sorry. I know how close the girls are. But without Bea there's no point in me going over the script and tricks on my own . . .' He sighed.

'You don't want to worry about Bea missing a few days' rehearsals, she's a trouper. She picks things up fast.'

'I guessed as much,' Mel said, 'though she's a bit of an enigma, is Bea.' He wondered how Blackie would take it, him discussing Bea when she wasn't there. But he thought he'd carry on. 'Bea's the real McCoy, a great performer who can win over the whole audience. But in reality, she blows hot one minute and cold the other. I never know how to take her.' He stared at Blackie who was listening intently. Mel gave a little hesitant laugh. 'I'll say one thing – she's a knockout in her stage clothes. They fit like gloves, don't they?' He remembered Blackie's eyes, like his own, had been out on stalks looking at Bea in the silver dress.

'You met her for the first time when we were abroad with ENSA. By that time I'd been travelling all over England with the Bluebirds. I promise you, Mel, she won't let you down. I know how much these shows at the Coliseum mean to you. Believe me, now Rainey and Ivy are taking time out, this programme means the world to her. She won't let anyone or anything get in the way of her making it a success. By the way, I've something to add about the act.'

Mel realized he'd been well and truly put in his place. He wasn't about to hear anything derogatory about Bea come from Blackie's lips. But whatever was Blackie going to say to him now?

'I read your notes, everything's good.' Mel sighed at the praise. 'But you'll not always be appearing in theatres. The Americans are in England now and I'm hoping to book in further work up and down the country at USA bases. You'll need alternative mind-bending tricks that won't rely on Bea disappearing beneath the stage. Give me a few details later on.'

Mel stared at him. Any work was good work as far as he was concerned. He realized Blackie was definitely putting a halt to any discussion about Bea.

'Sure, that's not a problem,' he replied. 'When you see Rainey and Jo, you tell them if there's anything I can do, just let me know.'

Blackie nodded and turned to the window. His hands were held loosely behind his back. Mel guessed he'd been given his marching orders. The conversation was at an end. He was just about to leave the office when Blackie moved and faced him again.

'There's a few days in the week ahead when the rehearsal rooms aren't in use. I'll book you in for them, is that all right? Bea should be ready to return then. I want the pair of you to show the public a polished act on opening night, which isn't that far away. There's going to be some important people in the audience, very influential. You know what I mean by that, don't you?'

Mel nodded. Him and Bea would knock 'em all for six.

'I know you have to think about getting back to rehearsals,' Rainey said. 'Thank you for looking after me.'

In each hand Bea balanced a white plate containing bacon sandwiches over a mug of tea. Rainey stood at the table and waited while Bea carefully set the food and drink down. Cigarette smoke swirled aimlessly in the air of the café and the dance music coming from the wireless on the shelf along with the customers' chatter made it diffi-cult for Bea to hear what Rainey was saying. She smiled instead. 'Suits you,' she said, tugging at the enormous blue-and-white striped apron dwarfing her friend. Bert had insisted if she wanted to help in the café, she had to be dressed for the part. At another table talking to a customer was Della. Her striped apron was folded down to her waist over a tight black skirt that was topped by a red frilly blouse. Her peep-toe high heels clacked across the lino floor as she returned behind the counter to slip dirty mugs onto the sink's wooden draining board. For such a small person Della walked very heavily. She must have sensed Bea watching her for she suddenly looked across and gave a small wave and a smile, her painted blood-red nails fluttering daintily.

'All I've done is let you share my room.' Bea pulled out a chair for her. 'Mind you, I think working in here has done you a power of good. What's with the aprons?' Bea asked. Then she remembered Bert talking about cleanliness being next to godliness.

'Remember when Bert went to that Lyon's Corner café in Southsea, a few days ago?' Rainey asked. Bea nodded. 'Well, he was quite taken with the waitresses wearing their frilly white aprons . . .'

'I remember Della telling him that no way was she walking about his café with a lace doily on her head!' Bea began laughing at the memory and her heart lifted to see a smile also creep across Rainey's face.

Since Charlie's funeral, Rainey had decided to give up her self-imposed exile in Bea's room and she was now helping out in the café. Bert had agreed it would do her good but he insisted she put her 'happy' head on as he didn't want her tears frightening his customers away. Bea had thought his words harsh and insensitive at the time, but they seemed to have worked, for Rainey was looking brighter with each day that passed.

'You don't have to work,' Bea said. 'Charlie left you well provided for.'

Rainey said tartly, 'Money or not, I can't mope about. Charlie wouldn't have wanted that and it's not good for the little one.' She held her hands protectively over her bump.

Bea saw Rainey's white teeth bite into the fresh bread and fragrant bacon. She took a mouthful of her own tea. Rainey was right, Bea needed to rehearse with Mel. Bea hadn't been idle while she'd been passing Rainey countless handkerchiefs to mop up her tears and listening to her friend telling her how much she missed and loved Charlie. Bea had memorized the instructions about the act, carrying it everywhere with her until the piece of paper began to fall apart. Bea had also gone out into the back yard of the café amongst the weeds and practised the songs she was to sing until she was sure even the garden's wildlife was sick of the sound of her voice.

She had also rehearsed how she would handle the sword scene, realizing she could bring so much more to the act than Mel's written instructions. She knew she must see Melvin again but her mistrust of him lingered.

Rainey was talking; Bea had missed some of the conversation but she smiled as Rainey said, 'Loving Charlie was the best thing that ever happened to me. But I didn't know how blessed I was when we three girls were on the road together with all our hopes and dreams ahead of us.'

Chapter Twenty-Four

'I didn't think I'd be up for it when Mum came round the other week with the invitation,' said Rainey. 'And I never thought Blackie would splash out for these frocks.'

'Compared to what we used to wear, these are like glorified day dresses,' said Bea, 'but let's face it, you'd never get into any of the form-fitting stuff we wore before.' Bea watched Rainey cup her hands beneath her baby bump. 'Anyway, Blackie's got the contacts to provide nice materials and sew them together. He couldn't have his girls running around in rubbishy outfits, could he?'

Ivy chipped in. 'Actually, we're no longer Bluebirds, are we?'

'Doesn't matter,' snapped Bea. 'You know what I mean.' The slight rankled.

'Don't let's bicker, it's too hot for that.' Rainey moved to stand in the open doorway of the Sloane Stanley's kitchen that looked out on its grass-covered garden and the huge elm tree that provided shade. 'Not long now before you open at the Coliseum, is it?'

'First week in September,' Bea said.

'Are you ready?' Ivy asked.

'Ready as I'll ever be,' Bea answered. She didn't like talking about stage work when the other two were around. She told herself over and over that they had wanted a rest from the hustle and bustle of show business, so she shouldn't feel guilty for forging ahead with her own career. But she did. And now the three of them were waiting in the kitchen while people bustled about preparing food and teas for the guests. They were waiting for the announcement that they were to sing and for Blackie to play their introduction.

Of course, Rainey hadn't wanted to sing, said she didn't have anything inside her to give. Bea had said, 'Don't be so bloody dramatic, you think Charlie would thank you for refusing to sing at a mate's wedding? Especially someone like Syd Kennedy, who'd been a godsend to you when you first came to live in Gosport?'

'I couldn't believe it when Mum's invitation came through the post,' Rainey said. 'Who'd have thought Syd Kennedy would be getting married?'

'You didn't expect him to go on hanging around like a lovesick puppy for Jo to change her mind, leave Blackie and hitch back up with him, did you?' Bea thought Syd Kennedy had mooned around after Jo for long enough. Why, he'd even kept on writing to her all the time they'd worked abroad with ENSA.

'I don't know what I thought,' Rainey answered. 'I just thought he'd always be there.'

Bea shook her head. 'Men don't just "be there", they move on. Especially when the woman they'd cared about gets engaged and announces her wedding to someone else! But he'll always be a friend, he's a nice man.' She stood in front of Rainey and pushed her bra strap back beneath the shoulder of her dress. Her voice went down to a whisper, 'You all right?'

Rainey nodded. Bea was proud of the way Rainey was beginning to get back to some semblance of a normal life after Charlie's death. She gave Rainey a big smile.

'Wonder why he specially asked us to sing "The Bluebird Song"?' Ivy flicked her dark hair back from her face.

'Why does anyone ever ask for special songs? Memories, you daft ninny!'

Bea gave a wry smile. 'Syd was good to Rainey and her mum when they first arrived in Gosport. They still got a friendship that'll survive all kinds of hardships.'

'You'd make a damned good politician, our Bea,' said Ivy. 'Sometimes you spouts a lot of sense.'

Bea glared at her and moved over to the small mirror propped against the window frame. There were people she'd never seen before in the big hall next door. Not a great deal of people, mainly just friends and relations of Syd and Jenny. That was his bride's name, Jenny. The fact that both Jo's name and Jenny started with a 'J' was the only similarity between them. Jenny was a shy little thing who seemed to hang on Syd's every word. But he fussed around her like she was made of china. Bea wondered what his new bride thought of being introduced to the woman her new husband had asked to marry and who had refused him.

Of course, Blackie had been invited as Jo's partner, which Bea thought was a smart move, especially as Blackie seldom left Jo's side. Bea, herself and Rainey had no partners to bring but Ivy had arrived with Eddie, who was of course a friend to Syd. Syd had asked the three girls to sing the Bluebird song as the evening's entertainment. For old times' sake, they had agreed.

Earlier, Rainey had been talking to Mr and Mrs Harrington, who still ran the newsagents in the village of Alverstoke where Jo had worked. Bea kept her eye on Rainey, but from a distance. Rainey was doing fine.

Bea smiled to herself, thinking of the practice that had gone into the simple folk song. It was special. The first song they had ever sung together. 'Where The Bluebird Goes' had won them a place in the Fareham Music Festival and had set their feet on the ladder to fame.

'Pass me my make-up,' Bea asked. She took the drawstring bag from Ivy and touched up her lips with Vaseline, glad there was still some colour left from the lipstick she'd applied earlier.

'You look gorgeous,' said Ivy.

'I know I do,' grinned Bea.

'Eddie reckons you're the dead ringer of Jane in the *Daily Mirror* – you know, the blonde with the little Dachshund dog, the forces' favourite pin-up who keep losing her clothes!'

'You wait until I get hold of him,' said Bea. 'I'll thank him for the compliment then knock his block off. I've no intention of losing my clothes for anyone!'

'Shh!' said Rainey. She had poked her head round the kitchen door and was listening intently. 'Syd's talking about us.'

'Are you ready, girls?' Bea left her make-up bag on the draining board.

Blackie began to play so she grabbed Rainey's and Ivy's hands and with a smile on her face she pulled both girls out to sing before an audience once again.

Chapter Twenty-Five

'I suppose I ought to think about going home to Albert Street to live,' said Rainey.

Bea hadn't long been back at the café. Eddie had dropped her off then gone home to his own family. He'd taken her to London to Parlophone's studios, where she'd recorded the two big songs she was promoting when the show opened at the Coliseum at the weekend. It had seemed funny singing alone. Less than a week ago, she, Rainey and Ivy had travelled up by train from Portsmouth Harbour station to fulfil their recording commitments at the BBC studios.

Rainey was sitting gazing out at the spare bit of ground beyond Murphy's the ironmongers. 'If we don't sell it, you don't need it', said the sign in the window, next to the one that stated, 'Please don't ask for credit as a refusal often offends.' Bea couldn't read the signs from the high window overlooking the shop, but she knew them off by heart.

'I don't mind you being here with me. You won't be on your own when I'm out at nights over Portsmouth,' Bea said. 'There's always someone around. If you go back to live at your mum's place, you'll be alone while she's at work every day.'

'I don't want to feel I've outstayed my welcome,' Rainey turned and stared at Bea. Her beautiful green eyes looked as if they might overflow with tears at any moment.

'You did that ages ago,' laughed Bea, trying to lighten Rainey's mood. It worked; Rainey treated her to a lovely smile.

'I feel bad about causing the split between us. If it wasn't for me, we'd still be the Bluebirds and Blackie would be sending us all over the place to sing.'

'Bit late to worry about that now. Our records will still be released as The Bluebirds. Anyway, we're each of us all happy in our own ways.'

'But Bea, are you sure?'

'Listen, I've had Eddie rabbiting on in my ear all the way up to London about Ivy. Ivy this, Ivy that. Ivy and Mum are getting on so well together; Gracie's calling Ivy Mum-Mum now . . . Ivy got what she wanted, my brother. And he's as happy as a pig in muck about it. He worships the ground she walks on, so what's not for her to be happy about? You got a little one on the way, a new life, a new beginning. Me? I've got a record coming out more or less the same time I perform in a new show.'

'You take each day as it comes, Bea, I think you're marvellous!'

'Pssht!' exploded Bea. Then she began laughing. 'Oh dear, I sounded just like Mrs Wilkes then, didn't I?' Bea had fond memories of their music teacher from St John's School who had first discovered the girls' singing talents.

'She's not Mrs Wilkes now she's married, is she?'

'Whoops! I forgot. Anyway, she left a message with Blackie that they'll both be at my opening night.'

'That's great,' said Rainey. 'But I still think you're marvellous.'

'And you're going to tell me why?'

'Because you were the one most affected by us splitting up; you were the one who had the most to lose by my selfishness . . .'

'Yes, and I was the cow shouting at you after you announced your pregnancy . . .' Bea went over to the window and put her arms around Rainey. 'You're a daft cow an' all, you are.'

She took a step backwards. 'Blimey,'' she said, touching Rainey's bump. 'It's certainly come between us,' she grinned. Then she bent down to Rainey's stomach and called, 'Who are you, a little boy or a little girl?'

Rainey giggled. 'The doctor can't tell me that, but the nurse says I'm doing fine when I go for check-ups.'

'Well don't have a little boy; men are more trouble than they're worth. Have a little girl with the same colour hair as you. If you do have a boy, when I die I shall come back and haunt you for being so horrible!'

'Don't talk about haunting anyone. That reminds me, that psychic is back in Portsmouth.'

'I'm not going to see her. Helen Duncan spooked me enough last time.'

'Did anything come to you about those two alphabet letters, the beginnings of names, she said, of the woman who was trying to warn you of something?'

'No, and I don't even want to think about Helen Duncan and her omens.'

Bea was making light of it but she didn't let on to Rainey that every night thinking about the letters M or S kept her from sleep. Almost as much as wondering how to keep out of Mel's clutches.

'You are happy now though, aren't you?' asked Rainey.

'Apart from hating the bloke I'm working with,' Bea replied.

'Is he still touching you up?' Rainey asked, looking worried.

'Every chance he gets. He's like an octopus. And don't think I haven't had a go at him, I have. He just laughs at me. He says there's plenty of other girls who'd go on stage with him and be a lot nicer to him than I am.' Bea was quiet for a moment. She felt her tears rise and she wiped her hand across her face, smoothing the dampness away. 'He knows I need that job.' She let out a big sigh. 'He's telling the truth, Rainey, loads of girls would like a good-looking bloke like him pawing them about.' Bea pushed her hair back from her face. 'But not me, he reminds me of that sailor . . .'

'Have a word with Blackie, why don't you?'

'How can I?'

'You open your mouth and tell him how Mel makes you feel.'

'Don't you see that's something I can't do?' She stared at her friend. Oh, if only everything about this was as straightforward as Rainey seemed to think it was.

Furrows appeared on Rainey's forehead. 'Why not? You know how easy it is to talk to Blackie?'

'Not for me, he'll think I'm causing trouble. He'll say I'm

being highly strung. He won't believe it upsets me the way it does . . .'

'I'll tell him!' Rainey turned away. Bea grabbed hold of her shoulder, pulling her round to face her.

'No! You mustn't do that.'

'Why?'

Bea took a deep breath. 'I knew you and Ivy would never breathe a word about what happened to me round the back of the Fox because we were on our way up and our audiences had to believe we were pure young girls.' She paused and took another deep breath, not wanting to confess but knowing she had to. 'I made your mum promise not to tell Blackie. She's kept her promise to me. How do you think Blackie's going to feel about your mother when he discovers all this time Jo's kept that secret from him?'

'What on earth is that?'

Mel smiled at Bea before he answered her question. She'd arrived at Blackie's auditorium just as he was putting together the long-handled lever that would fix to the side of the box so he could push it in, sliding it along and thus crushing anything that was in its way.

'The audience will think I've squashed you,' he said.

'Squashed me flat?' Bea's eyebrows rose alarmingly. 'I've got some news for you, I'm not getting in there – it looks positively dangerous.'

He shook his head. 'It's not really. But we have to have an alternative trick that doesn't involve you disappearing below the stage. Blackie's lined up some shows at American bases after the run at the Coliseum and in an ordinary room or canteen without a stage there's no trapdoor.'

He loved the way she stood there looking at him. A slight figure in a summer dress and high heels, her hair windswept because she'd just come off the ferry.

'Are you crazy? We open on Saturday. I'm here today for a last practice to make sure everything goes well, and you want me to start learning something new?'

He walked up to her and put his hand on her shoulder. She felt soft and warm. She shrugged him away and folded her arms in front of her. She was trying to look aggressive so he stepped back and laughed.

'We only need a quick practise for Saturday night. It's perfect as it is. But a new trick needs lots of preparation. Come and look and I'll explain it to you. I've also written out all the details so you can take the piece of paper away and study it.' He grabbed hold of her hand and before she could pull away again he moved her in front of the oblong box on legs and castors.

'Two sides are rigid wood,' he tapped the back and one side where he had inserted the lever to enable him to move it inwards. 'This side looks like wood but is in fact very, very strong elasticized material that will give when anything is pressed against it.'

Bea ran her hand all around the box. 'The front is open with just a small curtain,' she said. 'And if you close the top,' she pulled it down, 'which is also made of wood, where will I go?' She looked at the lever that would push in one side until it met the other side and frowned. 'Where will I go?'

'Move back away from the box and tell me what you see.'

'An oblong box supported on four legs. And I can see right through the legs to the other side, there's no reflective mirror here, it really is four legs with a long box on top.'

'Shall we have a go at making you disappear?'

Bea blew out her cheeks. 'I can't see how you can do it,' she said.

Mel loved her when she was like this. It was as if she was a child, inquisitive yet naive.

'Look inside the box,' he said.

She leaned right over and began touching the black

material inside the box. He was bending over too, enjoying the smell of her freshly washed hair and the scent of California Poppy. Bea sensed him close to her and moved away.

'Don't do that,' she said.

He knew very well that she didn't like him getting close to her but it gave him pleasure.

'What?' he asked, mocking her.

'You know what I mean,' she said and glared at him. 'Don't stand so close to me.'

'Well, can you see how I can make you disappear?' He waved a hand around inside the box. Bea shook her head and her blonde curls tumbled around her shoulders. One day, he thought, one day, you will be mine, Bea Herron. But he didn't speak, merely lifted up the thinly covered inside bottom of the box revealing a space big enough for her legs to be hidden when the cover was replaced.

'Wow!' Bea exclaimed, stepping back and gazing at the outside of the box. 'Looking at it from here you'd never tell it has a false bottom. But there's not enough room for all of me down there, where does the rest of me go?'

He opened the front curtain, and then began sliding in the side of the box until it was almost flat with its twin end. He then showed her how the elasticated side gave way just enough for her to sit without any of her upper body and head being visible because it too was covered by a small black curtain.

'Legs here, top part here,' he said. 'I can then pull back the front curtain and *voila!* you have disappeared. I then twirl the box on its castors around a couple of times to prove to the audience that it's empty and pull the curtain across, pull out the lever releasing the side panel while behind the curtain you are wriggling your lovely legs from the bottom of the box. I tap on the top, pull back the curtain and help you out. One squashed beautiful girl made whole again. What do you think?"

'I think I'll need a lot of practise removing the bottom without exposing the trick to everyone," she said. 'If I can do it quickly and manage not to bulge out the elasticated panel, it will work. Otherwise they'll guess what's going on.' She paused. 'I think it would work better without shoes and a dress I can move in.'

'You could always wear glittery tights and a bra-top,' he said.

'I told you when I said I'd work with you that no way will I dress in some kind of slutty leotard like Margo wore . . .' He knew he was frowning at her. 'Margo! Or Suze, or whatever her name was that ran off when you were abroad!'

He took a deep breath and said very calmly, 'But you'll do it in a dress?'

'Yes, and we can practise today, if you like. It's a good trick. I think it'll work well.'

Mel stared at her. He was just beginning to forget about Suze, the girl lying in a makeshift grave in the desert. Now Bea, the silly cow, had brought all those memories to the surface again.

Chapter Twenty-Six

Before Bea started up the steps of the stage door entrance of the Coliseum at the end of Edinburgh Road, Blackie pulled her to a standstill.

'How do you feel when you're top of the bill?' he asked, pointing to one of the posters pasted at intervals along the wall of the old building. Bea looked at the two-colour offering.

Tonight's Entertainment
Overture
Hip Hip Hooray Twelve Beautiful Girls, The Act That
   Glorifies The Stage
The Three Thomases Celebrated Acrobats
Bella Bond, English Songstress
Horace and Horace, Musical Comedians

Interval, Refreshments
Monarchs of Music, Foot Tapping Pleasure
Caroline's Dogs
Joan and Arthur, Adagio Pair Apache Dance
Mel and Bea, Deception and Desire

'The poster doesn't even give our full names,' Bea moaned. She didn't want him to know how excited she was at seeing her name on a playbill once again.

'By the end of tonight everybody will know who you are.' She looked at Blackie and smiled. He grinned back at her. 'Can you hear it?' he asked.

'What am I supposed to be listening for?' Oh, God, not another air raid, she thought. Not tonight of all nights. Blackie led her to the corner of the building.

'If you can't hear it, you must be able to see the huge queue waiting to buy tickets.' Bea's heart lifted at the sight of so many people filling the pavement and snaking around the other corner.

'I promise I'll do my very best to make you proud of me, tonight and every night,' she said, squeezing his arm. Bea meant what she said. He'd given her a chance to show the public what she could do, and she wouldn't disappoint him.

'I know you will,' he murmured. At the stage door Blackie waved to a couple of men carrying furniture and had a few words with the door manager. Bea was happy to be back in the Coliseum. The Bluebirds had played here early in their career.

She and Mel had had a morning rehearsal here the day before yesterday.

Bea took a deep breath, there was always a difference in the smell of a theatre on an opening night to its atmosphere during the day when the actors were in rehearsal. To Bea it hinted of excitement mixed with a tiny slice of fear with a longing and the desire to know what a difference the first night's show might bring.

As far as she knew, friends and family with complimentary tickets were already seated inside the theatre. Her brother had offered to drive her round to Portsmouth but she'd declined his offer. She preferred to travel on the ferry. She wanted to approach this first night with a clear head and sitting in a van with chattering members of her family, although she loved them dearly, wouldn't give her time to think, to compose herself.

Blackie had met her at Portsmouth Hard to walk up Queen Street. He understood her anxiety about appearing in front of paying customers once more. She wished she could confide in him about her fear of Mel. That was out of the question, of course. Blackie was aware both she and Mel were using each other's talents to further their own careers. But without telling Blackie the whole story, including the sailor's attack on her, he would never understand just how deep her fear of Mel was.

Blackie and Jo were good together. Jo loved him without question. He was still surprising her with charms for her bracelet, the latest of which was a tiny gold wedding ring. He'd explained it was a symbol for the real one he hoped soon to put on her finger after the period of mourning for Madame and Henry was over. But although he loved her to distraction and they shared a happy life together Bea was aware he would be mortified to find Jo had kept even one secret from him, let alone several.

Jo had been like a mother to Bea, keeping her safe when they were all on the road together, helping her cope with her addictions to alcohol and food – props that had enabled Bea to face life after the attack. All that sordid mess would come out, of course it would. She sighed. No, this problem she had with Mel and his behaviour was something she would have to sort out on her own.

Bea heard a whimper and felt something brush against

her leg. A white poodle sat on her foot trailing her leather lead. Bea bent down and patted the dog's head. 'Hello, Daisy. Where's your mum?' she asked. People milled about them. The dog gazed at her soulfully. Bea picked up the lead. It was mucky, it had probably been trailing in the dirt. Bea recognized the dog as one of Caroline's pets. She never allowed her dogs to be out on their own – they were far too precious to her act, to her. Daisy was one of the younger dogs. All Caroline's pets were named after flowers. Bea tickled the dog's ear. Daisy was now firmly wedged on her foot.

'Found a friend?' Blackie asked. He looked down at Daisy. Just then a tall woman in a silk dressing gown almost careered into Bea. The worry on her face was obvious but her eyes lit up with relief as she saw Daisy.

'My baby,' she cried, falling to her knees and putting her arms tight about the white dog. The poodle barely moved noted Bea. 'Thank you, thank you, I thought she was gone forever,' she said dramatically as she peered up at Bea.

'I didn't find her, she found me,' said Bea. 'You must be Caroline? We're on the same bill.' She handed the lead to the woman, who took it.

The woman stood up and said, 'The lack of changing space means my dogs and I have to share with other acts. I put leads on all my darlings but someone must have left the door open. It's really not good enough. Bloody Hitler,' she exploded.

Bea realized she must have looked confused at the woman's outburst.

'The damage dear, the flooding in the main dressing rooms, we all have to muck in together . . .'

Bea looked at Blackie who steered her away from the woman who was still exclaiming her thanks.

'That's something I've just found out. A bomb had damaged a water main and there's flooding to some of the premises. You have got a dressing room,' he said. 'It's just a bit different from what you've been used to . . .'

'That doesn't matter, I can mix in,' said Bea. 'Last time we played here, we shared with the chorus girls.'

'You're only sharing with one other person,' he said. 'Mel.'

She didn't utter a word as Blackie led her through a maze of cluttered rooms full of noisy people. He paused outside a room with its door closed, knocked loudly and hearing no reply, twisted the handle and let the two of them inside.

There was a large oval floor mirror, a dressing table with a triptych of little mirrors, a small corner hand sink, a sagging sofa, a couple of kitchen chairs and an ornate wooden screen. A blanket had been nailed over a window to act as both curtain and blackout protection.

Mel's large carpet bag was on the floor near the sofa. He stored his stage make-up, cards and other paraphernalia in there. He'd obviously arrived and was probably checking on the stage furniture, ensuring the cabinet and sword were within easy access to the stage. His top hat and tails, his stage outfit, was laid across the back of the sofa so wherever he was he too was not yet dressed in costume.

Hanging over the screen were her two changes: the black glittery dress and the silver one. High-heeled shoes to match were placed neatly in readiness at the base of the screen. On the dressing table was a huge bouquet of calla lilies with a small card. On the floor next to the dressing table a tall vase held mauve Michaelmas daisies.

'The Michaelmas daisies are from me and Jo. We know how much you love them,' he said, picking out the card from the lilies and handing it to her. Her hand shook as she read the writing: *From Mel.* Bea deliberately didn't pass comment on the lilies but said, 'Say thank you to Jo for me, will you? That's exactly the kind and lovely gesture she'd make. It means a lot to me.'

'Are you going to be all right in here?' Blackie asked.

Bea's stomach was twisting itself inside out. The last thing she wanted to do was share a room with Mel. But she couldn't be a prima donna and complain when it looked as if all the other acts were making changing room sacrifices.

'Of course,' Bea said. She began opening her handbag and removing her make-up, hairbrush and pins, and putting them on the dressing table. At the bottom of her bag lay the tightly furled small umbrella. Bea looked at it. She knew she'd have no hesitation in using it on Mel if he started to take liberties with her, no hesitation at all.

Blackie looked at his watch. 'I need to leave,' he said. 'Things to do and people to see.' He smiled at her. 'Don't run off afterwards, Jo's laid on a bit of a do in our audition room.' He must have noticed her smile fade a little for he added, 'Don't worry, I know you want to be away before the last ferry. There'll be ample time for a few drinks to toast you on your success tonight.' He didn't give her a chance to refuse – well, how could she when she knew he and Jo were making a special effort for both her and Mel.

'Break a leg,' he said, kissing her on the top of her head then striding out through the open door. A few seconds later, Bea followed him. She had already decided she didn't want to take her clothes off in the same room as Mel, who could come back at any moment. She was looking for the lavatory, a cupboard, anywhere except behind that screen.

Bea discovered a broom cupboard down the hallway

stacked to its rafters with cleaning materials. Then she found a door that was hard to open, and when she did manage to set foot on the inside step she found a foot of water swirling around the furniture. The water was brackish and stank to high heaven. There were two more rooms ankle-deep in water on the ground floor where she was. She understood, then, the seriousness of the flooding. Up a flight of stairs Bea discovered three rooms. All, when she opened the doors, were packed to the gills with performers in various stages of undress. Noise and laughter and angry voices clashed. The smells of perfume and sweat swept out from each room into the claustrophobic hallway. She discovered another door but as she heard dogs barking inside she didn't even bother to open it. Hadn't Caroline already told her she and the dogs were sharing with other performers?

It was then she realized as headliners she and Mel had been treated very well by the management. There were only the two of them and they had a room to themselves.

She'd also seen that all the downstairs lavatories were out of order. Performers were expected to share facilities normally reserved only for patrons. This was indeed going to be an opening night to remember for everyone.

When she arrived back in their dressing room, she

found Mel holding a drink in one hand and his written instructions clutched in the other. He looked smart in his black tails, dickey bow tie and shiny shoes. She breathed in sandalwood cologne. His folded clothes were piled on the sofa.

'You'd better get ready,' he said. 'I was here earlier but went out to find something to drink.' He waved the hand with the paper towards one of the kitchen chairs where a bottle of gin, two small bottles of Indian tonic water and a jug full of water stood next to an empty glass. 'All I could get hold of,' he said apologetically. 'I tried to get you some orange juice. Do I look all right?' he asked.

She realized he too was nervous. She had friends, a family who lifted her spirits by wanting to attend tonight's performance. He had never mentioned anyone close to him coming for opening night to wish him well.

'Don't you have anyone coming to see you perform tonight?' she asked. 'Relatives or special friends?'

He shook his head. 'I have no family except a brother but I haven't seen him since he was a kid. I expect he's long forgotten me by now.' Then he asked again, 'Do I look all right?' He wanted approval, just like everyone else. She breathed a sigh of relief. If he was going to pounce on her, it wasn't likely to happen before they performed their act, or was it?

'Yes, you do,' she said. She could smell bergamot mixed with the sandalwood. It was a soothing, masculine smell.

'Anything for you, Bea,' he replied flippantly, and took a small sip from his glass. 'Help yourself,' he said, and nodded towards the alcohol.

'Thanks,' Bea replied. She didn't admit she rarely touched alcohol now, why should she? And he was clearly a liar. Why tell her he was teetotal then drink in front of her?

Going to the chair she poured herself some water from the jug. It was now or never, she thought, carrying it behind the large upright lacquered screen. She put the glass on the floor and began pulling and lifting both dresses over and into the safety of the small space. The black dress was the correct outfit for the first half of the act, and the silver one needed to be deposited by herself safely near the stage so she could change into it later after she had disappeared from the cabinet.

In remarkably swift actions she removed her day dress and slipped into the form-fitting black dress with the sham buckle at the front. She picked up her glass and drank deeply. She then stepped out from behind the screen and into Mel's unwavering gaze.

She slipped her feet into her black shoes before putting her empty glass back on the seat of the other chair. Her heart was thumping.

'Come here,' he said. Her insides changed to writhing snakes. Mel gave a small chuckle. 'Turn around.' Warily she faced away from him. Suddenly she felt his hand on the nape of her neck. She froze, her body rigid at his touch. Then relief swept through her as she realized he was pulling up the dress's zip that she'd been unable to reach.

'You're very tense,' he said. 'Are you sure you're not too nervous to go on?'

He twisted her body around by gripping her shoulder and ran the tips of his fingers over the make-believe buckle, then felt along the invisible Petersham belt around her waist. She realized she was holding her breath, willing him to touch only her waist and not move his hand higher towards a breast.

'Try to remember there must be no obstruction whatever when the sword enters.' He stared down at her, holding her very close. 'You'll soon get used to checking these things for yourself.' His breath was warm on her cheek. He wanted her to believe the only reason he had touched her was to make sure her costume wouldn't fail when the blade was thrust in. She gave a resigned smile. She'd discovered his little ruse.

Her reflection in the large oval mirror showed a shapely young woman with a cascade of blonde hair framing her face. More relief came as Bea saw her reflection didn't betray the fear she felt and she hastily moved away from him to refill her glass. She had already decided that after she had left her silver dress and matching shoes somewhere safe and ready to change into, she would wait at the side of the stage until their act was announced. If he chose to follow her there, fine, there would be other actors about; at least she wouldn't be alone in the same room with him.

He said, 'Are you sure you can cope? It's a big audience tonight.' He was playing with her. Bea was well aware his extremely gentlemanly behaviour was designed to lull her into a false sense of security.

After swallowing a mouthful of water, Bea ran her fingers through her curls and picking up her lipstick and carefully outlining her full lips said, 'When I get out on the stage I become another person. Don't you worry about me at all.'

Chapter Twenty-Seven

The adagio dancers knew their stuff all right. The gasps from the audience as the woman was thrown around by her partner during the Apache dance showed what a good act it was.

'We have to follow that,' said Mel. Even at the side of the stage Bea felt he was standing too close, invading her space.

Bea had tried peeking into the audience to see where her brother and Ivy were sitting. She knew it was a full house. The stage lighting dazzled her from where she stood so she was disappointed she couldn't make out any of her family or friends who had come to cheer her on. Not that it really mattered, for she felt they were out there somewhere and that was all that counted.

The applause for Joan and Arthur as they bowed to their audience was tremendous. As soon as the curtain came down upon the pair of dancers, the stage became a hive of activity.

'That was fantastic,' said Bea as the couple moved past her. Their reply was breathless, their bodies and faces wet with sweat from their exertions but Joan managed a broad smile. Bea knew the audience, still whistling and clapping, was really the only show of appreciation the couple needed.

Mel ran on stage to check the cabinet had been placed correctly and that it faced the audience. A small table centre stage held the sword in its elaborate sheath. A pack of cards sat beside the blade. Bea knew he had planned the placing of his props meticulously. She could almost feel his brain working, checking everything so not a thing could go wrong. Except her, of course, she could mess everything up by making some foolish mistake. But she wouldn't. Bea wanted this stab at fame just as much as he did. She had practised the songs until she was note perfect, the same songs that were now being released by Parlophone under her own name.

And then Mel was at her side. 'Everything is ready,' he whispered. He put on his top hat and smiled down at her. The theatre's orchestra played a short introduction and then the master of ceremonies introduced them. The red velvet curtains glided back and grabbing Bea's hand, Mel smiled at her before walking proudly to centre stage.

Taking a deep breath, Bea smiled for the audience, then smiled up at Mel and she had to admit he looked every inch the professional showman in his top hat and tails. The glitz and the glamour suited him.

It was her job to win over the audience and as soon as she opened her mouth to sing, she knew she had the theatre's patrons in the palm of her hand. Then came repartee between Mel and her that led up to the sword trick.

The audience were with her chanting, 'No, don't let him!' Of course, they wanted to see the good-looking magician stick a sword into the beautiful blonde who had just touched their hearts with her wonderful voice.

The shocked gasps and screams echoed around the auditorium as Mel pushed the blade to its hilt into her stomach. Bea screamed, she couldn't possibly be anything else but dead, could she, not with the blade protruding from her back? She sagged helplessly. Mel was supporting her while he spoke to the audience. To cries of horror he began slowly removing the sword, making conversation with the people sitting aghast in their seats. Finally, he made a great show of wiping the spotless sword without the audience realizing no blood had been spilled. Bea acted her part beautifully, lying dead on stage. Mel stood over her, giving the audience what they wanted, glamour and thrills. He put out his hand and Bea rose to her feet amidst cheers that she was safe after all.

Mel asked Bea if she'd help him with another trick. He made a great show of proving the cabinet on stage was solid but empty and there was no possible way she could escape from it. He wanted to get rid of her so he'd make her disappear, he told the audience. He asked them if they believed he could do it.

'No!' came the answer. He led her to the cabinet and she got inside, careful to step to the back over the mirror that hid her feet from the audience's view. He shut the door and padlocked it. He told the audience to forget about her for now, that he would show them mystifying card tricks.

Bea, inside the box, lifted the stage trap door that the cabinet stood above and in moments was beneath the stage and changing into the silver dress. The space below the Coliseum stage was large, fairly clean, only containing rarely used props and the flood water hadn't permeated that part of the building, one of the first things Mel had checked out. Bea emerged from a small door that led into a corridor that met the stairs leading to the circle. She hurried up the steps.

She carried her shoes, only putting them on when she stood outside the door she was to push open and emerge from singing her heart out. She waited for her cue, watching through the glass pane in the door as Mel had the audience awed by his card tricks which involved members of the audience eventually leaving the stage still wondering how he had managed to fool them. Mel then asked if the audience would like Bea to sing again. Of course, they did!

He used the key on the padlock and then opened the cabinet. He made a great show of her being missing. Then told them it was what he'd promised, to get rid of her. The audience was dumbfounded. Then a spotlight illuminated the audience sitting upstairs. Bea hastily ran her fingers through her curls and as the light shone on the door she pushed it open to emerge in a dream of a dress that glittered like silver dust. She stood in the spotlight soaking up the applause then began singing and she kept on singing as she walked down the long steep slope to the stage where Mel helped her up the steps to stand beside him.

The audience whistled, clapped, shouted. Bea laughed with them and asked them to sing along with her to a final song that she knew everybody could sing and loved, 'You Are My Sunshine'. Of course, they were all more than happy to oblige.

At the curtain call at the end of the show the clapping was so loud for Mel and Bea that Mel whispered to her, 'Well done. If Jerry dropped bombs now, we'd never hear them because the applause is so loud.'

Bea took the chance to change into her everyday clothes while Mel was packing away everything he needed for the next show on the following Monday. Her black dress and shoes had been retrieved from beneath the stage and she'd checked that they hadn't been harmed by her hurried change of costume. Mel had decided to leave all props and clothes at the theatre for the next performance.

More flowers had been delivered for Bea. She told the cleaners they could have them but to please freshen up the Michaelmas daisies as she wanted to keep them in the dressing room for as long as possible.

Later, she and Mel met up with Blackie and Jo to walk the short distance along Queen Street to Blackie's auditorium. There was a buzz in the air as other performers gathered to dine, or party the first night away with friends.

Everyone was excited and ecstatically happy the evening had gone so well.

'Eddie, Maud and Ivy are making their own way to our place,' Jo said.

'Do you really think they liked what we did?' Bea asked. She was full of high spirits.

'Everyone loved you,' soothed Blackie.

'And, had they arrived, Bert, Della and Rainey would have loved you, too,' broke in Jo. 'I didn't say anything before as

I didn't want to worry you but Rainey's not feeling well, so Della and Bert said they'd stay with her.'

Bea rounded on Jo. 'What's up with her? She was all right earlier. Aren't you worried?'

Jo narrowed her eyes. 'Having a baby isn't all sunny days and lots of fun,' she said. 'But there's no need to worry about every little ache or pain. If Della says she's fine, then she's fine. I trust Della.'

Bea knew she wasn't going to stay long at the gathering for she wanted to get back across the ferry to Gosport. Now, hearing about Rainey, she was more determined than ever to leave as soon as she could.

A small crowd had gathered on the pavement outside Blackie's auditorium. The blackout made it difficult for Bea to see who was there but she heard Eddie's voice and Maud's raucous laugh. Ivy was talking to a portly man, a stranger to Bea.

'Let's get inside,' said Blackie jovially, unlocking the door, and within moments the pavement was clear. 'Thank God there are no raids tonight, so far,' he said.

'Who's that tubby red-haired man?' asked Bea, waving a hand towards the man Ivy had been talking to. As Bea wouldn't be drinking, she thought Jo and Blackie could do with some help serving guests with alcohol and the tiny triangular sandwiches she'd spotted on plates in the kitchen.

It was so nice being amongst friends, Bea thought. Especially as she and Mel were the centres of attraction. Of course, she was worried about Rainey but Bea guessed Jo and Della, having had children of their own, certainly knew best. She decided to mingle for an hour or so then leave. It meant going across the ferry and walking along Mumby Road alone, but it wasn't something she hadn't done before in the dark.

'That's Cecil Edmunds,' replied Blackie. 'He's one of Basil Dean's associates. He's just returned from Africa. There was a nasty bit of business he had to clear up at one of the camps we played at.' Bea stared at him. 'I'll call him over.' He made to walk away but then thought better of it and returning, whispered in her ear, 'As your agent, I must tell you he's likely to make you an offer on behalf of Basil Dean. Think carefully about it. Basil Dean isn't someone one treats lightly.'

Before Bea had time to ask him more Blackie had slipped away into the small but noisy crowd. There were so many questions she would have liked to ask Blackie before he left. Bea spotted Mel coming towards her with a drink in his hand. He was joined by Blackie and Cecil Edmunds. She watched as the three men drew near.

An offer, she thought. What did Blackie mean? Basil Dean had a finger in almost every pie in the entertainment world. Surely he wasn't about to suggest she might like to go abroad again with ENSA? Bea sighed. If the war continued it was something she would love to do, but not at this moment in time. There was too much for her to worry about here. Bea wouldn't leave Rainey, certainly not before the baby was born. The two of them had become very close since Charlie's death.

'I'm very pleased to meet you, Miss Herron.' Cecil Edmunds' voice reminded Bea of melted chocolate. He took her outstretched arm, presumably, she thought, to shake her hand, but instead he raised her fingers towards his lips and kissed the palm of her hand. A soft kiss that didn't immediately make her want to snatch it away.

'Hello,' she said. He had small blue eyes that seemed to dart about, missing nothing. She withdrew her hand and studied him. He was short, round, and his red hair was thinning. She could smell Coal Tar soap.

Beside him, Mel glowered. If Blackie sensed any change in Mel's attitude, he was obviously ignoring it.

'Something's come to light at the air force base, the last camp in Libya we gave a show at,' Blackie said. 'Mr Edmunds is making enquiries . . .'

'What's this to do with us, Blackie?' Mel demanded, without letting him finish.

'I'll get straight to the point,' Edmunds said. 'A body has been discovered outside the perimeter fence. A woman, Susan Jennings, you may remember her as your partner . . .' he said pointedly, staring at Mel. The air about them, thought Bea, went suddenly cold.

'That's ridiculous. Margo,' Mel used her stage name, 'ran off with that airman.' He glugged from his glass.

'Apparently not,' Cecil Edmunds replied. 'She had identification on her.'

Bea put her hand to her mouth. She felt sick. How had this come about that the young woman had died and nobody had discovered it until now? Margo, Susan, dead? Surely there's been some mistake, she thought. Margo, Susan? Bea's heart started beating fast. Her head began to swim. M or S! Bea would have fainted, slid to the floor, had Blackie not pulled out a stool from beneath the table and guided her onto it. She flopped forward like a rag doll, but secure, because Blackie supported her.

'Oh, my dear, have some water . . .' She lifted her head to find a cup pressed against her mouth. 'I know, it must be a terrible shock. Especially if you were close to her.'

'But I wasn't,' Bea said, pushing the glass away Then she

relished the water's comfort as her mouth swallowed and began to lose its dryness. It ran through her mind what she had just said. She wasn't close to Susan Jennings. The woman was close to her, though! How much closer did the spirit of a dead woman need to be to warn her not to trust someone? Helen Duncan had given her a message from beyond the grave!

Surely not. She wasn't a believer in all that claptrap! But Helen Duncan had told her she was being given a warning from someone on the other side with the initial, M or S.

Bea shivered. 'Thank you,' she uttered into the kind but worried eyes of Cecil Edmunds.

'Just because you find a body of one of our artistes buried near a fence in a camp where we gave a performance, it doesn't mean one of us killed her,' said Mel. He drank down the rest of his drink.

Blackie stared at him. Bea saw a frown cross his face.

Cecil Edmunds said, 'I didn't say the woman had been killed . . .'

'Come on,' said Mel, 'you wouldn't be here if you didn't think someone harmed her! It reflects on ENSA, doesn't it? So you've come to pin her death on anyone you can. It'll take the heat off people thinking such a wicked thing could happen while we were out there cheering on the troops.' Mel looked at his glass, saw it was empty and strode away.

'Well,' said Blackie. 'We certainly know how Mel feels, don't we?'

'Look,' said Cecil Edmunds. 'This particular death is an ongoing case.' He turned to Bea. 'I haven't only come from Basil Dean to talk about sad things,' he said. 'This doesn't concern our friend over there,' he pointed to Mel who was pouring whisky into his glass. 'Mr Dean, who as you know is head of Ealing Studios, the picture company, has had his eye on you, Bea. I've already had a word with Blackie here and I'd like to arrange a meeting in London that will hopefully suit and be beneficial to all three of you: you, Blackie and Basil Dean.'

Chapter Twenty-Eight

The downpour came when Bea was nearing the train station at Portsmouth Harbour, almost at the ferry terminal.

She was eager to get home to the café. So much had happened in such a short time she wasn't sure whether she was on her head or her heels. Her first thoughts were for Rainey and the baby. She had so many things to tell Rainey, Della and Bert.

'Bloody rain,' she swore. Her dress was clinging to her body and her hair was hanging down her back, freezing her skin like icy fingers up her spine. She'd already dismissed using the small umbrella that Bert had given her. Not only was she already drenched but the dainty little thing would be more use as a sun shade than keeping this deluge at bay.

Her mind kept turning over Helen Duncan's words. She wanted to dismiss as utter rubbish everything she'd witnessed that night in Copnor. Except that she had spent ages on the ferry boat coming back to Gosport trying to pacify Grandad. Hadn't he said no one could have known it was his own fault he'd fallen foul of the gas when he'd ripped off his mask trying to get to the lad? Bea shivered. Perhaps the woman wasn't a charlatan after all?

She would also tell Rainey about Basil Dean and his request to meet her and Blackie in London. Cecil Edmunds had mentioned Ealing Studios. Ealing Film Studios! She'd tried to get Mr Edmunds to talk more but he'd said better to wait until they actually sat in conference in the meeting. And then there had been tonight, the first night of the new show!

Everybody seemed full of praise for her and Mel. Though she knew she'd find out what the critics thought when the daily newspapers were printed. It was awful finding out that Susan had died in such tragic circumstances. Mel had really got on his high horse about that, hadn't he? She wondered what had really happened to the woman – and where was the airman?

Bea swore again as her foot tripped against a broken paving stone. That was the trouble with the blackout. White safety lines had been painted on kerbs and pavements to hopefully show up in the darkness. Not much use when the lines were practically worn away by people's footsteps though.

Bea stopped hurrying and stood in the doorway of the cigarette kiosk at the edge of the road to catch her breath. A little bit of shelter was better than none at all. The rain made everything doubly dark and dreary and icy, she thought. Tonight the rain even smelled cold. Now, she was at the top of the short road that ran down to where the ferryboats docked. A red phone box was not too far away; she wondered if she could reach that for more shelter when she left the kiosk's doorway. She could make out cars and taxis taking passengers to the ticket office, wheels bumping as they collided with ruts in the road leftover from bomb blasts. The large shape of a double decker was disgorging passengers at the bus stop. She wondered how the drivers attempted long journeys when their headlight beams were doused to mere pinpricks of light. Bea knew the blackout was necessary but she hated it.

'Bea!' She heard her name being called. It was even difficult to hear properly with the rain noisily slanting down from the heavens. Staring hard back along the pavement when the figure became visible Bea groaned. Why on earth had she wasted time sheltering in this doorway when in another few minutes she could have been on a ferry boat?

'Bea, didn't you hear me shouting?' He was breathless. 'I've been chasing you practically since you left . . .' She stared at Mel, he was as drowned as she was.

'What do you want?' Her voice was grudging.

He pushed his fingers through his dripping hair and edged closer to her sheltering from the downpour. 'You shouldn't be rushing out of Blackie's in this lot . . .'

'It wasn't raining when I left . . .'

He grabbed hold of her shoulders. 'Don't split hairs with me. Tell me what Cecil Edmunds offered you.'

She tried to shrug her shoulder away. His fingers were biting into her wet skin.

'I don't know, he never said, it's just a meeting with Basil Dean . . .'

'A meeting that obviously doesn't include me? Why, you little tease! I give you a chance to work with me and you've done the dirty on me . . .'

He was shaking her now, his hands glued to both her shoulders.

'Don't hurt me . . .' Bea whimpered.

Her plea inflamed him. He was taller, stronger and her meekness seemed to empower him. He let go of one of her shoulders and slapped her across the face. Her head whipped sideways, her hair flying out, its wetness spraying across the kiosk's door.

'No!' Bea shouted, her voice swallowed up by the noise of the falling rain. 'No!' she cried out again. 'I'm not one of your bloody women . . .'

She felt his fingers tighten on her shoulder as he yanked her towards him.

She heard her dress rip under the strain of him pulling the thin material. She dropped her handbag, its contents sliding, spilling on the tiles inside the doorway and out into the rain as she grabbed the front of her dress trying to hide her brassiere and naked skin from his eyes. He let out a laugh that chilled her to the bone. The musky sandalwood cologne coming from his heated skin, the smell that before she'd thought so masculine, now choked her.

It was like being with that sailor all over again. She knew exactly what Mel was going to do to her in the relative privacy of that doorway . . .

Bea dropped to her knees and her hands felt about on the slickness of the wet tiles. Her stomach heaved as her fingers encountered spent matchsticks and dog-ends.

Then she had it, the little umbrella, clutched in her right hand. Mel was pulling her to her feet. 'Get up, you bitch,' he said. 'You're just like the others, flaunting yourself and then saying no.'

He towered over her. Her wet fingers slid over the button and she pressed.

It clicked. He must have heard the noise for he let go of her and stepped back. In the darkness the blade glittered. It was mere inches from his open jacket. Bea knew if he moved forward the deadly blade would pierce his clothing, his skin. He paused, barely breathing and he said again, 'You bitch!'

He jumped away from her off the pavement, backwards, then turned and ran.

The taxi mowed him down. The screech of brakes was followed by doors clattering open and people emerging from the vehicle, with voices raised. Mel lay on the road. He wasn't moving. Now people were yelling, rushing towards the scene and Bea was wondering where they had all come from.

She took a step forward and looked at Mel's body. The taxi driver was bending over him. The rain was lashing down. She shrank back into the darkness of the kiosk's doorway.

Everything suddenly cleared in Bea's jumbled brain. She knew what she had to do. She swept all her dropped items back into her bag, along with the little umbrella, then tucked her torn dress's shoulder material through her brassiere strap, so that it was no longer hanging down, and swiftly made her way towards the telephone box.

Bea was shaking but after putting in the pennies and pressing buttons she requested an ambulance to be sent to The Hard. She said there had been an accident. She was asked her name and address but instead simply gave her location and hung up.

She could now wait. Mel would have identification on him. The authorities would soon know who he was. Bea wanted more than anything to be inside Bert's café where the smell of bacon mingled with chip fat, and cigarette smoke curled towards the ceiling making her feel safe.

Watching the pinpricks of dull light announcing the arrival of a ferry that would leave the jetty within minutes for Gosport, Bea reassured herself her return ticket was still in the pocket of her bag. She didn't take another look at the scene of the accident.

She began walking down the slipway in the rain, towards the ferry boat.

Chapter Twenty-Nine

Rainey was sipping hot cocoa, her feet up on a chair and a blanket around her shoulders as Bea stepped into the café. Everyone had apparently been correct: whatever had ailed the expectant mum had now thankfully passed.

There were no customers, the bad weather having seen to that. Bert was mopping the floor. Della sat next to Rainey reading a *Woman's Weekly*, a cup of tea in front of her on the Formica table.

'Why is your dress torn?'

Rainey had set down the mug, was up off the chairs and standing in front of Bea, peering at her face before she slipped the blanket she was wearing over Bea's shoulders.

'My God,' said Della, 'you look awful.' She slid out of her chair and went behind the counter, coming back to Bea with frayed but clean towels in her hands. 'Shall I rub your hair dry for you?'

Bert said, 'I'll get you a cuppa.' He left the mop sticking up in the galvanized bucket, went to the sink and began washing his hands.

Bea promptly burst into tears.

An hour later Bea was still answering their questions as her friends digested and queried her account of Mel's attack and his accident. Over and over Della asked, 'Shall I telephone your mum and get her here?'

'Her and Eddie may still be over Portsmouth and he'll be angry that I didn't come back to Gosport in the car with them.'

'They won't be angry with you, my love,' Della stressed. She then foraged beneath the counter again and came up with a tube of cream-coloured liquid. 'I know you don't like wearing heavy make-up, Bea, but this is Pan Stik, film stars use this to cover flaws. Try it on that bruise.' She unscrewed the top and spread a little on her hand. 'See how it covers? It's good for bags under the eyes as well. Many's the time when I worked down the massage parlour I used this to hide the slaps I got from customers.' Della didn't often elaborate on the life she lived before she settled down with

Bert because she knew he didn't like being reminded of her former profession. Neither did Bea realize Mel's slap had marked her face.

Bea had changed into her nightwear and had stopped shivering at last. She took the Pan Stik gratefully. Beneath the counter at the café were all manner of useful things that might never see the light of day.

Again Della asked, 'Shall I get Maud?'

'I don't want mum worried; she had a bad enough time of it when that sailor . . .'

'This is different,' Bert insisted. 'I know you keep saying he didn't, but did he hurt you, love, besides that God awful bruise on your cheek?'

She answered, 'I was scared more than anything and I just wanted to be here, safe.'

'If the authorities contact you, you must tell them the truth,' he said. 'Tell the truth and shame the devil.'

'But it was my fault he stepped into the path of the car . . .' Tears threatened to spill again.

'I don't think they'll see it that way when you show them your dress.'

Bea must have looked guilty. 'You haven't already thrown it away, have you?' Rainey asked crossly.

'I shoved it in the bottom of the wardrobe,' she admitted.

'Did the blade pierce his skin when you pointed it at him?' Bert asked.

'No, of course not, but it must have scared him because he twisted backwards. I would never have hurt him. I just wanted him to leave me alone.'

'Everyone will realize that,' Della said.

'But what if he's dead? I walked away . . .' Tears sprang anew from her eyes.

'You telephoned for the ambulance, what more could you do? Miss the last boat home and sleep on the streets?' Della was getting cross with her.

'Tell you what I'm going to do,' Bert went out to the hallway at the bottom of the stairs and came back with his coat on and his flat cap jammed on his head. 'If you're that worried about the blighter, I'm taking a walk over to South Street to the police station. I shall tell them you reported the accident and I'll try and find out if he's all right.'

'You can't do that,' Bea insisted.

'I can't see why not. It's not like the police station shuts for the night, is it? And if I see a few of my mates over there they'll soon put me right. This is a "you scratch my back and I'll scratch yours" situation.'

Bea knew his 'mates', they were the coppers who ate for

free in his café and closed their eyes to his dealings in the black market.

Bea suddenly put her hand to her head. 'This is going to hit Blackie hard. There's no stage show tomorrow because it's Sunday but we're supposed to be performing on Monday night. I can't go on stage alone!'

After Bert had gone out in the rain, Della said, 'I think you should try to get some sleep, Bea my love. And you . . .' She waved a hand towards Rainey. Rainey now had a room of her own next door to Bea.

'I'd rather wait until Bert comes back,' said Bea.

Della gave her smile. 'You might be waiting a long time, love. When that lot and Bert get talking . . .' She gave Bea a hug. 'It's a wonder he didn't get me to make a pile of bacon sandwiches to take over there for them.' Della was quiet for a while then she said, 'You are a funny young woman. If some bloke tried it on with me like that, I certainly wouldn't be worried about him!'

After saying goodnight, Bea never thought she'd sleep. She tried to clear her mind and think instead about the other acts she'd watched from the side of the stage that night. The established acts were brilliant: the dancers, Caroline's dogs, the solo singer who was on the stage for the very first time

– she'd had a charming voice and received huge applause. The trapeze artists were wonderful, she thought, plenty of Oohs! and Ahhs! from the spellbound audience. The comics drew a blank, though, they weren't funny at all. They'd tried, but the kind of comedy they'd presented wasn't at all suitable for the audience. Saturday night Portsmouth audiences liked a good belly laugh. Such a shame, Bea thought. She wondered if Blackie would ask them to brighten up their act or perhaps he might even get rid of them, replace them with a comic who . . . Trying to think about other things wasn't working. In her head she could see pictures of Mel splayed on the road beneath the front of the taxi and they haunted her.

She was woken in the morning by Bert, with a cup of tea knocking on her door. 'C'mon,' he said. 'There's a lot to be done today.'

Hastily Bea scrambled up. She realized her shoulder was painful; looking down at it she saw she was covered in bruises and in places the skin had been broken by Mel's nails. Her jaw hurt. She remembered the slap.

'Is he dead?'

'Takes more than a knock to put a bugger like him out of action,' Bert said.

'One of my mates contacted Portsmouth Hospital.' Bert looked down at Bea's alarm clock and said, 'I should thir at this time he's sitting up in bed after a pretty nurse has taken him some porridge and toast.'

Bea stared at him. 'What? What d'you mean?' She'd thought Mel was seriously injured. She'd seen him lying on the road in the rain.

'Two broken legs, a few lacerations to his face and a broken wrist, and no doubt he'll play on that so one of them pretty nurses spoonfeeds him his breakfast.'

'Are you sure?' This couldn't be true, she thought.

'Coppers can get people to talk any time of the day or night. Why would they lie?' Bert picked up the tea and handed it to her. 'Drink this, it's good for shock.'

As she gulped it down, the mere action of drinking calmed her. Bert must have been reading her mind for he added, 'I'll tell you something else. Your name never came up after he was admitted. He reckons he simply didn't look where he was going, stepped off the pavement straight in front of the taxi . . .'

'How d'you know my name wasn't mentioned?'

'I asked if there was anyone with him when he got knocked down and was told he stressed he was quite alone, simply travelling across the water to meet a friend.'

Bea said, 'Why would he say that? It was because of me ⁀ stepped into the road. I telephoned for the ambulance.'

'C'mon love, use your loaf! He's hardly going to say he was assaulting his stage partner, one of the Bluebirds, is he?'

Bea handed Bert her empty cup. 'I won't forget I'm to blame for his accident . . .' she said.

She didn't get any further for Bert banged the cup down on the small table next to the bed and said, 'You were trying to protect yourself, don't make excuses for that bounder. Anyway, I haven't finished telling you what else I found out.'

She looked at him.

'That rogue is probably mixed up with that young woman's death out in the desert. He's not going anywhere at present,' Bert gave a dry laugh. 'He can't walk away from this, can he?' He saw she wasn't smiling, so he added after rolling his eyes, 'Anyway, today he's being questioned by the police. It looks like the airman has turned up and what he's saying doesn't match with Mel's version . . .'

'Surely Mel couldn't be involved . . .'

Bert didn't answer her. Instead he said, 'You'd better get up and come downstairs. Blackie telephoned earlier. I told him you was asleep and I wasn't going to wake you.' He looked at her alarm clock. 'You got fifteen minutes, I reckon, before he phones again.'

Chapter Thirty

Bea hastily washed and dressed. She didn't want to speak to Blackie, she really would have preferred to stay in bed all day to think about what had happened. She guessed Blackie would telephone her to say Mel was in hospital. Mel, no doubt, would have made sure Blackie knew about his injuries. That would mean there would be no shows on Monday. Normally there might be an afternoon matinee performance and another show in the evening. Either Blackie would have to persuade another act to step in, equally as good as Mel and Bea, which would be difficult to obtain at such short notice or . . . Bea didn't want to think about it. During the night she had woken several times wishing she could do something that would result in the act continuing . . . The show must go on, and all that.

And how would she ever be able to face Blackie , knowing

it was her fault things were as they were? She had however dabbed the Pan Stik on her face, blended it in, and was pleased with the result. The stiffness in her shoulder she could do nothing about.

She refused Della's offer of toast and another cup of tea and wondered how she could help Blackie out of a mess that was down to her. The phone rang. Bert answered it and after a short conversation handed the receiver to her. She tried to sound shocked when Blackie explained Mel had been run down.

'I'm trying to get hold of another magician so that you at least can go on stage and sing,' he said. 'Mel's going to be out of action for quite a while, poor chap. The trouble is, it's the beginning of the winter season and anyone decent is already working . . .' She heard him sigh. 'Already this morning I've had to cancel the comedians' contract. The manager of the Coliseum said he'd had complaints . . .'

'Blackie!' she cried, her heart going out to him. She hated to hear him so down and depressed – this man had, after all, given her, Rainey and Ivy their biggest chances in show business. That everything had unravelled for the Bluebirds hadn't been his fault. 'Blackie, I've had an idea.' She looked at the wall clock in the café and said, 'Could you hold fire for a coup of hours? I'll get back to you then and you can tell me if idea is a good one or not.' One of the thoughts she'd had in the early hours had begun to take form and she was becoming quite excited about it. But she needed help . . .

There was an intake of breath down the phone and Blackie then said, hesitantly, 'Two hours and you'll telephone?'

Bea nodded frantically then realized he couldn't see her, so she answered. 'Two hours.'

Blackie said, 'All right. I'm going to the hospital to see Mel. Can I give him your love?'

Bea squealed, 'No, don't give him my love. Just tell him Bea says she's sorry for the mess he's got himself into!'

Bea got off the bus at the Criterion picture house and ran, ignoring the pain in her shoulder, towards Alma Street. She'd already telephoned ahead and begged Ivy not to leave the house until she'd spoken to her. When she arrived Maud was just leaving for church. Bea kissed her and said, 'Just a flying visit, Mum.'

'It'd be nice if you stayed for dinner. We're having real food, you know. Not cardboard potatoes! Do you know that bakers are now renting out cardboard wedding and christening cakes because there's not enough ingredients for proper ones?' Maud walked away, moaning about rationing daughters who had little time for their mothers, then as if she remembered something, turned, her feet planted firmly on the pavement and shouted, 'You was blimmin' good last night, best show I've seen for ages.'

Eddie was still in bed, Gracie was in her playpen and Ivy, in the scullery, had just started peeling the potatoes for Sunday dinner. Maud always had a roast dinner on Sundays. Sometimes the meat was near invisible because of the rationing but Maud would never let a Sunday go by without the appearance of her fluffy golden roast potatoes.

Bea picked a sharp knife from the drawer and began helping Ivy.

'You sounded a bit mysterious on the telephone,' Ivy said.

At first Bea wasn't sure whether to tell Ivy the whole story just as she'd explained it all to Bert, Rainey and Della. But she was fed up with lies and half truths so everything came tumbling out. When she'd finished, she saw Ivy had tears in her eyes.

'Oh, Bea,' she said. 'You've tried so hard to get on in the theatre but everything's against you.'

Bea suddenly remembered that Basil Dean wanted to see her and Blackie in London, not that she knew what he wanted. 'There are still chances out there, Ivy, if we grab them with both hands. What I'm going to ask of you is a sort of pay back to Blackie. He was let down by us . . .'

'I didn't mean . . .' Ivy began, but Bea took no notice of her. Ivy's excuses wouldn't wash with Bea because deep down Bea knew Ivy felt guilty about taking time out from the Bluebirds to be with Eddie and Gracie.

'This idea of mine could get Blackie out of a nasty situation. He's never going to make a success of running Madame's business if things keep going wrong for him. He needs a comedy act and a new magician to take Mel's place. We can give him both. You and me!'

Ivy dropped the potato peeler into the bowl of potato skins. 'Are you out of your mind?'

Bea foraged around in the dirty water and handed the peeler back to her. 'No! And don't tell me you haven't been itching to get back up there on the stage and sing because I know you too well.'

Just then Gracie started to whine. Ivy went to the cupboard and took a Farley's Rusk out of the packet and carried it into the kitchen for Gracie to chew on. It did the trick for Ivy came back into the scullery with a contented smile on her face.

Bea said, 'Oh, yes, you make a lovely mum for that little girl but I know you, you want it all. You want Eddie, you want Gracie, and you want to be back in the limelight.' Bea shrugged her shoulder and winced because she'd forgotten it hurt. 'Is it because Eddie don't want you to go on the stage again?'

Ivy began to laugh. 'Don't be stupid, we've already had this conversation and he wants what I want. Most importantly he wants me to be happy.'

Bea threw a mangled potato into the pan of cold water. 'And what do you want, Ivy? Tell me what you want?'

Ivy walked up to Bea and put her arms around her. 'Like you, I want it all.'

Just then Eddie in striped pyjamas poked his head round the scullery door. 'Any tea?' His blond hair was all stuck up at the front. He looked at Bea and mumbled, 'Hello Sis.' He stared at her face for a moment like he wanted to ask a question, but didn't. Bea realized the Pan Stik hadn't fooled him. 'Any tea?' he asked again.

'Make your own,' chorused Bea and Ivy. Bea laughed and said, 'That's two of us who want it all, then.' She looked at the clock. 'I haven't got long, I promised to telephone Blackie and the time's getting on.' She pulled Eddie towards the stone sink and handed him the potato peeler. 'Finish doing these, brother dear, while I have a quick chat to your Ivy.' Bea wiped her hands and pushed Ivy into the kitche to talk. 'When you've finished, Eddie, don't forget to m the tea.'

Bea and Ivy sat at the kitchen table while Bea outlined her idea. Then she waited for the questions she knew would come thick and fast. The piece of paper with Mel's outline for the act was in front of Ivy.

'I don't know the routine,' said Ivy, twisting her long dark hair behind an ear. 'It's entirely different from our singing act.'

'You can learn it. We've memorized songs in less time. Tomorrow afternoon there's a matinee.'

'Doesn't give us much time. What about costumes?'

'Everything we need is already at the Coliseum. We'll improvise.'

'What if I make a mistake?'

'Then the audience will laugh even more.'

'I can't do card tricks.'

'No, but you can do something better, you can sing Billie Holiday songs and you are word perfect on those.' At Bea's words a smile touched Ivy's lips.

'Surely this act belongs to Mel? Isn't there some kind of law that protects his ownership?'

'Blackie will know the ins and outs of all that. I'm sure if e credit Mel, that'll be enough for him.' She stared deeply Ivy's eyes, 'After what he tried on with me, he's hardly o make a fuss, is he?'

Ivy said, 'I'm frightened I won't be able to do the act justice .'

'You aren't the only one who's frightened, Ivy, I'm scared stiff. But it's for Blackie, and for me,' she added. Then as an afterthought, 'And for you.'

Ivy stared into Bea's eyes, then she reached across the table and grabbed both her hands. 'Yes, I'll do it. One for all and all for one!'

Hearing Ivy say those words took Bea back to a frosty night outside St John's school, when the three teenage girls had vowed to stick together to work as one for success on the stage.

Bea felt tears rise and prickle the back of her eyes but she blinked them away.

'Thank you,' she whispered. 'Now I must phone Blackie and get him on our side.' Then her voice rose to a shout, 'Eddie, we need a lift to Portsmouth!'

She went over to the playpen, scooped up the little girl in her pink silk dress that Maud had made her from the shawl bought in Africa, and ignoring the wet biscuit caked to her face and hands and glued in her blonde hair, hugged her tightly.

'Gracie, because of your lovely Mummy Ivy, everything' going to be all right.'

Chapter Thirty-One

When Eddie drew his van up outside the Coliseum, Blackie was already waiting, keys to the premises in his hand. Not that he needed to open any doors, for a firm of Portsmouth builders were already inside the theatre, their plumbers dealing with the burst water main and its aftermath. He gave Bea a wave.

She was subdued. What if her great plan didn't work out? She'd known her brother wanted an explanation. Sunday was his day of rest, for being with his family. Especially since his building firm had been busier than ever lately, due to the government's promise that despite the war, house building was to be increased. He deserved to be told everything.

On the way over in the car with Ivy in the front seat pointing out things to a bouncy Gracie, like 'car', 'tree' and 'ssy cat', Bea recounted to him Mel's attack on her. When she'd finished, he stopped the van at the side of the road and turned to stare at her. She saw his eyes were very bright and didn't like to think of him being sad for her, but there was also anger in his tone.

'Why am I never around when these damn things happen to you?'

'You make it sound like it's a regular thing,' she said, trying for a humorous attitude.

He raised his eyebrows as if to ask, 'Isn't it?' She'd looked away. She knew the last thing he meant was that she brought disaster upon herself.

'Thank God Bert gave you that umbrella thing to protect yourself with.'

'Oh, I'm not keeping that,' Bea said airily to her brother. 'I'm giving it back to him to put in his collection. With all the worry that's caused me from pointing that sharp thing at Mel, I know now I could never hurt anyone deliberately . . .'

'Not even to protect yourself again?' Ivy's voice was querulous.

'No,' said Bea and shook her head. 'And d'you know something else?'

'What?' Eddie asked.

'I feel like I allowed that sailor to ruin part of my life. I know I was only fifteen or so but I'm not letting Mel de the same! I don't even hate him. He'll get what he deserves from someone higher than me. After all, what goes around, comes around. What he has done for me is to give me even more determination to get on with my life.'

Eddie had smiled at her then. He'd opened his mouth and she thought he'd been about to come out with some other little pearl of wisdom, but instead he said, 'I wish the pair of you all the luck in the world. Telephone me with Blackie's answer. By the way, I left a note for Mum. There'll be hell to pay if she comes home from church and no one's there for her Sunday dinner. I'm going to drop you both off at the Coliseum. Me and Gracie are going back to Gosport. Ask Blackie, and Jo, if she's around, to bring you back to our house later to eat.'

'So,' Blackie said, leading them both round to the stage door. 'What you've told me so far sounds as if it might work. But,' he paused while two men carrying a great length of thick hose passed them by in the narrow passage to the dressing rooms, 'I won't allow either of you to ruin my reputation.'

'Bearing in mind, of course, that neither of us has had a chance to even practise this different act . . .' said Bea quickly.

'I'll make allowances for that, you know I will.'

Bea, Ivy and Blackie were in the small room where only the night before Mel and she had got changed to go on stage.

'Cor,' said Ivy. 'Don't that dirty water make the place stink!'

'Don't worry,' said Blackie darkly, 'perhaps neither of you will be coming back to smell it again.'

Bea pulled a face at him. 'We know how much this means to you, the show must go on and all that malarkey! It means a lot to us as well, that you're giving us this chance to work together.'

Bea took down Mel's evening suit from over the screen and passed it to Ivy. 'Get behind there and put this on,' she said. 'I told you to study that script on the way over in the van. I know you were pointing out items of great interest to Gracie like pussy cats but have you memorized most of it?'

Ivy looked out from behind the screen. 'Looked at it? Memorized it? 'Course I have! But you just make sure you follow my ad libs because I'm doing it my way!'

Bea looked at Blackie and put her hand to her head in utter defeat. 'Oh, dear!' she said. Then, she took a deep breath and barked, 'Blackie, I need you to go backstage and put the cabinet in position on stage. Make sure it's directly over the trapdoor and facing the audience. Remember, directly over! It's not that heavy but maybe one of the builder's men will give you a hand. Also, will you take down this box of tricks,' she handed him the case containing the sword and sheath. 'Put it on stage on a small table just off centre. Please,' she added. 'Also, we need you to play the piano. I know you don't like playing without sheet music but the two new song sheets are in that box and I know you'll be able to start playing the other songs by ear when we begin to sing as you've played them hundreds of times. We'll be out as soon as we're changed.'

Bea heard him muttering something about who was in charge around here. And then he was gone.

Bea marvelled at the light-hearted atmosphere in the dingy room. It was so different from the ominous cloud that had hung over the place when Mel was in there. Please, please, let this work Bea whispered to herself. She looked at her black sparkly dress then at the Michaelmas daisies still fresh in their vase and they too seemed to give her hope.

The laughter began when the curtains drew back to reveal Ivy dressed in Mel's too-large evening suit. The legs had been rolled up, the arms pushed up, the top hat was aslant and the tails dragged across the floor of the stage. There was no one to give them an introduction so they introduced themselves.

A wolf whistle came from the third row as Bea spoke. Some of the plumbers and labourers had settled down for a free peek, their feet dangling over the seats in front, cigarettes hanging from their fingers and lips. Bea's smile grew even wider; they had an audience to play to. Blackie sat at the piano, unsmiling.

Ivy's patter came naturally. Tongue in cheek, she was echoing Mel's words, but there the resemblance ended. She could have been Tommy Trinder or Charlie Chester in her oversized outfit. But she wasn't, she was Ivy Sparrow, magician! Magician and funny man! She was the joke master who was going to get rid of her beautiful assistant. She got the men to chant, 'Oh, no you won't!' to her own 'Oh, yes I will,' then turned it around so they unwittingly said she could do it. That even raised a laugh from Blackie.

Bea played the straight man to Ivy's quips. It wasn't hard for her to follow what her friend was up to because Ivy made sure the audience realized she was the funny one and Bea was the glamour girl with the fantastic voice.

At the sword trick, Ivy made a big thing of not being strong enough to push the sword through Bea's body. So she sat on the table and used her foot against Bea' stomach to urge the sword in deeper. Blackie laughed out loud at that.

Because they both knew there was time to be made up because the comedians from the previous show weren't appearing at the Coliseum again, Bea and Ivy sang together. Their voices mingled sentimentally over old songs that had the workmen joining along and that Blackie could play without the music. 'Chattanooga Choo Choo' had them doing their old and practised dance routine and 'I Don't Want To Set The World On Fire' was obviously a favourite of the audience. Ivy caught Bea's eye and Bea knew she was communicating to her that she missed Rainey. 'All The Things You Are', sentimental and sweet, was followed by 'Ma, He's Making Eyes At Me', which had Bea off the stage making up to one of the plumbers in the audience and you could see he loved every moment. They finished with 'A Nightingale Sang In Berkeley Square', beloved and nostalgic. Then Bea was amazed at Ivy's very corny jokes that kept the men laughing. Some she recognized as part of Bert's café repartee.

Ivy, holding a pretend telephone to her ear said, 'Is that Mrs Jones on the line? Yes? Well you'd better get off there's a train coming!'

Ivy talking to the audience: 'I have a greeting today

for ninety-eight-year-old Emmy Parsons! Happy Birthday! That's from her mum and dad.'

And so the silly jokes went on. Bea wondered how on earth her quiet, reserved friend remembered so many ancient jokes that had the big beefy workmen in stitches.

Getting Bea into the box to disappear almost fell flat because the audience didn't want her to go – either that or they didn't believe the silly magician could do her job properly.

Soon though, Bea was escaping from beneath the stage and outside the swing door in the circle, already changed into her silver dress for her last entrance.

She pulled back the heavy door so she could hear Ivy singing her favourite Billie Holiday song. Ivy's voice was rich and breathy and had the audience spellbound. Bea thought proudly, this is what people want, to soak up the words of beautiful music, not to feel inadequate because they didn't understand the mystique of card tricks.

As Ivy's song ended, Bea opened the circle door. This time there was no spotlight, no introduction from the piano, just Bea. But as she walked down towards the stage and into the stalls, singing, the men began clapping and whistling.

*

Blackie said later in the dressing room, 'It's uneven. It's funny whilst giving the audience something to think about. Get some practise in. I'd like to see Ivy out of that blasted top hat and tails and into a pretty dress at the finale with you.' Then he added, 'The audience laughed in the right places, though, and the audience is always right. You go on tomorrow night.'

Bea grabbed hold of Ivy and began jumping with her up and down.

Chapter Thirty-Two

Eddie's eyes never left the Coliseum's stage. He was so full of pride he wondered if his shirt would go on taking the strain before his heart burst right out of his chest. Ivy's silly telephone gag had the packed house laughing. Even he knew it wasn't that funny and no doubt the people were laughing at her audacity in repeating it. It didn't matter, the audience were laughing, bums on paid seats enjoying 'Ivy and Bea, Magic, Mayhem and Music Extravaganza'.

For months now they'd carried on headlining the show. After Christmas it was all going to change. Contracts had been signed for Ivy and Bea to visit American air force bases up and down the country. He could cope with that quite easily because his beloved Ivy and his whiz of a sister had stated emphatically that they both wanted to be performing nearer home as much as possible. Middle Wallop, Beaulieu,

Chelmsford, Maldon, Sudbury, were some of the United States army air force bases where they had bookings.

'They're good, aren't they?' Eddie caught the wistful note in Rainey's voice.

'Shhh!' came a voice from the row behind. Eddie smiled at her and whispered. 'I shouldn't wonder when you've had that sprog you'll be joining them.'

Rainey's baby was due shortly and she was enormous! So huge all the family worried about taking her out of the house.

'Oh, I will if Bea gets her way,' Rainey replied.

'Shhh!' It was the voice again. Eddie smiled at her. Tonight there'd been an item in the *News*, about the acts appearing at the Coliseum. Bea and Ivy had had nothing but praise heaped upon them – practise and time had perfected 'Magic, Mayhem and Music Extravaganza'.

He thought about the front-page story about the young woman found dead in the desert and wondered how Melvin Hanratty was feeling after being remanded once again while yet more enquiries were made. The airman looked as if he'd had a hand in her death, so it was said. Everyone would find out what really happened and what sentences both or either of the men might receive in the new year.

'Want a bit of toffee? It's homemade.'

Eddie refused the paper bag that crinkled loudly beneath

his nose, handed from his mother, Maud, sitting at his side. He heard a tutting sound come from the row behind. Just as well he hadn't brought Gracie along to the show. Thank goodness Mrs Wright, their next-door neighbour, was looking after her. Gracie was a darling but she couldn't keep still for a minute.

Bea and his Ivy were singing now. For the hundredth time that night, he wondered how he'd become so lucky to have such a wonderful woman as Ivy love him. He'd die for her, yes he would. Though nobody dared to die before 5 January 1944, the day of Jo and Blackie's wedding. That Tuesday was going to be a day to remember. Eddie thought they had surely invited everyone they knew, including some posh people like Basil Dean, who had got quite pally with Bea.

So pally in fact that he wanted her to go with a party of actors including himself to Tunis, North Africa, as part of ENSA. But Bea had turned him down. He'd talked about his directing and producing, especially the film *Twenty-One Days*, which had starred Vivian Leigh and Laurence Olivier, and said Bea could do well in pictures. Ivy and Rainey were more excited than she was, however.

'If it happens, it happens,' she said.

It turned out Bea looked a lot like Meggie Albanesi, the love of Dean's life, who had died in 1923. Dean was still, after all this time, obsessed by the actress. Bea told Blackie she'd stick with the American lads, thank you very much! Eddie agreed with her. What he'd really like, if anyone were to ask him, would be to see the Bluebirds together again. Not that anyone would ask him – why should they?

He mulled that thought around in his mind while admiring his Ivy in her silver dress and matching high heels, the twin of Bea's glamorous outfit. His words came out quite clearly to Rainey as he tapped her gently on her arm. 'Mum would just love to get her hands on your baby, to mind, while you went back to sing with them.' He nodded towards the stage where Ivy and Bea were singing.

'Shhhh!' came the agitated sound from the row behind him.

Eddie looked around at a very large lady in an equally large hat who said loudly, 'Perhaps you don't like watching a brilliant act?'

For a moment Eddie was speechless, then he replied, 'Oh, I'm very sorry, but I do appreciate Bea and Ivy, more than you'll ever, ever know!'

Acknowledgements

Thank you to my agent, Juliet Burton and to my editor Therese Keating, who together made this a better book. Thank you, Ella Patel, for being a marvellous press agent and to all at Quercus who work so tirelessly for me.